W9-CYD-688

THE KILLER III

PQP529811

JACK ELGOS

THE KILLER
III
The Final Reckoning

Jack Elgos

YELLOWBAY BOOKS

Published by YellowBay Books Ltd 2013
www.yellowbay.co.uk

YellowBay Books Ltd
ISBN 9781490480534

Cover design by Emily Heaton

YellowBay Books is dedicated to edgy new writing.
Let us know what you think at **info@yellowbay.co.uk**,
Or visit Amazon and give the book a review

Contents

Prologue

Deep in his heart he'd known that, sooner or later, it would happen. His brief bout of freedom had come to an end. They'd tracked him down; they'd found him. Convinced his life was over he had waited on his knees for the bullet to the back of the head that never came. Instead, a helicopter landed. He was dragged inside and they were taking him back. Bollocks.

Belfast native Darren McCann, now known as Liam O'Neil, was an I.R.A. enforcer turned paid assassin working for the British government. His days were filled with violence, torture and cold-blooded murder and they were taking their toll on his mind and body. He had only just survived a terrorist suicide bombing on a bus, and his nights were filled with dark dreams. Then he met his angel, Montse, a pretty Spanish girl who was helping to heal his soul and gave him hope of a way out, an end to his nightmares – just as soon as he had completed his private mission.

Two down, two to go and then he was done. The four I.R.A. men who had ordered the brutal murder of his Ma, disguising it as a Protestant U.V.F. crime in order to recruit him to their cause for some reason he couldn't fathom, would all be dead. Then he was out, done, finished for good, and he would settle down to a quiet life in a tiny Spanish village with the girl he had come to love. But the last he'd seen of Montse was when she was being dragged away from him in handcuffs by the Guardia Civil.

A scarred British soldier sat opposite him in the helicopter. This man had swooped down from the sky to save him from the Spanish authorities, but he knew it was all a ploy to take him back to the clutches of Anthony Turner, his secret service handler. Over time he had come to like and admire the man, but now he was angry and any feelings of loyalty or friendship had gone. Why wouldn't they all just leave him alone; let him be? Why the Hell was he so important?

1

June 1983

The helicopter descended rapidly through gathering storm clouds, eventually slowing a little to hover momentarily in the threatening yellow glow before gently landing on the marked helipad. Liam sat, his grim expression unchanging, as he glared intently at the soldier opposite. The two men had spoken not a single word during the entire flight from eastern Spain.

As the rotors began slowing, the cockpit door was opened by one of two waiting soldiers. A huge sergeant reached in, grabbed his collar and pulled him out. He could do nothing to stop them because his hands were in cuffs. Immediately flanked by the squaddies, Liam felt each arm held by firm hands as he was propelled through the first drops of rain in the direction of a large wooden hut.

'Where am I?' Liam asked in a low voice. When there was no reply he tried again in a stronger tone. 'Where the fuck am I?' Still there was nothing, just stony glares from hard, uncaring faces.

'Bastards,' cursed Liam as he spat on the ground.

The door of the hut swung open at their approach and a third squaddie saluted their arrival. He knocked once on an internal door and his colleagues pushed their prisoner roughly into a small room before swiftly departing. Liam landed on his knees, unable to use his hands, and then fell over onto his shoulder.

'Oh dear, there really is no call for such barbarism,' said a familiar voice above his head before nimble hands quickly removed his restraints and he was helped to a chair in the first moment of compassion he had experienced since leaving Montse's bed that morning.

'Mr. Turner,' said Liam with a deep sigh. 'What a surprise.'

'I doubt that, dear boy, but I was beginning to think you were never coming home.'

'The thought did occur.'

'Yes, well, under the circumstances I can see why. We know that you had no way to contact us for quite some time so that's completely forgiven. I think the last two or three weeks, though, you really could have made the effort to get in touch.'

Liam closed his eyes and took a long, deep breath to control his rage. He was angry at this man. He was angry at the whole situation, but Turner had an unstoppable way of saying what he had to say and Liam was resigned to hearing him out. Besides, compared with the bullet he had been expecting, this was definitely the lesser of two evils.

'So, when did you find me?' he sighed, rubbing his arms to bring back the circulation.

'Oh, not for quite a while,' Turner confessed. 'We thought you were dead of course. At first we couldn't work out why you would be on that bus, but you had to have been on it because you weren't anywhere else, you see.'

'Logical assumption,' Liam acknowledged.

'Quite. So then we looked at the facts and reasoned that you must have discovered something partial about the terrorists but needed more information before letting us know. You were following the lead, so to speak.'

'That's about the size of it,' Liam agreed.

'Admirable, dear boy. Admirable. But then the bus blew up, didn't it?' As if on cue the sky roared with thunder and hail poured from the skies, hammering on the roof and thwarting any attempt at conversation for several minutes. Turner shrugged his shoulders and mouthed the words, 'British weather'.

As the din finally receded the Englishman continued. 'Apparently we are in for a glorious summer, but today just isn't playing the game.'

'And it's all about playing the game, isn't it Mr. Turner?'

'Very well said, Liam, but that's not something you're very good at you know.'

'Mr. Turner, my life is not some pawn in your stupid war,' Liam spat. 'I nearly did die on that bus, and what would it have been for?'

'Well, there are many schools of thought on that one, but let's leave the philosophical questions aside shall we? You nearly died; we thought you were dead and you decided to stay dead.'

'But you discovered I was still alive. How exactly?'

'Well, there weren't any bits of you.'

'What?'

'Bits, dear boy,' Turner repeated patiently. 'That was a very big blast and none of the bodies came out intact. We found plenty of bits of Arab types and identified two poor souls who seem to have been from the Spanish authorities, but we had quite a few pieces left over, so to speak, and it took us a while to fit them all together. We came to the conclusion they were American forces, deniable of course.'

'You found bits of deniable Americans?'

'Well, they were definitely deniable because nobody claimed them and the Americans do tend to deny more than most. It was all terribly gruesome. But there were no bits of you, do you see? Ipso facto, you were still alive.'

'Ipso what?'

'Latin, Liam. The facts proved that you weren't dead. Therefore you were alive.'

'Fuck.'

The deafening hail returned then and Turner decided to pretend he hadn't caught the profanity. He'd known this man for around two years and knew that it was futile to try to change him. Besides, he understood the frustration he was feeling. Circumstances had given the lad a chance to get out and he'd very nearly made it. In truth, he had been sorely tempted to let him be, allow him to stay dead, but there were too many risks involved. No way would this man rest until his mother's death had been fully avenged, which was fine by him. Everyone wanted the perpetrators dead. They were I.R.A. organisers at just the right level to interest Her Majesty's secret forces. The lowly soldiers, those who planted the bombs, could be dealt with by regular law enforcement. Those at the top were too well protected by the façade of politics and were out of reach, but these middle management types, the committee men, could be eliminated. It had to be done in just the right way, at just the right time and by just the right tool. This angry young man was that tool, but he had to be handled.

Turner could feel the controlled rage within Liam, and it concerned him. The lad couldn't bottle stuff up for long. It was going to have to come out sooner or later, and they weren't going to get very far until it did. He needed to release some of that anger now so that Liam would really listen and they could move forward. He knew just how to do it. As he waited patiently for the rain to subside he rose from his chair and slowly paced the room as he considered how much he wished he could get out too. He really detested his job and he detested what he was about to do, but he knew it was the right move.

'Montse,' he said when conversation became possible again.

'What the f…'

'That's how we found you. You do know she's a prostitute, don't you?'

The chair flew back and crashed against the wall as Liam jumped to his feet and Turner recoiled over his desk in genuine fear as the man lurched towards him. The door opened and a squaddie rushed in, but Turner quickly waved him away. This had to happen.

Fists clenched and his breath coming in short, harsh gasps, Liam fought hard for several seconds not to hit the man in front of him, their faces just inches apart. Finally he thumped the desk and backed away. 'I know,' he muttered through gritted teeth, 'but what the fuck has that got to do with anything? What in Christ's name are you trying to say?'

'She gave you up, Liam,' Turner said, his voice quiet and matter of fact, though his body remained tense in anticipation of an attack.

Liam staggered backwards at the words, his eyes widening, his breathing ragged as he struggled for comprehension. 'G…gave me up? Gave me up how?' he stammered. 'No, she can't, she couldn't, she…'

Turner remained silent, watching as Liam's face contorted with emotion, his eyes fierce, the veins on his neck fit to burst until his head began shaking slowly from side to side and his mouth formed a lop-sided grin.

'No, no, you've got it wrong. They took her off in handcuffs, for Christ's sake.' Liam's voice rose as he glared at the man opposite, though he kept his distance. 'She was crying, screaming, pleading with me to help and I couldn't do a fuckin' thing about it man. Not a thing, do you understand? Those bastards had me in chains and she was screaming. They had me in chains *already*, you stupid fucker.'

'Yes, Liam, she was arrested for your benefit, and by now she'll be back home.'

'No, you're wrong. I know you're wrong. That was real, man, that was real. I could see it in her face. I could see it in her eyes as she looked at me and I couldn't help her. I couldn't…' Liam's voice cracked as he tried to continue. 'She…I… I thought…'

'You thought she loved you, my boy?'

Though Liam was unable to form another word, the small nod of his head told Turner all he needed to know. He had released some of the anger, gained the upper hand, and the man would listen. It was a temporary respite but, for now, they could move forward. He'd been here before with this lad and he knew how to handle him, but oh how he hated it.

'She does love you, Liam, I'm pretty sure of that. I'm also sure that she didn't mean to give you up and probably doesn't know that she has. We used her, my boy, and I'm very sorry.' Turner raised a hand to forestall any further outburst. 'Sit down, Liam, you need to hear me out.'

Liam opened his mouth to speak, but decided against it, swallowing instead to counteract the tears pricking at the back of his eyes. He was emotionally drained. In the last few hours he had been dragged from bed, handcuffed, faced certain death, been reprieved, had his arse flown half way across a continent and found out that he'd been betrayed by the woman he loved. He couldn't make sense of it all and he needed someone to do it for him. He retrieved his chair, took a seat and waited. He just didn't have the energy for anything else.

Turner remained quiet for a few seconds more, allowing time for the young man to gather himself before enquiring, 'Are you ready?'

'Just get on with it,' Liam told him. 'I'm sitting comfortably. You may begin.'

'It took us some time to realise you were still alive, as I've said. All those bits, you remember.'

'We've dealt with the body parts, Mr. Turner. Let's move on.'

'Quite. Well, then it was a matter of trying to find out what happened next. There were no witnesses you see, but we knew somebody must have seen something. They always do, you know.'

'If you say so.'

'Oh I do. Definitely. Now there are several small villages round there so we sent out a couple of, well, spies I suppose you'd call them. That was a little tricky, actually. We're not well staffed with operatives who understand Català. It's really quite a failing at our end and we must address the problem. I've already suggested some new training initiative to…'

'Can we just get to the point here?' Liam urged.

'Yes, yes, quite right. Sorry. Well, that's really why it took us so long, but finally one of our men picked up something in Spanish about someone saying to someone else something about a couple of young lads and some rabbits and that they were scared to hunt again in the area where the bus blew up.'

'Alex and Esteban.'

'I'm sure you're right. It was a long shot and their names weren't important, but the fact that they had a sister who spoke English and was a… well a…'

'We've already agreed that she is a prostitute, Mr. Turner. Besides, that's a perfectly respectable profession in Spain.'

'Oh indeed, I am well aware that it's only we puritanical Brits who view it differently. Anyway, let's just say that her profession made her easy to get to and one of our men has an Irish accent, which she commented on because she had a friend who spoke like that, and, well, that was the clue we'd hoped for. He followed her home and a couple of days later I received a nice, clear photograph of you doing exercises in her garden.'

Liam sighed, a long, deep sound, as he shook his head. 'Simple as that, eh?'

'Yes Liam.'

'You made me believe she'd deliberately turned me in.'

'Yes Liam.'

'That was a fuckin' low blow.'

'Yes Liam. I needed to get your attention and I'm sorry. One has to do some very distasteful things in my job.'

'Does she know where I am?'

'No. She believes that you are still in Spanish custody.'

'I need to call her.'

'No Liam, you can't do that. Not yet.'

'Listen Mr. Turner,' Liam hissed, 'I'm sitting here all calm like, hearing how you tricked me and how you tricked Montse. I'm in a fuckin' shed in the middle of nowhere, which is the last fuckin' place I want be, and I assume I'm here because you have a job for me. Well, I'll tell you straight, I'm done. It's over. I'm going to call Montse, the woman who saved my fuckin' worthless life, by the way, and then I'm out of here and I'm going back. You've had your money's worth out of me and I'm through. You don't fuckin' own me and that's all there is to it. And if you don't fuckin' like the way I'm fuckin' swearing, then it's fuckin' tough because the alternative, Mr. Turner, is that I break your fuckin' face.'

'Mm,' said Turner as he scratched his head thoughtfully. 'We have a problem here dear boy, and it's a lot more than your excessive use of the profane.'

'Oh, what fuckin' problem you stupid old man? I'm out. It's over. Simple.'

'What's simple, Liam, is that you are simply wrong. We do own you. I own you and you went A.W.O.L. I had to get you back.'

'A.W.O.L? Fuckin' A.W.O.L.? You talk as if I'm a fuckin' soldier in your fuckin' army. Well I've got news for you old pal, I am fuckin' not. So fuck your stupid fuckin' army blather - and fuck you too.'

'You do have a contract with Her Majesty's government, Mr. O'Neil.'

'What, that stupid dotted line I signed on in prison? Fuck that. It's not worth the paper it's written on. I'm sick of Her Majesty's fuckin' government, sick right up to here.' Liam pointed a finger to the centre of his forehead as he spoke. 'I'm sick of England, sick of Ireland and their bleedin' wars and sick of being used by someone whose word doesn't mean shite. When has Her Majesty's fuckin' government honoured anything they've ever signed? They don't, and I don't see why I should.'

'Well honour is rather what I had in mind, Liam. Your honour. I had assumed you were a man of your word and that your handshake meant something.'

'My hand…' As Liam's voice died away, a shadow crossed his face.

'Yes, you should think on that while I take a short break. Quite honestly my ears are hurting from all this swearing and we haven't had any tea yet. I assume you'd like some biscuits too?

'What?'

'Biscuits. Would you like some?'

'What? Biscuits? Yes … what?' But Turner was already gone and the door had closed behind him. Liam sat alone in the small room. The pounding hail had passed and now a steady rain played on the roof, its mournful sound accompanying thoughts he would rather forget.

***

Ireland 1981

Darren McCann had no idea how long he had been in the Maze when Turner's arrival put an end to the brutal torture he had suffered from that madman McQuillan. One hand was useless, the bones smashed by McQuillan's hammer, and Turner brought medical aid, tea and biscuits. He also brought the news that would change his life – the truth that his beloved Ma had not been killed by the Shankill Butchers as he had thought, but rather that the I.R.A. had made it look that way in order to recruit him.

With the eventual acceptance of this fact Darren signed the papers Turner offered and followed him from the cell secretly back into the outside world. As they arrived at the door Darren looked towards the fence and knew it was his last chance, while knowing there was no chance at all. If he made a run for it now then he would die from a British secret service bullet rather than the prison guard bullet that had been organised to fake his death. Yet still it was an option. Turner had just two service men with him and he might make it. If he didn't… well, he'd been prepared to die in that cell so what difference did it make? Real death meant real freedom.

Turner watched the broken young man for a moment and knew the thoughts that were in his head. He wasn't surprised. Who wouldn't consider a way out after all he'd been through?

'It's now or never, Darren,' he said quietly as he held out his hand.

Darren tuned to the older man and looked at the outstretched arm. With his injured hand held tightly to his chest he slowly offered his other in return and Darren McCann, Butcher of Belfast, became Liam O'Neil, British secret service operative.

***

Shite! He was fucked.

Liam listened to the incessant rain as it pounded on the roof of some hut in God knows where and waited for his handler to return. The soft voice of his Ma played in his head – 'A man is only as good as his word, son.'

'Chocolate or plain?' asked Turner as he entered the room.

'What?'

'Digestives, dear boy. Which would you prefer?'

2

The Other Man

'More tea?' asked Turner the following lunchtime as they sat once again in the hut. He had decided to call a halt to yesterday's proceedings and sent Liam off to lodgings so he could rest and think. Today the rain had gone and the bright sun offered a hope of the glorious summer they had been promised.

'Aye, go on then, I will have another please,' Liam sighed, 'but when are we going to get to the point, Mr. Turner? I don't suppose you've gone and dragged me back from Spain just for small talk over cups of tea.'

Turner leaned forward slightly and, as he generally did, placed a hand gently on Liam's knee and squeezed a little. He lowered his voice to an almost conspiratorial tone. 'A new termination order has been issued Liam,' he offered.

'Is it…?'

'Not yet, Liam, no,' Turner interjected before he had time to name the two men he still wanted so badly. 'Here, take a look at this file.'

Liam took the cardboard folder, but laid it beside him on the table. 'Look Mr. T, I've accepted our deal. You're right, we did shake on it, but you promised I'd get all the bastards responsible for me Ma's death and, so far, I've only got half of them. You don't seem to be living up to your end of the bargain and I'll not look at anything else until you tell me what's going on.'

'Well that's hardly fair, old boy. Those men are earmarked for you, but we have to get them in the south. We can't have you going north now, can we? Far too dangerous for your previous incarnation, so to speak. We could have sent other operatives to get them where they live, but I've fought hard to keep them yours.'

'I didn't know that.'

'Well it's best all round, really. They all have to be deniable operations, and you're about as deniable as they come.'

'Couldn't I be just as deniable in the north? Darren has been dead and buried for a long time now. I'm sure he's been forgotten about.'

'Well, maybe. Time does have a way of dimming the memory of course. I'll tell you what, Liam. If you will be a good chap and take a look at that file, then I promise to re-visit the situation with Mr. Moore and Mr. McMurphy to see if we can expedite them. How does that sound?'

'Shake on it?'

'Indeed, Liam. You have my word,' said Turner offering his hand.

Liam held out his in return, but then withdrew it slightly. 'And I get to go back to Spain in the meantime?'

'Now Liam, I really don't think you understand what a problem your constant gadding about has been for us.'

'Regular contact, all protocols followed and I'm yours when you need me. No more gadding about,' Liam offered, his hand outstretched once more.

Turner sighed. 'OK, Liam, I'll see to it.'

They shook and Liam reached to retrieve the file. 'Right you are, then. Who's the lucky bastard this time?' he asked.

'Someone I think you will be unfamiliar with I'm afraid. He's pretty new on the scene.'

Liam studied the papers in front of him and shook his head. 'Dillon Kane? No, never heard of him. Who the fuck is he?

'Oh shit, sorry,' he continued quickly at the sight of Turner's disapproving glance. 'I've been away a while. Takes some time to remember to watch me language, you know.'

'Quite,' tutted Turner. 'Well, in the past few months, those Sinn Féin fellows have been desperately attempting to sway public opinion to their own cause. In short, I could say that Dillon Kane is simply a politician but, the truth is, the man is the head of the P.I.R.A. propaganda machine.'

'OK, where's the hit, and when do I have to leave... and, I'll just read the file, shall I'?

'If you would be so kind, Mr O'Neil.'

Liam lit a cigarette and read slowly, digesting the detailed information that Turner always provided. There were photographs, background, known associates and a schedule for the following week.

'A university in Newcastle Upon Tyne?' he queried at one point. 'What would yer man be doing there?'

'Garnering support for the cause.'

'The British support the R.A? That could never happen, surely.'

'They are targeting the young.'

'Aye, a bunch of bloody school kids.'

'Hardly that, Liam. University students are an intelligent, radical and fearless bunch. Just look at how they took on the American government over Vietnam. It is of very real concern to us that the P.I.R.A. propaganda machine could find a receptive audience in the minds of our brightest youth.'

'Holy mother of God,' Liam breathed as he returned to the file. He grimaced at the part outlining the number of bodyguards, which immediately preceded the instruction for an up close and personal kill of the target. That was going to be a little tricky, but he'd had worse odds. Still, a long, low whistle escaped him as he turned the page.

A few lines further and he stopped abruptly. 'What the f…'

'Liam, please,' Turner interjected.

'Oh, you expect me to take this calmly, do you? No way, never, not a chance in Hell. I always work alone and you know that. What the fuck is all this about some gobshite partner?'

'Liam, the bodyguards need to be taken out by a sniper at night.'

'I'm a bloody good sniper.'

'Yes, lad, I know you are. I don't doubt that you could take the three of them out, but then what? Do you imagine Mr. Kane will just stand there calmly waiting for you to stow your rifle and run down to terminate him?'

'No, of course not, but why don't I just take him out with a bullet as well? In fact, why don't I just take him out and leave the guards? It's not like you to order, what do you call it, collateral damage.'

'No, I agree, the guards are unfortunate, but the main target has to be dealt with by knife, you see,' Turner explained, his tone calm and matter-of-fact.

'No, I don't see. Dead is dead. What do you care how it's done?'

'Because that's how we'll make the point that we need to make.'

'What fuckin' point?'

'That, dear boy, is none of your business. We have agreed in the past not to talk politics, and this is a political point. Things have to be done in a certain way and that's all there is to it.'

'Oh shite. Well get someone else then. I don't do teamwork and that's that.'

'We could use someone else, that's true, but your knife-work really is unparalleled you know. You and that *Killer* of yours are the best I've ever seen. I take it you still have your weapon? I did instruct that it should be left in your possession.'

'Aye, I've got it,' Liam confirmed as he felt the comforting shape of the knife in his back pocket.

'Well, there you are then. You're the man for the job.'

'No.'

'Yes.'

'Fuckin' no.'

'Handshake, contract, honour, Liam.'

'Oh fuck.'

'I take that as a yes, then?'

'You take that as I've no fuckin' choice, have I?'

'Quite, and now that's agreed we'll have an end to the swearing. It's time for you to be reacquainted with your partner.'

'*Re*-acquainted?'

'Oh yes, you have met once or twice before,' Turner smiled as he reached for the phone. 'Please send the sergeant in,' he instructed.

3

Hurry up and Wait

Brian Gates, career soldier, special-forces trained, started his morning with a cup of coffee at his army digs and the promise of a weekend's leave now that he'd delivered that bleedin' scrawny Irishman back from Spain. He really didn't know what was so special about the man. He was short and thin and had a seriously bad attitude, but Turner seemed to need him and his was not to reason why and all that. He was a soldier and he did what he was told. Besides, he needed to keep in with Turner for a while until he had made his decision.

At 40, Brian knew his forces career was coming to an end and that he had to find other employment, but the offer he had recently received from Turner gave him a moral conflict. He had no problem with covert operations, and his skill as an S.A.S. marksman had seen him in many deniable situations, but he'd always been under direct army command. He couldn't be sure exactly what authority

Turner represented; 'Hush, hush,' was the only explanation he'd been given, but something just felt wrong about the shadowy nature of it all. Killing for the army was one thing, but he was now debating becoming a hired assassin and it troubled him. The money sounded good, though, and one thing was for sure – he needed money.

His marriage was on the rocks and he didn't know if it was down to his long periods of absence, which likely wouldn't be solved by a career in covert operations, or by their financial worries, which just might be. They couldn't go on as they were, though, with one argument after another that simply made him want to spend time away from her. The only answer he could see was a change of scenery. Things might be better if he could get her away from her mother.

'Soon mate, soon - I bleedin' hope so anyway,' he thought to himself, as he thumbed through the 'Island Living Property' magazine.

As if by magic, or possibly owing to the fact that Brian had read this page so often, the brochure opened at *his* page - the Ibiza page. He lit a cigarette and started to read *his* advertisement - again.

In classic Estate Agent double language the ad read:

Cala Llonga:

Elegant 2-bedroom apartment situated in the residential area Pueblo Esparragos with community pool, on-site cosy restaurant and minutes from a sandy beach.

This modern apartment has two entrances and includes a covered terrace overlooking the pretty bay of Cala Llonga, surrounded by verdant hills.

It also contains a sunlit living room with dining area and kitchen: fully-fitted to the highest quality.

Both bedrooms have built-in wardrobes and there are two stylish bathrooms, one of which is en suite.

All in all, the perfect holiday, or permanent home, which you can move into immediately.

Brian screwed up his eyes as he leaned back into his seat. The last part of the ad was the bit he didn't really like. 'Move in immediately? Well we could - if we had enough bloody cash to buy it, that is.'

He lit another fag and, as usual, began to pour over their finances again. He struggled through some calculations, maths had never been his strong point, and he still hadn't found the solution. 'Come on mate, there has to be a way,' he frowned as he studied the figures.

A loud knocking interrupted his train of thought. As he opened the door a smiling postie stood holding out a letter, pen and receipt book.

'Recorded Delivery mate, can you sign here?' He pointed at his pad.

Brian signed and took the envelope back to his table. As he tore it open and quickly read the paperwork his jaw dropped slowly to his chest. He couldn't believe the contents. 'That fuckin' bitch,' he scowled as he read and reread the divorce petition in his hand. 'You said you were off to your mother's for a bleedin' week's holiday - not going to Lawyer J Daggett's office for a fuckin' divorce.'

He tried in vain to tear the papers up, but he was so angry that all he managed was to crease them. 'Cow,' he screamed as he threw the documents on the floor and stamped on them.

'If she thinks she's getting half of my pension, she can fuck right off - fuckin' bastard bitch. As soon as I can, I'm off - and I'm not gonna let her know where either - fuck her and fuck the divorce. She'll have to live at that old battle-axe's house.' He spat on the floor, then instantly regretted it. 'Shit man, that's your own bleedin' carpet you're spitting on.'

The phone rang. 'Yeah, who the fuck's this?' he snapped.

'Bri, is that you mate?' asked the caller.

'Aye, it's Gates,' he replied in a friendlier tone as he recognised the voice.

'Sergeant, your weekend leave is cancelled. You are to report to hut E, thirteen hundred hours. Understood Gatesy?'

'Aye Corporal, I've got it. Clear as a fucking bell.'

Brian replaced the receiver, scowled and almost spat on his floor again. 'Don't be a bloody idiot,' he said as he gulped down the mouthful of saliva. It looked like the decision had been made for him. He'd already lost a brother to the army and now it seemed he had lost his wife too. If anyone was willing to pay for his services, and pay well, then they could have him. He was all out for himself now and fuck the moral conflict.

He had presented himself on the dot, thirteen hundred hours precisely, and now here he was in hut E, an hour later, drinking endless cups of tea and still waiting. He wasn't at any of the formal battalion units so he had to assume this was covert and that it was Turner who had summoned him. If so, he'd picked just the right day to do it.

'More tea Sergeant Gates?' asked the soldier.

'More tea? No thanks mate. I've been here an hour and done nothing but drink bleedin' tea. I've drunk so much I've peed three times already. Do you have any idea what this is about Corporal?'

'No Sarge, I was only ordered to have you wait in here. You'll be called when they're ready for you. Hurry up and wait - you know the army.'

'Aye me old mate, I do. Waitin' for the bleedin' brass is all I seem to do,' agreed the Sergeant in his broad Hartlepool accent.

'They're ready for you now, Sarge,' the young soldier finally announced, about half an hour later, and Gates stood to straighten his uniform before following the corporal down a short corridor and walking through the door that was opened for him.

He marched to the desk and stood rigidly to attention in front of the man he had expected to see while his peripheral vision caught the face of a man he had hoped never to see again. 'Sah, Sergeant Gates reporting as ordered, Sah,' he announced, deliberately ignoring the room's other occupant.

'At ease Sergeant, and please take a seat,' said Turner pointing to the extra chair he'd dragged across for the man.

Gates wavered a moment, but then sat on the chair as ordered. He remained completely at attention. 'What the fuck?' he heard to his left.

'Liam, sit down. Sergeant, please relax,' said Turner. 'This is not a parade ground and we are just here for an informal chat to get to know each other. Is that understood?'

'I already know this fucker,' Liam spat. 'If this is the gobshite you're suggesting I work with then you can go screw yourself. Seriously, Mr. Turner, what the Hell are you thinking?'

'And you, Sergeant, what do you think?' Turner asked as he ignored Liam's outburst.

'Sah?'

'How do you feel about working with Mr. O'Neil here?'

'Sah, I'll do as ordered, Sah,' barked Gates.

'That's not what I asked, Sergeant. I asked how you feel.'

'Permission to speak freely sir?'

'An informal chat, remember? Speak as freely as you like. I want to know your thoughts on the matter.'

'My thoughts sir? My thoughts are that the first chance this murdering Irish bastard has, he'll shoot me in the back of my head - Sir.'

'Mm, not off to a good start then are we? Have you two ever been properly introduced, by the way?'

'What?' came the reply in stereo.

'Yes, I thought not. Liam, meet Brian. Brian, meet Liam. Now shake hands, there's good fellows,' Turner instructed.

When neither man made a move, he continued. 'I can make that an order, Sergeant, if you prefer. As for you, Liam, simple good manners will suffice.'

Gates rose to his feet and extended his arm as he moved towards the other man who sat sullenly in his chair.

'Liam,' Turner prompted again.

'Ah, what the fuck,' Liam mumbled as he stood and stuck out his hand begrudgingly.

'That is no way to speak in front of a senior officer,' said Gates as he withdrew his arm.

'I'm not in your fuckin' army, son, and I'll speak how the fuck I like,' Liam spat.

'Gentlemen, please. Let's shake hands first and then we can move on to the other niceties,' Turner said, his face showing no trace of emotion. 'Go on. Shake.'

Finally the two men did as ordered before each retreated quickly to his chair.

'There, now, that wasn't so hard, was it?' Turner continued. 'Liam is quite right, Brian, he isn't in the army. However, as he knows full well, he is under my authority. You will come to realise that Liam has a colourful turn of phrase that all my best efforts have failed to curtail. Nevertheless, he is a man for whom I have a high regard, as I do of you Brian. You are the ideal pairing for this job.'

'What is the job, Sah?' Gates asked.

'Please address me as Mr. Turner. We're on first name terms, remember?'

'Er, yes, sir, Mr. Turner,' Brian agreed as he caught the smirk on Liam's face. Maybe they agreed on one thing at least. This Turner guy was definitely odd.

'Here's the file,' the older man went on as he passed Gates a copy of the paperwork that Liam had studied earlier. 'Now, would you like a cup of tea?'

'Yes, sir, er, Mr. Turner. Some tea would be nice,' lied Brian as he felt further pressure build on his bladder.

'I'll go and rustle some up then,' Turner said as he walked from the room.

The two men were on their feet simultaneously the moment the door closed. 'What the fuck is this?' hissed Gates.

'Fucked if I know,' Liam spat back. 'He must be fuckin' mad. He told me I needed a partner for this job, but he never said anything about you.'

'Well he never said anything about you either, you fuckin' Irish wanker.'

'You'd better watch your language there, Sergeant. He's your superior officer remember.'

'Fuck you,' snarled Gates before quickly retaking his seat as the door opened.

'Tea will be here in a moment,' Turner informed them. 'Now, let's study the job shall we?'

The three men sat sipping their tea together in an air of uneasy silence. Liam glanced across at the soldier and actually felt a little sorry for him. He knew the man must be feeling uncomfortable. Even he realised that chatting over tea and using first names were definitely not the norm in the British army. 'Fag pal?' he offered as he held out a pack of Capstan full strength.

Brian's hand moved slightly, but then hesitated as his eyes snapped back towards Turner.

'Go ahead old boy, feel free to smoke if you wish.'

'Sah than.. I mean – Mr. Turner, thank you sir.'

'Now, why the fuck would an old Tom Tit like you be thanking yer man over there? *I'm* the feller giving you a bleedin' fag, not him,' said Liam.

'Language please Liam,' admonished Turner.

'Sorry Mr. Turner, I keep forgetting - must try harder,' he whispered as a wry smile creased his face.

Brian accepted the cigarette and a light and appeared to relax slightly as he inhaled the strong tobacco. Liam studied him from the corner of his eye. The face was badly scarred and looked as if it had been through a windscreen a couple of times at least. 'How the fuck does a man get a bleedin' bake like that?' he wondered, though he said nothing.

'Fucking murdering I.R.A. bastard,' thought Brian for his part.

Anthony Turner took out his pipe and lit it slowly as he watched the two men before him. The tension in the room was all too evident, not that it was any surprise. He only hoped that the plan he had for the following day would sort the matter. He puffed rhythmically, his pipe soon resembling a steaming locomotive. 'Do you find any fault with the plan in general gentlemen?' he asked finally.

'No sir,' said Gates.

'Guess not,' Liam agreed.

'Then your problems are simply personal,' Turner continued, 'and yet you have worked together before.'

'Hah,' spat Liam. 'Call that working together? The fucker left me.'

'I was under orders, you Irish prick.' Gates rose from his chair as he spoke, and Turner was gratified to see him finally addressing the other man directly. 'Besides, I even asked permission to wait for you, though God knows why.'

'Yeah, OK then, tell me why?' asked Liam, standing to face his adversary. 'If you hate me so bloody much, man, why did you ask to wait?'

'I don't leave a man on the ground if I can help it. Any man, even if he is a murdering I.R.A. bastard.'

'Murdering, is it? Murdering? Well for your information I was under fuckin' orders too,' yelled Liam.

'And the fucker I was dealing with *was* the R.A. you stupid English twat. I hate them just as much as you do. And I don't murder, I terminate. Ask yer man over there.'

'True,' acknowledged Turner as both men looked to him. He felt strangely like a marriage guidance councillor and, even with the bad language he detested so much, he had to fight the urge to smile.

'A leopard doesn't change his spots, mate, and I don't care what you say,' huffed Brian, though his tone had calmed a little.

'Aye, well, you're entitled to your opinion. You're just wrong,' asserted Liam as he returned to his chair and picked up the paperwork once more. 'Looks like we're bloody stuck with each other anyway. There's no chance of you changing your mind, like, Mr. Turner?' he asked.

'None. You two are perfect and, if we can finally put last year's job to rest, I'm sure you'll get on famously. The sergeant here dropped you off, you did your job, things took a turn and you were late back. Nevertheless he waited, and only left because he had no option. The Republicans were closing in and he was under strict instructions not to get caught. Now that's an end to it, OK?'

'Whatever you say,' sulked Liam.

'Yes sir,' Brian confirmed.

A few hours and several cups of tea later, Turner finally dismissed the men with the instruction to re-convene the following morning. Gates marched from the room, but Liam hesitated by the door.

'There is something you wish to ask me?' Turner suggested.

'Aye, Mr. Turner. Are you really sure yer man's up to this, like? I mean, look at the feller's face.'

'His face? Do you mean his scars? He can't help them, you know.'

'Oh really? Well as I see things, if he'd have shown a little more backbone and fought back a bit harder, he'd have never got 'em in the first place. Those scars he's got tell me a story; that he's either soft or he's easy but, either way, I don't want to put myself in a position where my life depends on someone who allows himself to get cut up like a side of bleedin' pork. If you need anyone, it's the feller who gave him those scars, not him.'

'But you have scars yourself Liam, so does the same apply to you? There's a new one on your lip, I see.'

'That was just a bit of shrapnel from the bus,' Liam informed him, but he fingered the deep, crescent shaped mark on his cheek. 'The fucker who gave me this one is dead.'

'Ahh, so that makes all the difference does it? Would it interest you to know how Sergeant Gates received his scars?'

'Aye, it might.'

'Well, seven years ago he was unfortunate enough to be on patrol in the suburbs of Londonderry. His squad was ambushed, cornered, and the men soon found themselves under heavy fire. The sergeant ran to take cover and return fire by the side of a parked car, but just at the very moment it blew up. You see, the scars were not acquired in a simple fist-fight. He got them from an exploding Ford Escort.'

'You're sure about that?'

'Oh yes. According to the file it said Ford Escort on the boot lid.'

'No, not about the bleedin' car, ya spanner, the scars. Are you sure that's how he got 'em?'

'Indeed, it's all very well documented, and there's one more thing. Following the initial bomb blast the sergeant was shot four times, once in the chest and three rounds in the stomach - and he *isn't* dead. That's four times, Liam, in one sitting so to speak. And that makes the man one very tough cookie indeed, at least that's as far as my thinking takes me. Does that alter your opinion, lad?'

'It might. See you tomorrow Mr. Turner.'

God how he hated bombers, Liam considered as he walked back to the small barracks assigned to him for his stay. Cowardly bastards the lot of 'em, though he had yet to get his head round the suicide crew he'd been with on that bus in Spain. He supposed he couldn't call them cowards if they were willing to die themselves. No, he really didn't know what to call them.

That was in the past, though. His future was what concerned him now and, for the next week at least, that involved a British soldier called Gates. He couldn't bring himself to like the man, but it did seem that they had more in common than he had realised.

4

A Bit of Pugilism

Liam and Brian arrived at the hut within seconds of each other the following morning. They nodded briefly in acknowledgement before taking seats as far apart as they could in the small waiting area until the corporal arrived and apologised profusely that they were out of tea.

'Thank fuck,' Gates murmured as the young lad left.

'Pissy anyway,' said Liam.

'What?'

'His tea. Don't mind it when Turner makes it good and strong, but that guy's tea is pissy.'

'Yeah,' Gates agreed. 'I'm more a coffee man meself.'

'Me too.'

Turner's head appeared round the doorway. 'Are we ready gentleman? We have places to be today.'

'Yes sir,' Gates acknowledged smartly and the three men walked outside.

'I'll organise some tea as soon as we get where we're going,' Turner informed them. 'Apparently we're out. Mind you,' he lowered his voice to a whisper, 'it's no great loss. I wouldn't like to tell the lad, but his tea is a little weak.'

He caught the smile that passed between his two companions and was pleasantly surprised. At least they weren't at each other's throats today.

A short journey in a battered jeep brought them to yet another innocuous looking hut and they entered to the sound of a heavy thud as a body hit the canvas of a boxing ring in the centre of the room.

'Oh dear,' Turner mused. 'It looks like we've missed the main event.'

'A boxing match?' asked Liam. 'That's what we're here for?'

'He's the regimental champion,' said Turner indicating a large man standing over the prone body in the ring. 'From Scotland they tell me, come to give us an exhibition.'

'And we've missed it? Oh great timing. Now there's no action.'

'Oh, I wouldn't be so sure my boy. There are still the unarmed combat lessons to come. That's quite a speciality of yours, isn't it Liam?'

'Aye,' Liam answered cautiously. 'Why are we here Mr. T?'

Turner turned to face his men. 'Well, you see, I've been asked to make sure that you're physically fit after your absence before we send you out into the field again. I need to assess the sergeant here too. I assume that's acceptable to you Brian?'

'Yes sir,' Gates answered emphatically, his eyes glinting in expectation. He looked across at Liam and noted the anticipation on his face. Clearly they both had the same idea. Turner was going to pit them against each other in the ring and they couldn't wait.

'Good. We'll just watch while these young lads go through their paces and then you can get ready,' Turner instructed with a smile as he looked back to the ring, his ears catching the hissed conversation behind him.

'I'm going to have you, Paddy.'

'No chance you fuckin' monkey hanging prick.'

There were around thirty recruits of varying abilities and the training session made for enjoyable entertainment for the next hour until Turner asked if they were ready. It seemed they were, if their expressions were anything to go by. 'Good,' he informed them. 'I think I've made my choices. I need to be sure you can handle the odds, do you see? It could be four against two, you know, and we have to be sure.'

'What?' asked Liam. 'What the Hell are you talking about man?'

'Sir?' Gates queried.

'Well if there's a problem and you can't take the bodyguards as planned, then it could be three of them against the two of you. Mr. Kane, our target, doesn't seem to be particularly handy, but I suppose he might have a go as well if his life were threatened.'

'The two of us?' Liam asked in amazement. 'Together?'

'We're not fighting each other, sir?' Gates joined in.

'Why on earth would you want to fight each other?' Turner asked, his confusion apparently genuine. 'You're on the same side and I need you to prove yourselves.'

'Prove myself, is it? What the fuck?' Liam spat at him. 'I've proved myself time and again you stupid idiot. I'll not be doing any proving here, and that's a fact. If there's any proving to be done, you can do it yer bleedin' self.'

He started to walk away, but Turner's calm voice behind him brought him to a halt. 'If that's what you want, Liam.'

'Mr. Turner, no sir,' Gates began, but Turner had already removed his coat.

'Hold my pipe would you, Brian?'

Liam was back at his side in an instant. 'Calm down, Mr. T, I was only joking,' he assured him.

'If that's your idea of a joke, Liam, I, for one, am not laughing. Are you suggesting that I'm past it?'

'No mate, it's not that, it's just… Oh come on, man, I was kiddin' around.'

'Maybe for the unarmed combat, I'll admit, but I think I've still got a bit of sparring left in me. Sergeant, a recruit if you please,' Turner called to the Scottish instructor as he marched to the ring and a young, fit looking squaddie was summoned to face him.

'You're a fucking cunt,' hissed Gates as he glared at Liam. 'Embarrassing the old bloke like that. I suppose you're gonna enjoy watching this are ya, eh me bonny lad? Fancy seeing him make a fool of himself by getting the shit knocked out of him do you, ya Paddy twat?'

Liam said nothing. His head, lowered in shame, did the talking for him.

Turner was now disrobed and the instructor was lacing up his gloves as the two men watched with the rest of the recruits from the side of the ring.

'I thought he'd have been in worse shape than that,' Brian whispered.

'Aye, me too. All that pipe smoking and professor type clothes.'

'There's a bit of a belly, mind.'

'It's not much of one though, is it? And look, he's got some fair old biceps on him, so he has,' Liam noted.

'Yeah, but still. The man's fucking ancient and you're still a fucking cunt.'

'You've made your point,' Liam hissed. 'Shite.'

'Just do your best lad, and remember there's no shame in losing old chap,' they heard Turner say to the young recruit facing him as they touched gloves.

'Oh fuck,' said Liam.

'I can't bear to watch,' Gates agreed.

The young opponent looked hesitant, glancing at his instructor to check that he was really supposed to be doing this, but he received the nod and the sound of his mates' taunting finally spurred him to action. He started slowly, trying a couple of air jabs as Turner kept his feet planted in one place, his guard up. The lad moved in closer and aimed a couple of strikes, but only connected with arms that successfully fended him off. He darted in again with another jab, but his opponent's glove fielded the blow.

'Come on Dinger, stop pissin' about,' came a shout from one onlooker, while others contributed whistles and jeers.

Dinger sprang on his toes and tried again, jab after jab, but he couldn't find his target. Frustrated now, he began to skip about, electrified by the energy of youth. He came in for the kill, attacking with a flurry of blows… and then he was on his back.

The room was silent for several seconds before a lone voice said, 'Fuck me, and with just a single left hook.'

'Language Liam,' Turner said calmly, his feet still in the same place on the canvas, before the room erupted and drowned out his voice with cheers while a dazed Dinger struggled to his feet.

Turner threw off his gloves, jumped nimbly to the ground and walked towards them. 'Thanks old boy,' he said as he collected his pipe from Brian's motionless hand.

'Holy shite, where did that come from?' Liam asked.

'My friend, you should never judge a book by its cover,' Turner said calmly.

'So what were you, then? S.A.S, a Para, a marine, some sort of special forces bleedin' ninja trained killer Mr. Turner?'

'You can ask all you want old chap, but I couldn't possibly comment. Let's just say I am an old soldier, and we'll leave it at that shall we? Now I think you owe me that proof.' The crowd parted respectfully as he walked away.

Brian and Liam stood together in the ring some minutes later waiting while Turner was conversing with a group of recruits.

'You up for this, Nancy boy?' Gates asked.

'Guess I'll have to be, but it's you I'd rather be facing, like.'

'Yeah, well, we've got no argument there.'

Turner entered the ring with three of the youngest trainees and held up his hand. 'Gentlemen, this is to be a free-style, gloves off bout. I want you all to give it your best but, if we could avoid any fatalities or serious injuries, I would be most grateful.' He produced a small whistle. 'Whenever you're ready gentlemen,' he said, then blew a short, shrill blast and retreated quickly from the ring.

The three opponents advanced as one and, as Gates moved to meet them, Liam thrust out his leg to trip him. In the same movement he took out one of the lads with a swift punch to the chin. The second received an elbow in his eye while the third sustained a broken nose from a head butt. By the time Gates was back on his feet Liam stood victorious over the three recruits.

'Now who's the Nancy?' he grinned.

'Cunt,' hissed Gates, but Liam ignored him.

'Proved myself have I then Mr. Turner?' he asked the man standing at the side.

'Unfortunately so,' Turner assured him and the smile fell from Liam's face as three far more impressive looking men, and one very large Scottish sergeant, were entering the fray.

'Oh fuck, now, yer man there. Him I didn't fancy,' murmured Liam.

'Me neither,' Gates agreed.

'Sure you're up for this, you monkey hanger?'

'As long as I've got someone at my back,' Brian spat, and there was no time for further discussion as the whistle sounded again.

Six men circled each other slowly for several seconds until one of them let impatience get the better of him. He lunged directly at Liam who took him straight out with a swift upper cut. 'Just evening the odds,' he announced, but his words were cut off as a large Scottish fist came within inches of his face, avoided only as Gates leapt and grabbed the instructor round the waist, forcing him backwards. Liam had just a second to recover before the two remaining recruits were on him, one at his front, the other attempting a strangle hold from the rear. In one movement

Liam thrust his elbow backwards, catching the guy in the solar plexus, and dipped his head to bring it up sharply under the other lad's chin. There was a sickening crunch, and both men were down.

As Liam steadied himself he took a quick step sideways, only just avoiding Gates who came flying backwards towards him as he was thrown from the Scotsman's arms. Brian bounced from the ropes, straight back on his feet, as the lad who had sampled Liam's elbow quickly recovered and threw a well aimed punch at Gates. He wobbled, but countered with a thrust and then tripped the lad, jumping on him the next second and the two were rolling around on the ground like Greek wrestlers.

Liam didn't have time to pay attention as the Scottish sergeant approached. He was taking his time. No impatient lunges for this experienced soldier and Liam found himself retreating to the ropes, step by step, as he held his fists in readiness. His small stature usually played to his advantage. Opponents were caught off guard by his speed and his lack of height regularly gave him an edge when it came to the head butt straight up under the jaw. Trouble was, he doubted he could reach this guy's jaw. The fucker was huge.

He felt the ropes at his back and knew he must strike. One, two, three he caught the sergeant in the ribs, but it seemed to have little effect. Huge fists came back at him and he took a couple of painful blows in the face as he felt his lip split. He sank to his knees, but then ducked quickly under the man's arms, finally getting himself off the ropes. The sergeant was quickly back on him though, moving nimbly for such a big man. Another heavy punch caught him in the gut and the wind left his lungs as he felt his legs begin to buckle. This wasn't going well. Bent double now he took the only course open to him and surged forwards, his head crashing into his opponent's belly. He was gratified to hear a grunt and see the man sway, but was then amazed as he fell, face first, to the ground with a thud.

Gates had him round the ankles and Liam cast a sideways glance to see the third recruit out cold. The first eager young man was now back on his feet and repeated his lunge at Liam, but one swift punch had him out of the game again. Now, with just the huge sergeant remaining, Liam jumped on his back while his partner retained a hold on his legs. Gates was taking a few solid back-kicks to the chin, but he didn't let go and Liam finally straddled the Scotsman, forcing an arm under his huge neck and pulling his head back. For several seconds he kept the strangle hold until, at last, he was rewarded by a thumping sound on the canvas as the sergeant finally admitted defeat. The whistle blew and Liam relaxed his grip.

'Medical attention for this lad,' he heard Turner say of the recruit he'd taken out with his head. Gates' wrestling partner was rising groggily to his feet while the over-eager lad was sitting up looking dazed. Liam dismounted the Scot and offered his hand to help him up while Brian stood pulling jaw-grinding faces to check that nothing was broken from the kicking he'd received.

'Excellent,' Turner announced.

'Aye, you've got something there for a wee lad,' agreed the large sergeant as he shook Liam's hand.

'You too Jock,' Liam acknowledged. 'Where did you learn to fight like that?

'The old tenements in Easterhouse, Glasgow. Grew up with three older sisters,' he grinned back.

'Can't have been any tougher than Hartlepool,' Gates offered as he joined the conversation.

'Lord help me,' laughed the Scot. 'I've been taken out by a midget and a monkey hanger.'

'I think you'll find you were taken out by teamwork, dear boy,' Turner suggested. 'Thank you so much for your help, sergeant.'

'A pleasure, sir. You've got good men there, but I'd say you've also got a bit of a problem,' Jock suggested.

'I am aware of it,' Turner acknowledged, 'but we are making progress.'

'Well, good luck sir, and I'll leave you to it,' the Scot offered in parting.

As Brian moved away to collect his clothes, Liam asked, 'What now Mr. T? I guess you've had your proof.'

'Well, Liam, I would suggest that you had earned a pint, but I don't know if you're old enough to drink.'

'What the f...?'

'You proved your physical fitness and your fighting skills to me, but you also proved yourself to be immature and childish, tripping your partner like that. I believe that

Sergeant Gates proved himself to be the better man and I have seen enough for one day.'

As Liam watched Turner walk away he felt the sting of the words and knew that his plan had backfired. His intention had been to let Turner see that he didn't need Gates, but it hadn't played out that way and the dismissive way that his handler had finished the conversation was so unlike him that he knew he'd had a serious fall from grace. Bollocks.

Gates was returning and had Liam's clothes over his arm. He threw them at him and turned to walk away, but Liam called him back. 'Buy you a pint?'

'What, so you can throw it in my face? That trip was a low fuckin' trick.'

'Look mate, I know you could just have let me get the shite kicked out of me back there and I reckon I owe you a drink at least. Why did you do it? You could've just left me.'

'Someone had to do something. Your legs were going that quick I expected to see you on your back crying *Mama, Mama*, you Nancy prick.'

'Ah fuck you. It was a genuine fuckin' question. If you don't want to tell me, then…'

'Self-preservation,' Gates interrupted. 'He'd have had you, but then he'd have come for me. That was one big fucker.'

'Well you've got that bang on, so you have.'

'Besides, us northern boys got to stick together and I'll give you one thing, you're quick on your feet. I reckon I can do this one job with you, just don't expect us ever to be friends.'

'You're on. So, will you be fancying that pint about now?'

'Just the one?'

'Two would be better.'

Turner watched from a dark corner of the room as they headed off in search of the Mess and allowed himself a small smile of relief. It had all unfolded just as he'd hoped it would and he knew that Liam had learned a valuable lesson. Despite what he had led the men to believe, this pairing wasn't his idea at all.

***

'He's gone off script too many times, Anthony,' his colleague had said to him the previous week as they sipped brandy in the extremely private gentlemen's club.

'You are aware of the jobs he's done, aren't you Michael?' Turner had countered. 'Who else could we have sent to terminate Mad Dog O'Brien in that way?'

'That was a bloody one, I admit.'

'And on top of that I had to order that he be left behind, but he found his way back to us.'

'Eventually, but he didn't make contact. He broke all protocols.'

'Yes, and he was severely reprimanded for that. You stood him down for months, testing him with boredom. Yet still he continued to work for us,' Turner had said, his voice rising from its normal, quiet pitch.

'And this latest episode in Spain?'

'He was blown up by a bus full of suicide bombers. No one knew that was coming and I'd like to know how you would have handled it.'

'Okay, Anthony, okay,' Michael had accepted. 'I agree the circumstances were strange and I know you value the lad.'

'He's the best I've seen, but he needs his motivation. He needs to know that he will get the buggers who had his mother killed. I apologise for my language, but I assure you that Mr. O'Neil would express it in far stronger terms. You have seen the file. You know his history. I am absolutely sure that if we don't get him back in the fold then he will pursue his own agenda.'

'Then we will have no option but to terminate him.'

'And, if you do that, you will lose one of the most valuable assets that we have. It would be a bloody stupid move. Now, can I retrieve him from Spain or not?'

'This is his last chance, Anthony,' Michael had relented with a sigh. 'It's only your reputation and belief in him that is saving him right now, but he must be watched. It's a two man job the next time or you can forget it.'

***

Brian Gates' file showed that he had fought in several covert operations in different African countries, completed four tours of Ulster and been involved in a year-long, highly deniable undercover operation in the province. This made the sergeant the obvious choice for the retrieval mission from Spain and for the Dillon Kane job on his own turf, but Turner had known he needed to force the issue of trust between the two men. He just hoped that it would be enough, and to see them walking off together was the best news he'd had in many days.

'I could really do with a decent cup of tea,' he decided. 'Now, I wonder what on earth a monkey hanger could be.'

5

Cars, Houses and Monkeys

'Home?' Liam asked the next morning as he put aside his cup of weak tea. It seemed like the corporal had replenished supplies. 'You mean I get to go back to Spain?'

'Derbyshire,' Turner informed him. 'You'll be back in Spain soon enough, I promise.'

'Three days, sir?' Gates asked for confirmation.

'Yes, I don't think we can achieve anything further here. You know the plan and you know your rendezvous point. You may have the intervening time off.'

'Thank you, sir. There are some matters I could do to deal with at home.'

As Gates left the room Liam was about to follow, but Turner called him back. Shite, was he in for a lecture about tripping Gates? The subject had been avoided during the brief morning conference, but he felt it was unfinished business.

'Dear boy, I am confused,' Tuner said. 'Why do you call the sergeant a monkey hanger?'

'Because he's from Hartlepool,' Liam informed him with relief at the unexpected subject.

'And that means what, precisely?'

'Are you seriously telling me you've never heard that term before?'

'No old chap, I can honestly say that I have never heard that expression in my entire life. Is it an Irish saying for a rifle marksman?'

'Irish? No mate. It's an English expression,' Liam began with a smirk. 'You see, back in the Napoleonic wars a French ship sank off the coast of Hartlepool. The only survivor was the ship's mascot, a bedraggled little monkey who washed up on the beach wearing a French uniform. The locals who found him hadn't ever seen a Frenchman before and thought he could be a spy, so they held a trial for him on the beach. Because the monkey couldn't answer their questions they reckoned that he must really be a spy. So, the poor little feller was sentenced to death and hanged from the mast of a fishing boat. Apparently, Mr. Turner, that's a true story. Ask Gates if you don't believe me.'

Turner shook his head in disbelief and let out a small laugh. 'Tall tales. So it's one of those odd friendly terms, then?'

'Can be,' Liam agreed. 'We're not friends, Mr. T, but the man's not as bad as I thought he was. For a Brit, of course.'

'That's a great relief, my boy. I really can't express strongly enough how crucial it is that you work well together on this job. Crucial. Do you understand what I'm saying?'

'Mr. Turner, I rarely understand what you're saying,' Liam had laughed before he noted the almost sad look on the other man's face. 'Don't worry, Mr. T, we'll be fine,' he assured him.

Liam walked from hut E, wondering what could be so crucial about this particular job, and looked for the army transport he expected to take him back to the manor house that the government had provided for him in Derbyshire. There was nothing, and he was about to go back inside to ask how on earth he was supposed to get home, when he heard the sound of an engine approaching. A sleek Jaguar saloon pulled up in front of him and the corporal, he of the pissy tea, exited with a salute.

'That's my car,' said Liam in surprise.

'I believe so sir,' said the corporal.

'It's in Spain.'

'Sir?'

'I left that in Spain.'

'I wouldn't know about that, sir. Mr. Turner told me to valet it yesterday and bring it here this morning.'

'But it wasn't even at the same side of the country. I was in the east and I abandoned that in the west months ago. How the fuck does Turner always find everything?'

'Sir,' said the corporal, lowering his voice, 'I have found it best not to ask how Mr. Turner does anything.'

'Aye, you have a point, Corporal,' Liam acknowledged. 'Thanks, mate.'

Liam drove off to find the first main road. He wasn't actually sure where he was and needed to get his bearings. Then it was to the manor bound. It wasn't a bad little place, but oh how he would prefer to be going back to Montse. He longed to make contact with her. She must be frantic with worry by now, but he had given Turner his word. Ah well, if everything went as it should he could be on his way back to Spain very soon.

6

Newcastle - the Hotel - the Window - and the 'Right' Irishman

Liam pushed open the hotel door and the two men stepped swiftly inside. Turner had provided the key and neither man queried how it had been arranged. They hadn't had to check in and could never be identified as having been there and that was all that mattered.

Gates moved quickly to the window and assessed his vantage point. 'Perfect,' he announced.

'Looks like an easy shot to me,' Liam agreed, 'but you're the expert. At least that's what Turner reckons. Can't see why we'd need such an expert for this, though. It's only a few shots across the street.'

'I am a fucking expert. You may be handy with your fists, me bonny lad, but no one matches me with the sniper rifle. Besides, there's no such thing as an easy shot in the dark and in this weather,' Brian informed him as yet another clap of thunder shook the sky. June was proving to be a very stormy month and the rain hailed down.

'Yeah, well, even if you're the best, the cream, the king, a super-fuckin' star, just remember one thing will ya?'

'What's that then?'

'To hit the right fucking' Irishman. Don't want you mistaking me for one of them fellers.'

'Well keep out of the bleedin' shadows so I can see you, then I can't get mixed up can I, you cocky fuckin' tosser,' Brian spat at him. 'Anyway, I always hit what I aim at.'

'You'd better be right or I'll come back here and tear yer fuckin' head off, then take a shite down the bleedin' hole.'

'Look, you do your job and I'll do mine. There's just one thing I don't get.'

'What?' Liam asked.

'Why I don't just take out the target as well as the bodyguards. I don't see why you're needed.'

'Because any useless tosser can just shoot someone, but it takes a feller with real balls to do someone up close with a knife.'

Brian sighed. 'You're a right twat, Paddy. I meant, why is the knife necessary? Dead's dead.'

'I know, but Turner says the top brass need to make a point. You know, like you can't come preaching to our kids and, if you do, you'll be sent home in tiny pieces.'

'Christ.'

'Aye.'

Gates began preparing the scope on his Dragunov while Liam checked and cleaned his back up 9mm pistol. 'Clinical cleanliness always,' he whispered to himself as he repeated the mantra of his old trainer, Collins. The constant checking, cleaning and oiling of his weapons had served him well over the years and he'd never had a single weapon jam on him. Next he turned his attention his trusty knife, *The Killer*, stropping the blade up and down against leather and checking the metal against his thumb. He couldn't even feel the small cut he gave himself, so sharp was the weapon. He was ready.

'How much longer till dusk?' Brian asked

'Still about an hour I'd say. There's a kettle and some coffee here. Fancy a cup?'

'Aye, if you're offering.'

Drinks in hand they went over the plan one more time. It was simple enough, as long as Turner's information was accurate. Dillon Kane and three guards would arrive at the hotel opposite under cover of darkness. Liam was to lie in wait and, once Gates had taken out the guards, kill Dillon Kane in the most brutal way that time would allow. They hadn't factored in the storm, but the upside was that it seemed to be keeping everyone at home and the streets were quiet.

'It's time,' Liam announced as he stubbed out a fag and prepared to leave, 'and remember, I'm the fuckin' good guy.'

Once outside, Liam pulled up his collar to combat the strong wind and rain, then sprinted across the road and up a short driveway to take his place against a cold, wet hotel wall just to the side of the main entrance. 'Won't be long now Dillon, pal. You should've stayed in Ireland mate,' he tutted to himself as he considered the man's cheek. 'Think you can just come and stir up trouble, do you? This is their country for fuck's sake and you should've known better. The Brits aren't gonna have a sense of humour about shite like that.'

A couple of cars passed by as he shrunk back into the shadows and waited. Christ, he hoped this weather hadn't made them change their plans. It really was severe. Turner said it had been raining coal and crabs down south, which he would have disbelieved had it been anyone else telling him. Half an hour later he was soaked to the skin and beginning to worry when a pair of headlights rounded a corner, momentarily blinding him. As he focused again he could tell it was a dark coloured BMW, as the information had suggested, and it was slowing. This had to be them.

The car pulled to a stop just at the roadside and he watched as four figures got out and hastily raised umbrellas in preparation for a dash up the path to the door. Liam had just seconds to worry that the umbrellas would obscure Gates' view before one of the men went down. The sniper rifle was silenced anyway, but the rain drowned out even the smallest sound of gunfire and it looked as if the man had just slipped. A second guy appeared to trip over him and then a third, looking round in concern, lurched forward and hit the floor alongside his friends. That left just one man and his brolly staring in confusion at the men at his feet.

He registered the fact that something was seriously wrong here and his self-preservation instinct kicked in. He began running back to the vehicle, but a window shattered and the car body was raked with gunfire. As he turned back to try for the hotel door an unseen foot sent him crashing, head first, onto the hard, wet tarmac. The shock of the fall momentarily dazed him, but he quickly shook himself and attempted to get back on his feet. He couldn't move. Something was holding him down and, as his head was jerked upwards, a strong hand was clamped across his mouth and he found himself staring into a dark face.

'Dillon Kane,' Liam hissed, 'are you fuckin' stupid or what skin? You should know better than this. You just can't go strolling around here pal. The Brits have ordered me to send you back home in pieces.'

Dillon's eyes flew wide open in panic. He'd been assured that this visit was secret. No one but the boys knew; he'd been guaranteed that.

'What? Wha... what?'

Liam looked down at the trembling figure beneath him. 'Not to worry, Dillon old son, I'll try to make this quick, but you see, I've been told to make it bloody too. Sorry mate.'

Through terrified eyes the target watched in horror as the man holding him down pulled a knife from his pocket. He pressed the button and its blade sprang out, intensifying his fear a thousand-fold. He was unable to tear his eyes away as he stared in petrified fascination at the lettering he could just make out down the side of the weapon. MATADOR. Killer. It might as well have spelled THE END.

'Cat got yer tongue, has it?' hissed the voice in his ear. 'Well I suppose some final words are in order. Goodbye Dillion Kane - I'll see you in Hell, so I will.' Liam stared deep into the eyes of his captive as he dug the blade slowly into the side of his neck. 'It'll be over in a minute mate, so don't you worry.'

The last sounds Dillon Kane ever heard were muted gurgles as he began choking on his own blood. The final image he took to the afterlife was one of his killer's face and its evil grin as the man began slowly carving from one side of his throat to the other.

Liam crouched over the bleeding, still twitching body and, only now, did he risk a quick look around. The original plan had involved getting Kane swiftly out of sight round the side of the hotel before the kill, but the storm made that unnecessary and the whole scenario had unfolded without drawing any attention. Still, he needed to be away from here right now and, as he rose from the body, he thought he heard something above the rain and then felt a sharp sting as a single bullet tore through his jacket and skimmed across the top of his shoulder.

Ignoring the pain he was instantly down, bent at the waist and running towards the hotel on the opposite side of the street.

He bounded up the stairs and burst into the room. 'What the fuck are you doing, you maniac?' he screamed at Gates, who was hurriedly packing away his rifle and the rest of his kit.

'Leave it. We've got to get out of here now. And keep your voice down you idiot.'

'Leave it?' Liam yelled before taking a deep breath to control himself. 'Leave it?' he repeated in an angry whisper. You fuckin' shot me.'

'No,' Gates hissed as he placed the last of his equipment in his bag, 'you stood up into the shot I took at the movement behind you.'

'What fuckin' movement?' Liam asked as he recalled the sound he thought he had heard.

'Look, it was probably just a shadow, but we've got to get out of here and we've got to go now.'

Liam grabbed for his bag and the two men headed off, down the stairs, out to the side street where they had left their vehicle and were on the road within seconds, Gates at the wheel. They drove in silence for several miles.

'Look, if I'd been shooting at you, you'd be dead,' Brian finally offered.

'Maybe,' Liam acknowledged. He'd been thinking exactly that for the last few minutes, and he had heard something the moment he felt the shot. The thing was, as he dwelled on it now, he was pretty sure the sound had been that of a bullet whizzing past his ear. That didn't mean that Gates hadn't seen something behind him, but he looked across at his companion with unease.

'Is it bad?' Gates asked.

'Nah, just a graze,' Liam assured him as he wished he could tell what the other man was thinking, because he wasn't at all sure what to make of his own thoughts.

The silence in the car returned, accompanied by the storm which continued to rage around them. The rain finally lessened as they made their way south and Brian indicated the illuminated sign of a *Little Chef*. 'Fancy something to eat, bonny lad?' he suggested.

The friendliness seemed forced to Liam's ears, but it could just be paranoia.

'Look, you can stay here and sulk if you like,' Gates continued, 'but I'm starving.'

'Aye, all right,' Liam agreed as the car pulled into the park.

'Gimme a full English please, Tracey,' Brian requested of the waitress who greeted their arrival.

She seemed momentarily confused before realising her nametag had given her away and this little pleasantry eased her initial fear. She was used to all sorts of hard looking men walking into this place, but these two had so many facial scars between them that they looked scarier than most. The one who had spoken seemed friendly enough, but the other was wearing a dark mood on his face and a blood stain on his shirt that she really didn't want to know about. 'And what do you fancy my luv?' she asked him as casually as she could.

Still deep in thought Liam had been caught off guard a little. 'Erm, for me? Oh yeah, bacon and eggs, over easy, please darlin',' he requested.

Tracey frowned at him. 'How's that for your eggs d'ya say hinney?'

'Oh right. Aye, sorry darlin' I was miles away. I meant to say a couple of eggs and bacon please luv.' He smiled at her then and saw her relax. To Brian's equally puzzled expression he explained, 'Spent some time in America, and they have a strange way with eggs over there, so they do.'

'Tea, bread and butter?' Tracey offered and the two men nodded as they took their seats. They were the only customers and Tracey appeared to be the only staff.

'So, bonny lad, job done and with no problems. Just a quick in and out eh?' said the sergeant.

'If you call getting shot in the fuckin' shoulder no problem, then yeah, I suppose it was,' replied Liam as he pulled out a fag.

'Oh stop yer bleedin' moanin' lad, you're like an old woman. Jesus, it's only a bleedin' crease.'

The two men smoked in silence, then ate their meal in silence and then smoked some more. Liam glanced across at the sergeant who was staring out of the window, any semblance of fake friendliness now absent.

'You thinking about shooting the feller you're supposed to be protecting?' he ventured.

Gates jumped at the question. 'Fuck off,' he hissed. 'I *was* protecting you. I've just got things on my mind, OK?'

'What things?'

'Private shit. None of your fucking business.'

'Well, maybe it is my business if it means I end up with a bullet in my shoulder,' Liam suggested as he detected a genuine despondency in the man.

'It's got nothing to do with that. Jesus, man, you're sounding like a dripping tap.'

'Well, I'm gonna keep on drippin' until you tell me what's up 'cause, one way or another, I don't think you're fit for duty. Listen, if you need to get something off your chest, run it by me. I'll not be tellin' anyone.'

Gates stared at him as he stubbed out his cigarette. Finally he sighed. 'It's the wife, all right? The bleedin' bitch buggered off. She's gone and left me.'

'Ah, Jesus, and sure that's bad news. Sorry mate. Another feller is it then?'

'No idea bonny lad. All I know is I got the divorce papers a few days ago. The cow had her lawyer post 'em to me.'

'Shite, that's fuckin' cold, you know. So, no chance of getting back together then eh?'

'No chance in Hell. Besides, if she's gone this far she can fucking well keep away as far as I'm concerned.'

'So sign the papers and get rid of her then. What's stopping you?'

'Horror stories lad, horror stories,' said Gates as he shook his head from side to side.

'What do you mean mate?' asked Liam.

'You know, the sort of tales you hear about blokes getting totally skinned in bad divorces.'

'So you reckon she'd get everything then, do you?'

'No mate, there's not that much for her to get. But, the thing is - well I've seen a little flat you see, and I want it, but I don't want her, or her fucking dragon of a mother, getting their hands on it in a bloody divorce settlement.'

'Ahh right. So you've only just bought it then eh?'

'No bonny lad, you're not listening. I don't have it yet, but if I can scrape the money together I'll buy it, and I don't fancy the idea of a bleedin' divorce judge forcing me to split it with her.'

'So, why don't you just go ahead and buy it and keep it secret from her then.'

'I know. The thing is, I don't have the money just yet.'

'So take on an extra job then. A bloke like you can always get work in security or something.'

'Aye lad, you're right - this is something I've been mulling over for the past couple of days.'

'So do you have a job offer then?' asked Liam.

'Maybe lad, maybe. Anyhow, how about another cup of tea, then we'll get off eh?'

Liam looked up to call Tracey, but stopped as he saw a large man holding her firmly by the arms. 'Now that doesn't look good,' he whispered to Gates. 'Did you see that feller come in?'

Gates glanced over his shoulder and shook his head. 'Looks like a domestic, I reckon. Best stay out of it.'

Liam narrowed his eyes and watched as the man prodded the waitress with his finger and mouthed what looked to be threats. He rose slowly to his feet and felt Brian's hand on his arm, but he shook it off. 'If you can stand by and watch a woman get threatened, then that's up to you, but I can't,' he said quietly as he moved towards the scene.

'Oh fuck,' Brian said under his breath. He doubted Liam would need any help in a one to one, but he'd better be ready just in case.

The man seemed oblivious of his approach as Liam saw the fear on the girl's face. 'Oi, what's your bleedin' problem pal?' he demanded.

The man instantly released Tracey's arms as he spun on his heels to face Liam. 'Who the fuck are you?' he snapped. 'Don't tell me you're her new bloke. She's kicked me out for a short-arsed pillock like you?'

'I met this lady tonight,' said Liam evenly.

'Then fuck off before I flatten you, you little tosser. This is mine and Tracey's business - it's got fuck all to do with you.'

Liam stood his ground and repeated slowly, 'I - asked - what - your - problem - is - pal?'

'You, you're my fucking problem - now fuck off.' The man again turned to face Tracey. 'And you're not getting the fucking dog back either. In fact I think I'll drown the little bastard.'

'Oh no, not Jasper. Please Donny don't, please,' she begged him through tearful eyes. 'There's no one else. I've told you. It's just, oh Donny, you know it's not working out.'

'Oi, you had better walk out now while you still can mate,' Liam insisted.

'Please go, hinney,' Tracey whispered. 'He's got an awful temper. You've got no chance.'

'Yeah, that's the only thing she's got right,' Donny grinned as he raised his fist and swung at Liam.

In one movement Liam caught the fist in his hand, head butted the guy and swung him round with his arm up behind his back. Then he let him fall to the ground in a crumpled heap. He was out cold. 'You okay there, are you luv?' Liam asked Tracey without taking a breath.

'Y…yes,' she stammered.

'Don't worry, he won't be back,' Liam assured her as he bent to grab Donny's legs and began to drag him to the door. 'And don't you bother yourself to help,' he yelled over at Gates who sat, casually smoking.

'No intention of it mate,' Brian assured him. 'You seem to have it all in hand.'

When Liam reappeared a few minutes later he had a small black puppy in his arms. 'Jasper?' he guessed.

'Oh yes, thank you,' Tracey whimpered from the comfort of Brian's arm round her shoulder. 'I don't know whatever possessed me to get mixed up with him in the first place. He was so jealous and I never gave him any reason.

'Look, you'd better go,' she continued. 'My boss will be back soon and Donny might have called the police. Your meal is on me.'

'There'll be no police,' Liam assured her.

'You stay safe, love,' Brian added as he ignored the offer of a free meal and threw several notes on the counter. 'If this man here says Donny won't be bothering you again, you can believe him.'

As the two men walked from the café they left a young waitress cradling a puppy in her arms and crying softly.

'So, where'd he go?' Brian asked as soon as they were out of earshot.

'Forget him, just like you forgot to help me,' Liam snapped.

'Hey man, that wasn't our fight.'

'So you can sit back and see a woman get treated like that? Or have you just got a downer on all women because of your wife?'

'Well, you may have a point there. You reckon she was cheating on him?'

'Don't know. Not my business, is it? But there's just no excuse for hitting a woman, that's all.'

'Okay, I get it. You sure he won't be back?'

'Aye, I'm sure,' Liam said as he climbed behind the wheel and they drove onto the A1 heading south.

The Brotherton turning was just behind them as a dull, rhythmic thudding came from the rear of the car.

'We got a flat?' asked Brian.

Liam ignored him.

'Hey, have you gone deaf laddie? Can't you hear that?'

'Aye, I can hear it,' Liam agreed as he turned off at Ferrybridge and pulled into a dark lay-by under the A1 bridges, 'but that isn't a flat tyre.'

'So what the hell is it then?' asked Brian as he followed his partner out into the early dawn and walked to the back of the car where Liam opened the boot.

'Oh fuck,' whispered Brian as he looked into the bloodied face of Donny. 'You're not right in the head man.'

'You basta…' Donny began as he tried to sit up, but he was immediately silenced by the snub nosed .38 that Liam held to his head.

'Got nothing to say for yourself then?' asked Liam.

'Wha…what?' Donny stammered. 'Listen, man, I had to keep her in line. A good slap every now and then never did anyone any harm…'

…and this time he was silenced by Gates with a hand to his throat. 'Fuckin' wife beater,' he spat. 'I reckon you were right about him mate,' he said as he turned to Liam, 'but I'd say a bullet was too good for him.'

'And I'd say you'd got a point,' Liam agreed as he pocketed the pistol and replaced it with *The Killer*, holding it under Donny's chin. He slowly slid the back of the blade up the side of his face and then turned it to make a small cut on his cheek. 'Just a little something to remember me by,' he offered, 'and I'll be checking back on that wee girl in a few days. I do not expect her to have seen you again. If she does, you're a dead man and that's for sure. Do I make myself clear?'

Donny nodded slowly as Gates pulled him from the boot and set him roughly on his feet. 'I'd suggest the M62 west mate.'

'Or the A1 south,' Liam added, 'because the north-east has just become fuckin' dangerous ground for you. I'm sure you get my meaning there. Do you, eh, sonny?'

Again Donny nodded. Gates pushed him away and the two assassins watched as Tracey's ex-boyfriend stumbled off in the morning light.

'Looks like he's heading to the southbound lane,' Gates noted a few moments later as the figure disappeared from view.'

'Aye.'

'I don't reckon he'll be calling the police.'

'No, I wouldn't be thinking he would.'

'So we can go now?'

'Aye.'

'That was an interesting night,' Gates said as he climbed into the car, 'and my feeling is that Turner never needs to know about the extra curricula activities.'

'Probably best,' Liam agreed as they headed out on the road once more.

7

A Well Deserved bit
of R & R

The debrief had been completed and Turner was happy with their work. The papers were full of the gruesome discovery of four bodies outside a hotel in Newcastle. The Irish connection had quickly been identified and the police were looking at political motivation.

'Just what we were after,' Turner said over his tea. 'You two work well together.'

Neither Liam nor Brian had commented and the meeting came to a close. Gates left straightaway, but Liam hung back.

'I think you need to forgive the sergeant,' Turner offered, guessing at Liam's concerns. 'His explanation for the shot that grazed you was perfectly rational. Even you admit you stood up at just the wrong moment.'

'I know, but I just can't shake the feeling that it wasn't an accident.'

'I would say, Liam, that if a marksman of Sergeant Gates' calibre had wanted you dead, then you would be dead. Besides, what possible motivation could he have had?'

'He doesn't like me much. Maybe he just wanted to make a point.'

'It's possible, but I suggest we accept the official explanation and leave it at that. Besides, the job is done and there is nothing in the foreseeable future that would put you together again.'

'About that foreseeable future, Mr. Turner. Did you clear it for me to go back to Spain like you promised?'

'I am a man of my word, Liam, and you have a week.'

'Thanks, Mr. T. A week will do nicely,' said Liam shaking the older man's hand and taking his leave.

The following afternoon he was driving off the Pride of Bilbao ferry, the deep metallic blue of his Jaguar glistening in the strong Spanish sunlight. The engine gave a muted growl as he gunned the sleek car in the direction of Catalunya, a small farm and a girl called Montse. He was nervous about the reception he would receive. He had tried to call several times in the last twenty-four hours but there had been no reply. Maybe it was the phone system, which wasn't that great in rural Spain, or maybe there was no one home. Ah well, he would know soon enough.

The journey seemed to take forever, but by early evening he was finally driving down a long farm track and approaching the house. A dim light shone from the kitchen window, which gave him hope as he pulled up and switched off the engine. As he opened his door he heard 'Qui es?' from somewhere inside the house.

'Montse, lass, it's me,' he called out nervously.

He heard a bolt slide back, which immediately saddened him. The door had never been locked before and it was clear the occupant was scared. Slowly the door opened and the business end of a double-barrelled shotgun poked out. He moved to stand directly in line with the weapon, making himself clearly visible to the person holding it. He saw the gun begin to shake and then the door flew wide. The weapon was tossed aside and Montse stood unsteadily for a second before crumpling to her knees and covering her face with her hands.

'Oh lass, I'm so sorry,' Liam said as he moved quickly to her and placed his hands on her shoulders.

'Darren?' she finally managed, and it was wonderful to hear his old name on her lips, albeit through her tears.

'Aye love,' he said softly as he raised her to her feet.

She looked at him for a second and then threw her arms round his neck. 'I thought you were dead,' she cried.

The dawn light was barely hitting the window the following morning and Montse was already packed. The previous day had been spent in explanation and apology, the language changing rapidly between English and Spanish, as they each rushed to fill the other in on what had happened. Darren was relieved to hear that Montse had been released from custody as soon as he had been extracted from Spain, though she hadn't been told any of the details. The police had accused her of harbouring a fugitive, but had let her go with a warning and she had spent the next days, nearly two weeks now, locked in her home and grieving for the man she feared dead.

The passion that followed had been a hurried, fumbling affair, born of need and desperation until finally Montse had calmed and they made love again, eventually falling asleep in each other's arms. Now she was up and scared once more. Her brothers, Alex and Esteban, had also been released by the police with just a warning, but they weren't grieving. They were angry and blamed Darren for everything and he could hardly disagree there. Thankfully they had been away at a party when he arrived, but were due back some time today. The plan was to be long gone before they came home and it was just 7am when the pair set off in the car, heading for La Seu.

Darren looked across at Montse and smiled sadly. The poor girl seemed terrified. She had thought her lover dead, she had to escape the wrath of her brothers and now the only safe place he could think of to take her was into the arms of E.T.A. freedom fighters. He would understand if she was simply wishing she had never met him.

'They don't bite,' he had assured her. 'The Spanish government may label the whole lot of them as murdering terrorists, but they're not animals you know.'

'Well, all right,' she finally acquiesced, 'if you think it would be appropriate and acceptable for me to meet them.'

'Acceptable? Now why the Hell wouldn't it be? They're as much family to me as you are and I'm sure they'd love to meet you.'

She hadn't seemed convinced and Darren spent most of the journey chatting about nothing in particular while Montse said very little. Eventually they turned off the main road and headed up an overgrown dirt track. After a mile or so even that petered out and they left the car to make the rest of the trek on foot, trudging ever upwards into the middle of nowhere. Darren considered that he spent an inordinate amount of his time in the middle of places that looked like they didn't exist. Montse even commented at one point that she couldn't see anything or anyone, but Darren assured her that, soon enough, someone would see them.

The sound of an engine caught his ear from just beyond the small hill in front of them and Montse looked at him in panic. 'Is it them?' she asked with wide, frightened eyes.

He reached to take her hand and hold it tightly. 'Just keep still now, love,' he instructed her. 'They will have been watching us for some time until they could tell who we were. I haven't been here in quite a while and I would guess that they think I am dead.'

'Just like me,' she nodded.

'Yes,' he agreed, 'except for them it's not new. I've been dead before.'

'Darren, you are a confusing man.'

'Ah, yes, that's another thing I forgot to mention. Here they don't call me Darren. Here it's…'

'Meester Bootch,' came an excited squeal as a jeep barrelled over the hill, slid to a halt in a cloud of dust and an ancient looking woman jumped from the cab with the agility of someone half her age. 'You are alive.'

Darren's face was covered in wet, gummy kisses as Montse looked on in amazement. This wasn't what she had expected. This woman looked like her grandmother as she babbled on in an odd mixture of Spanish and the guttural sound of the Basque language. Darren just stood and grinned: he couldn't get a word in. Then, the next moment, the grin disappeared and his head spun to the side on the receiving end of a good, solid slap.

'Twice,' the old lady shouted. 'Twice you rise from the grave. My heart will not take this again, Meester Bootch. Do you hear me? If you die again you will stay dead. And who is this?' she yelled as she pointed a bony finger at Montse, though her eyes remained fixed on the man in front of her.

'Erm, well, this lady is the reason I did not stay dead this time, Mamma,' Darren muttered, his head hanging low in apparent shame, though the smile playing again on his lips suggested the lie.

'Then I should slap her too,' the old lady announced and Montse took a step backwards before thin, wizened arms surrounded her and she was pinned in a surprisingly strong grip as wrinkled lips came close to her ear. 'Thank you,' they whispered.

'So, you will not introduce us?' the old lady demanded as she released her hold and returned her attention to Darren. 'I expect better manners.'

'Sorry Mamma,' Darren grinned. 'Montse, this is Rosa. Rosa, I present Montserrat de la Vall dels Llops.'

'Catalana?' Rosa asked.

'Well, obviously I would have preferred a Basque woman, but then I already have the best Basque girl on earth, don't I?' Darren put his arm around the old lady's shoulders. 'This is my girl, Mamma. I have brought her for your approval.'

'We shall see,' said Rosa sternly, but she offered Montse a wide, toothless grin before kissing her on both cheeks. 'I will make my decision over lunch. As will the others. I have summoned everyone.'

'How many others are there?' Montse asked him as they sat in the back of the jeep a few moments later.

'Quite a few,' he whispered as the vehicle lurched over the unforgiving terrain. 'I don't know this driver, though.' He indicated the man at the wheel who was receiving an incomprehensible rant from Rosa. The poor guy had just seemed bemused by the events of the last five minutes but had finally decided to ask what was going on.

'Looks like she doesn't want to explain the return of her Prodigal Son,' Montse whispered back. 'That woman is terrifying.'

'She has her moments,' Darren agreed.

Rosa was preparing a light meal with a fruity red wine as a battered old 4x4 came hurtling down the dry dirt track to the house. Seconds later the door burst open and six dishevelled, heavily armed men rushed into the room, stopped and stared slack-jawed at Darren.

Montse caught her breath and tried not to make her fear obvious, but these men were exactly as she had pictured E.T.A. terrorists. One had an eye-patch, another was missing half an ear and the others, while not displaying any disfigurement, just looked plain odd.

'Mr. Butch, my brother, is that really you?' asked eye-patch, finally breaking the silence.

'Aye, it's me all right, you brutal Basque bandit.'

Montse watched in fascination as half-an-ear lunged forward and nearly knocked Darren off his feet with the force of his embrace. Then all seven men were hugging and kissing and swearing in a sweaty lump that made it impossible to distinguish who was who until tiny Rosa forced her way into the middle of the testosterone mass and slapped each one of them on the face.

'Manners,' she yelled. 'Where are your manners?'

The men disentangled themselves and grinned. 'Sorry Mamma,' one of them mumbled.

'Mr. Butch, I am ashamed of you,' Rosa scolded. 'There is plenty of time for this reunion later, but you should introduce your guest.'

A long, low whistle escaped eye-patch as he noticed the woman for the first time and asked, 'My brother, who is this beauty?'

Darren walked forward and took the frightened girl by the hand. 'Lads, this is Montse. This is my girl,' he said simply.

'Captain Antonio Rodriguez de la Vasco,' announced eye-patch with an exaggerated bow, 'but you can call me Vassi.'

'Hector,' half-an-ear informed her.

'Sixtro,' announced a third man with an attempt at a sweet smile that was anything but.

'And my sons José, Roberto and Little Valentino,' supplied Rosa to complete the line-up. 'Now we shall have some lunch and become acquainted. Mr. Butch has much explaining to do.'

Montse sat quietly as she listened to her man telling his compadres what had happened to him since he had left them months earlier in a bus full of "Arab types" who turned out to be suicide bombers and blew the bus to bits. Seven heads nodded at that point. They knew of the explosion and had assumed Butch was killed along with all the others. He apologised for not getting word to them that he was still alive, but they quickly understood that he must "stay dead" in order to protect the family that had saved him – two young lads and their sister. All eyes turned to her then and she blushed as Darren came to the part about her nursing him back to health. Then the heads shook in unison and disbelief as he finished the tale with her arrest and his own kidnap as he was spirited back to England.

'Phew' whistled Vassi. 'That is some story, my brother. Señorita, you are more than welcome at this table,' he offered in Montse's direction.

'Th…thank you,' she stammered.

'Relax, my dear, relax,' Rosa urged.

'She has been watching too much TV, Mamma,' Darren explained. 'She thinks you are all murderers.'

'Murderers?' spluttered Hector through a mouthful of wine. 'We're not murderers. Anyone here ever murdered anyone?'

All heads were shaking vigorously as a variety of denials fell from their lips.

Montse smiled at this welcome news. 'I'm sorry,' she said shyly. 'It's just that when the news mentions E.T.A. it always tells of unknown killings. I am embarrassed that I believed that. It is good to know that you are not all killers.'

'Oh, we're all killers, all right,' Sixtro butted in, yet again failing as his attempt at a sweet smile came across as an insane grin. 'I personally took out four Guardia Civil in one go, but I am a freedom fighter not a murderer.'

'Absolutely,' agreed Vassi.

'Freedom fighters,' echoed Roberto.

'We only kill those who deserve to die,' Valentino assured her.

'Yes, yes, I see, of course' Montse acknowledged with a wan smile as she looked at Darren for help.

He returned her glance with a creased brow, half smile and a small, embarrassed shrug of his shoulders. 'Me too,' he mouthed at her.

'And look what they do to us,' Hector joined in. 'I lost my ear fighting for freedom.'

'You lost your ear robbing a bank,' Darren corrected. 'Just couldn't dodge the bullets fast enough.'

'It was still for the cause,' Hector pouted.

'Bank robbery?' asked Montse.

'Long story,' Darren offered. 'I'll tell you later.'

Vassi caught the confused look on Montse's face. '*You* are not to worry Señorita,' he assured her. 'As *una Catalana* you are perfectly safe in our company - unless of course,' his one eye squinted slightly as he stared at her, 'you are an undercover security agent. So tell me truthfully now - you are not a member of the Guardia Civil, or the Polícia are you?'

Montse swallowed hard and violently shook her head. 'No, no I am not. I promise you I am not - I swear.'

'Oh stop it Vassi,' snapped Hector. 'You take no notice of this mad-man sweetie. He is only teasing you.'

'I just need to check that she wouldn't fold under questioning,' Vassi continued, but he was laughing now.

Montse felt Rosa's protective arm around her shoulder and she finally began to relax. All the banter was confusing but she had been around enough men to know that making jokes at her expense was their way of accepting her. 'I have been questioned and I didn't fold,' she told them and was rewarded by Darren's look of pride.

'And that is that,' announced Rosa. 'These men will torment your life out if you let them, my dear. If you would like to slap some sense into all of them I will make sure that they stand and accept their punishment.'

'That's okay,' Montse said as the first genuine smile spread across her face. 'I have two brothers.'

'Talking of which,' Darren butted in, 'we need to stay here for a few days but then I must leave. Will you see Montse home safely after I've gone? I could do to keep away from those bothers for a while.'

'You must leave again so soon?' Vassi asked.

'I still have unfinished business. I've only got two of the men responsible for killing me Ma and there are two more left.'

Rosa tutted as she spat on her floor. 'Putasemea. Find them. Kill them slowly, my son, then come home safely.'

'Aye Mamma, don't you worry. They're both gonna get exactly what's coming to them.'

As Rosa caught the sad look on Montse's face she changed the subject. 'Would you like to see your room my dear?'

'A double bed, I hope,' Darren interjected.

'My son, I may be old but I am not ga-ga yet,' Rosa assured him as she took Montse by the arm and led her from the room. As the door closed behind them Montse could hear the men cursing at the injustice that had been done to Darren's mother and offering their help in getting the bastards.

At the end of the week Roberto drove Darren and Montse back to where they had left the car. Someone had been down to secure it in their absence but now, as they approached, they heard the horn blowing. Darren jumped from the Land Rover, looked at the Jaguar keys in his hand and then at Sixtro sitting at the wheel and revving the engine.

'How the fuck…?' he began, then thought better of it. Asking Sixtro how he had managed to start the car without the key would have been a stupid question. The guy was the best car thief and the best driver he knew.

The back windows rolled down then and Vassi poked his head out, brandished a pistol and yelled '*Aiai.*' Hector's head followed.

'No, my brothers, we have been through this already,' Darren told them. You cannot come with me. This is a job for one man alone or an army.'

'We have an army,' Vassi suggested.

'I know. I know you do,' Darren agreed, 'but this is my fight. Come on now, get out. You know I'm right.'

'How long is this going to take you, brother?' Vassi asked as he regretfully left the car. 'You have been after these men for what, two years now? It doesn't seem to me that the English are helping you much.'

'You have a point and my patience is wearing thin,' Darren agreed, 'but I gave my word that I would return and I have other work to do. Look, you just get my girl home safely as we agreed and I will be back as soon as I can.'

He hugged each of his comrades before they headed back to the Land Rover to leave him with Montse.

'Really Darren, how long will it be?' she asked, tears in her eyes.

'Sooner than you think, my love. I wasn't joking there. My patience is almost at an end and I do have a bit of a plan, but I can't go back on my word.'

'Your word is very important to you, isn't it?'

'It's everything, Montse. A man is nothing without his word.'

'Please stay safe,' she begged as she hugged him to her.

'I promise,' he assured her with a kiss to her forehead before jumping in the car. The dust cloud from his wheels almost hid her from his view as he drove away, but he could just make out her waving arm in the rear view mirror. He really needed to pull his plan together quickly and then come back home for good.

8

Goin' Home

·

'Back right on time. Well done, Liam,' Turner commended him as they sat in the drawing room of the Derbyshire manor house. He sipped his tea and drew deeply on his pipe. 'Did you put everything right with your lady friend?'

'Aye, Mr. Turner, it's right enough, but she was a bit shocked to see me, like.'

'I'll bet she was, dear boy. Well, assuming you continue to perform your duties to our satisfaction here, I have arranged that you can have one week off in four to go a-courting, if you like. How would that suit you?'

'Hey, Mr. Turner, that would be fine,' Liam beamed.

'There is one proviso, though. If a job comes up at any time then you must drop everything else. Is that understood? You must always be in readiness.'

'Readiness isn't the problem, Mr. Turner. I'm always ready, you know that, but you also know what it is I'm ready for, and that's not happening.'

'McMurphy and Moore, I assume.'

'Aye, that's right. I've only got two of the bastards who had me Ma killed, but there are two left and you promised that I'd get them.'

'And you will, my boy, you will. But it's all about timing, and then there's the cost of course.'

'The cost? What cost?'

'Well you aren't cheap, you know, and it all has to be accounted for higher up.'

'Accounted for? What, like book keeping or something?'

'Yes, quite, at least on the surface. It's all very political and not something I like to be involved in. We don't mind spending money, but we have to make it look good in the accounts. We need to keep Mrs. Thatcher happy, you see. Long term planning and all that. The more we can justify our expenditure, the more money we will receive. You, however, are quite difficult to justify.'

'What the f…'

'No Liam, I refuse to let you ruin my tea with your foul language. No one minds paying out for missions and you are pretty cost effective, but every time you go A.W.O.L. it costs a fortune to find you and that isn't cost effective. Behave yourself and you will get what you want, but you have to be patient.'

'I am behaving myself.'

'Are you? I wonder.'

'What the f… What are you on about?' asked Liam as he searched his brain for any recent transgression. 'I've been good as gold since you kidnapped me.'

'Liam, really, that's a bit strong old boy. No one kidnapped you.'

'Well what the fuck would you call it then?' Liam asked indignantly.

Turner raised his hand. 'OK, we'll not go into that, shall we? What's done is done, and you can see it any way that you like. That is in the past, but what I want to talk about is what happened yesterday morning.'

'Hey, I wasn't even here yesterday morning. I didn't get back until last night. Whatever happened, it wasn't me, I swear.'

'Really? That's strange, you see, because yesterday morning the switchboard at headquarters received a call on a secure line. One of those used purely for confidential information. One of those that is highly classified.'

'It wasn't me. I'm tellin' you, Mr. Turner, I didn't call anyone.'

'Does the message "Ask Paddy to call Mr. Druid" mean anything to you, Liam?'

'What? Who?' Liam closed his eyes and put his head in his hands. 'Oh fuck,' he said slowly.

'Aha, I thought so. That number is for our operatives only, Liam, and they all know how to identify themselves. It sent our poor little Nancy on the switchboard into quite a flap, I can tell you. Off she went, scurrying for the code book, but she couldn't find anything and she didn't know what to do.'

'Oops.'

'Oops indeed, Liam. So, when I arrived from Ireland in the afternoon I was immediately summoned. "Do you know someone called Paddy?" they asked me. My speciality is you Irish boys, Liam. How many Paddys do you think I might know?'

'Quite a few?' Liam guessed.

'Indeed I do. So why, do you think, when someone has broken protocol and given out a secure number, my immediate thought was that it would have been you?' Turner puffed deeply on his pipe and leaned back in his chair. 'I'm waiting, dear boy, and this had better be good.'

'It's not really,' said Liam as he squirmed in his seat. 'I think I fucked up.'

'For once, Liam, I would say your language is entirely appropriate.'

'It was when I was in New York last year, doing that McKee job, and there was this young lad and he really helped me out, like, and I just gave him that number so he could contact me if he needed to. I'd forgotten all about it. Oh fuck.'

'See what I mean? Not cost effective at all. We don't mind paying out thousands for a job well done, but we do not like having to change all of our secure numbers and going to the considerable expense and trouble of getting the new numbers to our operatives, some of whom are in very deep cover.'

'You have to change all of them?'

'All of them.'

'Oh fuck, Mr. Turner, I really am sorry.'

'Yes, well, I think it's Nancy who could do with the biggest apology, Liam. You absolutely ruined her day.'

9

The Call

Later that evening Liam sat looking at two pieces of paper on his desk. One was a crumpled scrap with a New York phone number scrawled on it. The second was a neat, official document with lots of columns and lots of headings for days, amounts, details, justification etc.

'Justi-fuckin'-cation,' Liam spat at the wall. 'Fuck me.'

Turner had left the document with the instruction that they all needed to be more accountable for their expenses. Phone calls on his home secure line were a justifiable expense, apparently, but they could be monitored. Well, fuck that.

Liam glanced at the clock. If he had the time difference correct then it would soon be time to call a certain lad in New York to find out why he had rung and fucked up poor Nancy's day. He glanced at his "secure" phone and shook his head. A call to New York from a public box was going to cost him a fortune, but no way was he going to try to justify this on a fuckin' expenses sheet. What a load of bollocks.

He jumped in his car and headed to a public phone box, calling in Harding's Off-Licence en route where the genial proprietor provided as many 10 pence pieces as he could. Liam hoped it would be enough. His pocket bulging with coins, he placed the call.

'Hello?'

'Tommy?'

'Hey Paddy, that you buddy?' came the excited, and unmistakably American, voice.

'Aye lad, it's me. Everything OK? I heard youse were trying to get in touch with me.'

'Yeah, right, I've got some news.'

'Well make it quick, Tommy. That last number I gave you is no good now so I'm on a public phone.'

'Is it safe to talk?'

'Oh, aye, it's untraceable, but we just need to make it quick.'

'Oh, sure, well, hey, you remember that fella Jimmy Mal?'

'Which one? The real 'un or that poor sod that shit himself?'

Tommy's laughter crackled down the line. 'Jeez, that poor old bastard. What was he again, some sort of school teacher? Just a guy with the wrong name, right?'

'Right. Him or the other one?'

'The real one, man, that's what I'm sayin'. Do you remember him?'

''Course I fuckin' do. What's this about, Tommy, and quick like?'

'Well you can forget him 'cause he's A.F.U.'

'A.F.U? What's that mean? Speak English mate.'

'Jeez man, you said to make it quick, so I was using short hand, wasn't I? A.F.U. All fucked up, you know.'

'All fucked up how?'

'Jeez, Paddy, ganked, iced, ghosted, wasted - um, suppose you could say the Mick's a deadman.'

'He's dead? Jimmy Mal? How do you know he's dead?'

'How do I know? 'Cause it was us, the Druids, that hosed him. We did it.'

'You've killed him?'

'Yeah man, that's what I'm telling you, an' we done him for you.'

'How? How the Hell did you manage to get to him Tommy?' asked Liam. This was momentous news.

'Oh, it wasn't no biggy really. Me an' the boys had nothin' on one night and he just came in the bar, so we decided to follow him about town. Y'know, see where he went, and what he did, that kinda stuff.'

'And?'

'And,' continued Tommy, 'after an hour or so we got kinda bored, so I pulled in front of him ready to go back to The Sunbrite for a beer or two, and you'll never fucking guess what happened next Paddy.'

'Go on then mate, I'm listening,' Liam urged as he piled coins into the phone. The cost seemed unimportant right now.

'Well, there we were driving along and minding our own business, with him following us, when a stop light turned red.' Tommy paused a moment for effect, then carried on with his story. 'An' this fuckin' dork of a driver he's usin' don't see us, or the fuckin' light - and the man rear-ends the fuckin' T-Bird. So me an' the boys jump out and, well the truth is, there wasn't much damage, just a minor fender bender, a few scratches, a broken tail light and a little scrape is all really.'

'Fuck the car Tommy, what happened next?'

'Oh, yeah right, well, there we were and we're just standin' an' lookin' at the rear of the car, and the front of the limo, when the back window rolls down and Jimmy sticks his head out, starts shoutin' and bawlin' and givin' *me* all sorts of shit and abuse - even had the cheek to tell me to watch where I was drivin' to.'

'So?'

'So, I walk up to the side of the limo to give him some shit back, and that's when him and the other fella in the car start to get really aggressive. He reaches inside his jacket - so I whipped out my .38 - and shot Jimmy right in the fuckin' head. Link an' Mono took out the other guy. Then

I put a couple in the driver just for fuckin' up our T-Bird and we left. Nothin' much else to say really. End of story.'

'Jesus fucking Christ. You and the boys really did him, right there in the bleedin' street?'

'Yeah man, that's what I'm tellin' ya. It was like the stars all aligned. I mean, that's a busy street right there, but there was no one on it. It was just perfect, man. Couldn't resist. I think there was one old dear coming round the corner, but we were outta there by then.'

'Jesus. With a fuckin' .38? What happened to your .22 mate?' asked Liam in shock.

'The .22? Oh, I pawned it. You were right there Paddy, the .38's a much better gun.'

'Holy shite, Tommy, I'm bleedin' stunned to be hearin' it mate. Hey, can you prove any of this?'

'Prove it? Why do I need to prove it? You sayin' you don't believe me Paddy?'

'No, no lad, 'course I'm not. It's just that, um, well, you see, the people I work for might pay for this. It's what they might call a justifiable expense.'

'A what?'

'Never mind. But they'll need proof.'

'Yeah, sure I can prove it. It's in all the papers. Jeez, you really think you could swing us some dough for this?'

'No promises, but I think so. You got a safe address to send it to? And don't go sayin' the fuckin' Sunbrite bar.'

'Sure, I've got a P.O. box. You got a fax number?'

Liam reeled off his number, remembering that not long ago, when he was in America, he didn't even know how to use a fax.

'Fucking cool man. Hey Paddy, I got a better idea. Why don't you just bring it? Be good to see you again bud, and we could have a few beers for old times' sake.'

'Me in New York? Don't think so Tommy. Bit of a history there remember? It's not that I don't want to, you understand. In fact I'd love to bring my girl for a visit.'

'Oh yeah, sorry man, wasn't meaning New York. But when I knew I'd be calling you I got an idea. You ever been to Virginia?'

'Virginia? No, why?'

'Link's a good old southern boy. He's from down that way, still got family livin' in a place called Dinwiddie, near Richmond. You could fly into Richmond International and we could drive down to see you. I'm sure we could all stay at Link's cousin's place. Be nice to meet your woman too. What'ya think bud?'

'Dinwiddie? Is that really the name of a place?' asked Liam.

'Yeah man, wild eh? They got all kinds of weird names down there. You only have to listen to Link's accent, it's all kind of y'all, y'know, an' y'hear - remember?'

'I remember Link all right, but I thought his accent was the same as yours. Youse lot all sound exactly the same to me,' teased Liam.

'Mine?' asked Tommy in mock shock. 'When I suggested you comin' across to meet up with us an' goin' down to Richmond, ya know what he said?

'No, what?'

'He said that he'd be grinnin' like a possum eatin' a sweet tater.'

'What's that mean?' asked Liam.

'No fuckin' idea bud, but he was smilin' when he said it, so I'm guessin' he meant that would be somethin' nice to look forward to. So, what d' ya think?'

'I think a trip down there sounds good.' Beeping from the phone interrupted him and Liam stuffed his last few coins in the slot. 'Gotta go, Tommy. Get that fax over to me and, don't forget, use a fuckin' *public* fax machine, like the library or somewhere.'

'I will Paddy, don't worry, I will.' And the line went dead.

Later that evening Liam's fax machine rang and, at the final beep, he tore off the paper, took it into his study and sat to read the document.

FAX ------ TRANSMISSION Cramer's Cafe. 3003 Indian Blvd NYC

Handwritten along the top of the fax sheet were the words. Hey Paddy, here's that newspaper report I told you about, had to photocopy it first, hope you can make it out OK.

Tommy. PO Box 3641. New York, NY. 10008.

New York (AP) – *Gang wars heat up in New York Police Commissioner Joseph F. Davis said this morning that the slaying of three men on Sunday in Yonkers could be gang-related.*

He said at least one of the men fatally shot in a car had been "targeted." He didn't elaborate further. A police spokeswoman said this evening that there were no updates available, except that the investigation is ongoing.

Just before noon on Sunday morning James Malcolm Brennan, a local businessman, and Anthony Moran, chief fundraiser for an Irish-American charity, were shot multiple times. Both men were pronounced dead at the scene. Daniel Patrick Griffin, charity worker and driver of the car, died of internal injuries in the early hours of this morning.

According to an eye witness the fatal shootings occurred following a minor road traffic accident where four to five men, dressed in dark clothing, were seen to open fire on the occupants of the limousine. Detectives are attempting to track down a large, dark coloured sedan, possibly a Lincoln, in which the assailants were seen making their getaway. No arrests have been made at this time.

END FAX

Liam poured a stiff whiskey, lit a fag and exhaled. 'Fuck me, Tommy, who'd have guessed?'

He placed a call to Turner and asked for a meeting the following day. 'You've only just beaten me to it, lad,' his handler informed him. 'I was going to call you. We have a job.'

10

The Problem

Turner sat blowing gently on his tea for a moment before taking a slight sip. 'No, Liam, the floor is yours,' he said, cutting off Liam's demands for information on the new job. 'You called me so let's hear what you have to say first.'

'Oh, okay, but it's not me Mr. Turner. I want you do something for some friends of mine.'

'Does this have anything to do with that Druid phone message?'

'Aye, it does. Here, read this.' Liam tossed the fax to Turner who read it slowly.

'My, my,' he said at last. 'So Brennan has finally met his maker. Now you see Liam this has turned out exactly as I told you it would. Do you remember?'

'No, remember what exactly?'

'Well old chap, when you returned from New York after the McKee termination, you seemed plagued by the idea that you had somehow failed. And, as I recall, I told you not to worry. And here's the proof that I was correct. That chappie Brennan has got himself shot to death by a rival gang. A fitting and poetic end for the man I must say. Now, what does this have to do with pagan rituals?'

'What?'

'Druids.'

'It's the Druids that did it.'

'Okay, Liam, let me rephrase. Who are the Druids and what do they have to do with you?'

'Well, here's the thing, like. When we did that debrief after America and I told you how I'd messed up with McKee and killed him before I could get the gen on Jimmy Mal, and then I got the wrong Jimmy Mal and he fainted in his own shite and…'

'Liam, that was more information than I required last time and I do not need it again. Let's accept that the poor man had an unfortunate bodily mishap and move on.'

'Yeah, okay, well this kid, Tommy, from the Druids is the one that tried to find Brennan for me. He was with me when I got the wrong guy and then he helped me get out of America when the whole McKee thing had gone to rat shit.'

'You didn't mention him before.'

'Didn't think you needed to know.'

'Liam, dear boy, when will you learn that I need to know everything?'

'Well I'm tellin' you now.'

'But what are you telling me, exactly? This fax just reports that a rival gang has killed Jimmy Mal.'

'And you believe everything you read in the papers, do you Mr. Turner?'

'Au contraire mon ami. I believe nothing. What I am beginning to discern, however, is that this rival gang was, in fact, your friends The Druids. Is that so?'

'Aye, that's so. They did it for me and I've told 'em you'll pay 'em for doin' it.'

'You did what?' Turner spluttered as he took a drink of his tea. He wiped the drips from his chin, placed the cup on the desk and raised his hand. 'Liam, my boy, no, no, no, you can't go saying things like that.'

'Well I've said it.'

Turner closed his eyes, drew a deep breath and shook his head slowly before adopting his patient face. 'Sanctioned, dear boy. Jobs have to be sanctioned. We can't just go paying a bunch of American hoodlums for shooting somebody just because they felt like it, now can we? Her Majesty's government really is quite fussy about these things. Even more so now that we have this new open accountancy policy. It's vital that everything is documented, do you see.'

'No I don't fuckin' see. This was sanctioned, Mr. Turner, and you know that. I was sanctioned and I failed.

All they did was finish the job and they did it for me. If you can't fuckin' justify that in all your fuckin' documents then you can fuck right off.'

'Liam this is absolutely intolerable,' Turner almost shouted as he slammed his fist on the table. 'I will not listen to your foul language a second longer and I will not have you telling me what is and isn't justified. You have no right. You are my operative and you will do as I say. Is that clear?'

Liam was taken aback. It was so unlike the mild mannered Englishman to raise his voice that his words had the effect of a good punch from any other man. 'Okay, okay, Mr. Turner, calm down man,' he said finally. 'I'm sorry for the language and all that, but this whole paperwork shite is a load of bollocks.'

Turner sat back in his chair and puffed on his pipe as he regained his composure. 'Between the two of us, Liam, I am in agreement,' he offered, his voice miraculously low and level once more. 'It's just that Mrs. Thatcher is quite unlike any of her predecessors. Economic forces, supply and demand, cost effectiveness, these are her main concerns and we have to comply. Now, go and make a fresh pot of tea, there's a good lad, and we will move on to your new job.'

***

'Reconnaissance? Why can't I just go and get him?' Liam's voice was urgent as he blew on the fresh cup of tea a few minutes later. 'Come on, Mr. Turner. You can't just bring up McMurphy's name and then tell me I can only watch him. Jesus Christ, he's one of 'em. He's one of the bastards who done for me Ma.'

'I know, dear boy, I know, but he just doesn't seem very active these days. We don't know if he's still pulling the financial strings or if he has been replaced. Personally I think he is still very much involved, but we need to be sure and you, my lad, need to make amends.'

'I need to make what?'

'Amends, Liam. We had an operative who had put himself in a position to watch him, but things went a bit strange last week and we thought he might have been rumbled. Then, this whole phone number debacle that your friend, Mr. Druid, caused a couple of days ago meant that we had to get word to him and that could have been the last straw. We are pretty sure he was compromised and we had to pull him out immediately.'

'Oh fuck.'

Turner just shook his head at yet another profanity. 'Yes, well, things could have been worse. The timing is quite fortunate as Mr. McMurphy is going away on holiday, so nothing is lost right at the moment, but he will be back in a month and you are to go and observe. You will spend the next three weeks in surveillance training, then you can have your week in Spain, and then you are going to Ireland for precisely seven days to make your preliminary report.'

Liam stared at his handler, but said nothing.

'Is there a problem, Liam?' Turner pushed as the silence continued.

'Well I don't know. Precisely seven days? It all seems so…' he struggled to find the appropriate word, but it wouldn't come.

'Calculated?' Turner offered.

'Aye.'

'Well that's exactly what it is. Everything has been worked out in the tiniest detail by our efficiency department.'

'Oh, for f…'

'No Liam, we are not starting that again,' Turner forestalled him. 'A study has been carried out and the head auditor calculates that it should take no longer that seven days to acquaint yourself with the terrain, carry out the surveillance and return home.'

'Oh he does, does he? Well, I hate to disagree with yer man's maths work there Mr. Turner but, if I've no bleedin' idea how long this'll take, how the Hell can he?'

'Well, to an accountant, it's all so very simple Liam. He calculates ferry crossing times, mileage, days for reconnaissance, days for surveillance and time to get home. There's even a petrol allowance. See for yourself. It's all on this sheet.

Liam took the offered paper and briefly studied it.

'And this here top feller of yours, can you tell me exactly how many terminations he's actually carried out?'

'Terminations? Good grief man, none of course. He's an accountant not an assassin. Besides, this isn't a termination; it's surveillance only.'

'Well that makes it even worse. A termination is done, dusted, finished. Surveillance could take forever. How the Hell can I know if a target's going to do something on a given day, for Christ's sake? What am I supposed to do; ask McMurphy if he would kindly oblige me by sticking to my fuckin' timetable?'

'Liam, yet again you are jumping in without knowing all the facts. You have a dossier and you need to read it. Our previous operative has strongly suggested an important round of financial meetings just as Mr. McMurphy returns from holiday. Since McMurphy is the finance chappy, he should be there. If nothing has happened with him in seven days, then nothing is going to happen at all and we will have our answer. McMurphy has been replaced.'

Liam scowled. 'If he's been replaced, does that mean he's no longer on the list and I won't get a shot at him?'

'I can't answer that, Liam. All I can say is that I, for one, am convinced that he is still very active.'

'Well I, for another one, am gonna' stick around long enough to fuckin' well prove it.'

As the older man winced, Liam grinned. 'Brace yourself, Mr. Turner, because I want you to give a message to this fuckin' auditor/accountant of yours. Tell him, from me, that this job will take as long as it takes. I'll read your dossier Mr. T, but this,' he held up the itemised sheet, 'with it's fucking petrol allowance is going to get torn up and used to wipe my arse after I've had a shite. Fuckin' gobshite accountants. Bollocks, the lot of 'em. Tell 'em that from me, will ya?'

Turner swallowed hard and was visibly pale. 'I, er, well, that is, I can certainly let your feelings be known, my boy, but you surely can't expect me to repeat that word for word?'

Liam laughed. 'No, I guess not. Okay, Mr. Turner, I've had my say. Just try to keep 'em off my back, will you? You can't honestly agree with all of this accountancy rubbish.'

'No, no, indeed I don't. Off the record the fellows at the club are calling it jobs-worth.'

'Aye, I'll drink to that,' Liam acknowledged as he reached to a cabinet and produced a bottle of Jameson whiskey, poured himself a glass and then added a small tot to the other man's cup. 'There you go, Mr. T, a wee drop of Ireland's best. It'll help you relax.'

Turner stared in horror at his tea and the whiskey floating in it. 'What on earth have you done?'

'Man, your face looks like a slapped arse,' Liam laughed.

'Well, old boy, to disagree over a timing schedule is one thing, but to ruin a fellow's tea? That's simply not on.'

'So you don't drink alcohol in your tea then?

'I most certainly do not. Such an uncivilised thing to do.'

'So, when you do drink, what's your poison then?' asked Liam.

'Well I do on occasion take the odd snifter you know, but that would be a fine, decent cognac.'

'Never whiskey?'

'If forced, it would be a single malt Scotch whisky.'

'Ah, go on, try it man. It might surprise you. Come on, let's drink to getting one step closer to McMurphy.'

Turner winced but clinked his teacup against Liam's glass and took a tiny sip with his eyes closed.

'So?' asked Liam. 'What do you think? Good, isn't it?'

'Oh I can tell you what it isn't,' Turner spluttered. 'It isn't a Le Reviseur Naploean Cognac.'

'You hate it?'

'Well, I wouldn't go that far, no. It's, er, it's good stuff Liam.'

'So let's have another then.'

Turner glanced at his watch and stood hurriedly. 'No, really, thank you but I need to go. Listen, you read this dossier.' He picked up the file and glanced through it. 'Tomorrow morning you will present yourself at the destination specified - overleaf,' he instructed as he passed the file across. 'No more arguments.'

Liam accepted the file dutifully and walked the older man to the front door. Turner was nearly at his car when he retraced his steps. 'The others in the car when your friends got Jimmy Mal, they were part of the NORAID problem?'

'I think so,' Liam confirmed. 'Why do you ask?'

'Exceptional circumstances,' Turner explained. 'It's a phrase that is being used a lot by the higher ups at the moment. An "exceptional circumstance" completion of a previously sanctioned termination. Mm, I might just swing it for your friends with the appropriate wording,' he mused. 'Read that file thoroughly,' he concluded, and then he was gone.

11

One Teacher + One Blackboard + Lots of Big Words = A Right Load of Bollocks

"Surveillance Training" should have been called "Stating the bleedin' obvious" as far as Liam was concerned. He and a handful of other recruits endured three weeks of boredom at the destination "specified overleaf". Half the time was spent in a room with a blackboard that made him feel like he was back at school. The teacher was a patronising little man who constantly wrote things on the board, read them out, repeated them, smiled in a "have you got that now" way before putting a ring around a word. With a stupid flourish he would then add an equals sign and turn back to the class with a "this is really important" expression and then add another word to his list before going through the whole procedure again. Liam was dutifully nodding to confirm he understood that *clandestine* equalled *surreptitious* but that *surreptitious* could equal *suspicious* and that *suspicious* was a bad thing requiring the newly chalk ringed *normalising*, which was now being linked back to *balancing*, which is where they had started hours ago. It was mind-numbing.

He had complained to Turner in a phone call, but received little sympathy. Apparently, the regular training officer was indisposed, but this replacement had been highly recommended. 'Well he should be highly fucked off,' Liam had offered before the usual reprimand for his language silenced him. He had sulked away from the phone and gone outside for a fag. He couldn't even smoke in the room because one of his class-mates was allergic. 'Allergic, my arse,' he mumbled.

Things weren't quite as bad when they had "in the field practical training" and he even learned a useful trick about shop window reflections, but it was mostly a load of bollocks. There were two things that made it bearable, though. He would soon have another break in Spain and there had been one very interesting fact in the documentation that Turner had left for him. His surveillance was to take place in Garvary near Derry, a little town where he had spent holidays with his Ma and his Aunt as a child. He knew the area well, but he had kept that fact to himself. He would not require the days allotted in his bleedin' "time schedule" for *familiarising*, yet another word ringed on Mr. Condescending's blackboard. Oh no, those days would be spent in an entirely different pursuit.

Eventually the tortuous weeks came to an end and he was once more in Spain. Montse had organised a meal with her brothers and their resentment of him was thawing a little, but it was still uncomfortable. It was worth it, though, for the time they had alone. They spent hours in bed, making love and talking.

'Why don't you just leave now?' Montse asked him. 'You said it would be soon.'

'Aye lass, I know, but I'm still committed until I've got the last two bastards.'

'And you want to get them.'

'More than anything, but I'm beginning to believe it'll never happen. There's so much red tape.'

'What is red tape?'

'Paperwork, bureaucracy, even accountants for Christ's sake. I can't do anything unless someone can put a tick in a bloody ledger. Turner's on my side, I'm sure of that, but I don't know how much longer I can wait.'

'Maybe you need a beeline.'

'A what?'

'Beeline. It is correct, no? I heard it the other day. It means when one choice is no good so you make another choice and go quickly.'

'Ah, I see.' Liam smiled fondly at the woman who lay in his arms. Her English was excellent and the odd slip in her wonderful lilting accent just added to the charm. 'You're sort of right, but I think you mean a plan B. Mind you, a plan B with a beeline is not the worst idea I've ever heard.'

'You are confusing me.'

'Sorry Montse, but our language is like that. It's food for thought though.'

'You are hungry now?'

'No lass. Listen,' he said, recalling his conversation with Tommy, 'do you think you would like to visit America?'

'America? Oh yes, I would love to see America. Is this in your Beeline plan?'

'Yes, love, it's in my Beeline plan.'

***

Liam had made an important call before leaving the surveillance training course and it had been a relatively simple affair. The man on the other end of the phone had quickly understood the coded message arranging a meeting in Spain and he had said little in reply. Now the two men sat opposite each other in a quiet cerveseria and conversation was no longer a simple matter.

'If I could trust that no one was listening, I'd just sort all this with you on the phone,' Liam said in frustration. 'It would be a lot quicker.'

'I c...c...can't help it y...y...you know,' offered Laa Laa. 'It's when p...p...people l...l...l...l...l...'

'Look at you?' suggested Liam.

'Yes.'

'I know mate.' Liam smiled. This was one of the good guys. He'd helped him out before and he was helping him now. 'You're worth the effort, you know, and it's really good to see you again.'

'It's g...g...good to s...s...see you too B...B...B...B...B...'

'Butch?'

'Yes. Is th...th...that your n...n...name today?'

'Aye, it'll do. Most of me mates in Spain call me Butch, though my girl calls me Darren. Liam's probably the safest though.'

'It's so c...c...c...conf...f...f...'

'Confusing? Aye, you're right there. I've got too many bleedin' names and now I need another. I can't have the Brits finding out that Liam O'Neil has gone to Ireland without their say-so and Darren and Butch can't go at all. So you think you have someone who can help me then?'

'Yes, when y...y...you're in Ireland ag...g...gain.'

The two men spent the next half hour having a five-minute conversation and the plan was made with code words to alert Laa Laa to Liam's movements as soon as he arrived in Ireland. A bit of reminiscing followed and then Liam headed out. It was the end of his break and he needed to be back in England again right on time. He was, as Turner had suggested, on his best behaviour.

***

'It seems a bit loose to me,' Liam observed as he looked at yet another dossier in front of him.

'I agree, dear boy,' said Turner as he sucked on his pipe. 'It's not my work, you see, but we have to act very quickly. If not, two more of our Irish operatives could be seriously compromised.'

'Is this my fault again?'

'No, this time you are blameless, but we must shut the fellow up.'

'So, just have him killed then.'

'Unfortunately it's not that easy. For one thing, he is a rather well-bred Englishman who just happens to live in Ireland. For another, his wife's cousin sits in the House of Lords.'

'Really?'

'Yes, it's frightfully inconvenient.'

'How annoying for you.'

'Quite, so all we can do is scare him a bit.'

'Why me, then? I don't really do scare tactics, you know. I'm more an ultimate solution kind of guy.'

'Yes, and that's what concerned me when you were suggested. Still, it shows that you are being trusted again, but can I trust you Liam? Do you promise that you won't terminate the man?'

'If that's what's required, then you have my word, but there's not much detail. I mean, his home address is really handy, but "avoid wife if possible"? What's that supposed to mean? There's not even a timeline, and I thought it was all about time and motion these days.'

'Liam, my boy, you will hear no disagreement from me, but this is a rush job. The man wasn't even on our radar until a couple of days ago and we know nothing about his personal habits or his marriage. As far as we know, the wife isn't causing any problems and we have no reason to want her harmed. If you can find him alone and keep the wife out of it, that would probably be best and that's why the timing is loose, to give you that chance. However, if you discover that they are an inseparable couple, then you might have to give the wife a fright as well.'

'I don't like the idea of a woman being involved.'

'No. Quite. You will have to use your best judgement. You did very well with your latest training, apparently, and you got an A+ from the instructor.'

'Must have nodded in all the right places,' Liam suggested.

'What?'

'Nothing. You were saying?'

'Well, as you are already going over for a reconnaissance mission it made sense to use you for this job as well. We can kill two birds with one stone, so to speak.'

'Terminate.'

'What?'

'I can terminate two birds with one stone. Wouldn't that be the right phrase here?'

'Oh Liam, that really is quite good,' Turner laughed. 'Terminate two birds, well I never. I will use that at the next strategy meeting. It should give everyone quite a giggle.'

Liam sighed. 'So, I still leave tomorrow as planned, but now there's no definite return date?'

'Quite, so that should make you happy I would think. One in the eye for the time and motion people, wouldn't you say?'

'Indeed I would Mr. T.'

As Turner took his leave he was still chuckling to himself about terminating birds and Liam smiled as he closed the door after him. He might just allow himself a good laugh too. This "loose" arrangement couldn't have come at a better time and, tomorrow, he could start on his Beeline plan.

12

Northern Ireland

Liam left the Jag over in Britain and arrived in Larne as a foot-passenger. With the exception of a hoard of screaming kids, the ferry ride had been uneventful and the sun was shining brightly as he strolled casually along to the car rental office.

'Good morning sir, how can I be of help today?' smiled the young man on reception.

'Mornin' to you too mate,' he replied. 'I'm here for a week or so and I'll be needing a car for a bit of sight seeing. Don't suppose you have something a bit sporty, do you?'

Half an hour later Liam was driving away in a gleaming new Ford Capri and following the signs for Ballymena. Once on the main road he put his foot down a little. Hmm, it was definitely no Jag, but it was no slouch either, Liam considered, and it was perfect for the job. It had a good, large hatchback and Liam made a mental note that this might come in useful some day. For now, though, he just needed to blend in and look like a tourist.

This was the first time he had been in Northern Ireland since his escape from prison and he couldn't afford to stand out. He knew Turner was pushing the issue for him and, despite his protestations, he did appreciate it. If they waited to get McMurphy in the south, it might never happen. So, here he was back in the north and that was another reason he was on surveillance and scare tactics only for now. 'Testing the water, dear boy,' Turner had said and he had to agree. He knew his appearance had changed drastically over the last couple of years, especially with all the scars he'd picked up in Spain, and he was unlikely to be recognised. Still, he needed to be careful. He headed out to Derry and his old haunt of Garvary. Best to get some of his work out of the way first.

Liam found himself a nice B & B for the evening and at dawn the following morning set off into the beautiful countryside. He parked the car, retrieved a rucksack and set off walking up a long, winding trail. At the top of a hill he sat and had a picnic, looking like any other backpacker admiring the magnificent scenery. It really was wonderful and that pretty little cottage down in the valley was so quaint. He placed an open bird watching book next to him and then pulled out his binoculars. He truly did like birds and certainly would never want to terminate any. There wasn't much diversity of species here, but he might get lucky and see an osprey.

He trained his glasses on something he couldn't identify and watched as it swooped towards the cottage where an old, battered Vauxhall stood alone on the rough path. He followed the bird as it flew away, then caught another in his view and saw it glide over the little rooftop. Bird after bird came and went but, after four hours of watching the little buggers, his arms were aching and he still hadn't seen an osprey. Two common doves were performing an amusing mating dance in a tree when they suddenly flew off in alarm as a Ford Fiesta approached the cottage. At last. Liam shielded the top of his binoculars so that the lens would produce no glare. 'Cloaking,' he mouthed to himself in amusement as he remembered the chalk ringed word on the idiotic blackboard.

The car stopped, a man emerged and Liam felt the bile rise in his throat as he recognised the form of Martin McMurphy, one of the co-signatories on his Ma's death warrant. 'Fuckin' bastard,' he hissed under his breath. 'Think yourself lucky, old son. I could be shooting you right now if only Turner would let me.'

After just three days of bird watching Liam had confirmed the intelligence garnered by the previous operative before Tommy's unfortunate phone call had put an end to his surveillance. McMurphy had indeed recently acquired himself a girlfriend called Fiona who lived in a remote cottage. How convenient. Even more conveniently, Fiona went out every afternoon from two until five and, purely coincidentally of course, that's precisely when other cars came and went. This was obviously the site of clandestine meetings and, with some photos to back it up, would prove that McMurphy was definitely still in the game. 'Fuckin' waste of my time,' Liam muttered to himself. 'Anyone could have figured that out.' So, he could tick that off then. 'Confirmation,' he grinned as another chalk ringed word floated through his brain.

By the following morning he had phoned a coded message to Laa Laa, checked out of the B&B and was on his way to Ballycastle. 'Sorry Mr. Accountancy man,' he said to himself as he deliberately went off-script again. 'This is definitely not on your itemised list.'

13

The Broken Radio and the Man from Kilkenny

On the outskirts of Ballycastle, just before the town centre, he pulled over, parked on the roadside and gazed along a row of old shops, quickly seeing what he was looking for. *Gerald Foley. TV and electrical appliance repairs.* He scanned the street for any signs of trouble, but this wasn't a dangerous place. The shop he was about to enter, on the other hand, just might be. Still, this is what he was here for and he took a deep breath before leaving the car and crossing the road.

A small bell jingled as he opened the door and he glanced at the innocuous interior. A musty smell filled his nostrils as he saw the lone occupant, a man in his seventies, stooped over an even older looking kettle that he was repairing. Could this really be the right place?

'Good afternoon young feller, how can I help you?' the man asked.

'Mr. Foley?'

'Aye son, that it is. What can I be doing for you?'

'I'm here to have a radio repaired. Mr. Joshua Flanagan of Kilkenny sent me,' explained Liam.

'Can I take a look at the radio then son?' asked the old feller.

'No, I don't think you understand, *Mr. Joshua Flanagan* sent me - from *Kilkenny.*'

'Well now, that's a long way to be travelling just to have a radio repaired, so it is.'

'Aye, but he sent me, you see. *Mr. Joshua Flanagan* that is.'

'Well, can I be taking a look at his radio then?' asked the man in rather a fluster.

'No I don't have the rad.., Er, look, never mind I think I must have the wrong address.'

The noise of someone hurrying down stairs behind a thick curtain had Liam nearly back at the door before a voice stopped him.

'Was it Kilkenny I heard there, from Mr. Flanagan?'

Liam looked at the new arrival, a man of around forty who was quickly drying his hands on a rag.

'Aye,' said Liam cautiously.

'And what would his full name be, then, this Mr. Flanagan of yours?'

'Joshua Winston Horatio.'

'Ah, 'tis all right, Da, I'll be seeing to this feller,' said the new man with a broad smile. 'He'll be coming through to the back with me.'

'Will I be mending the radio, then?'

'No, Da, not today,' his son told him. 'You'll be fixing that kettle for Mrs. O'Shaughnessy. She'll be needing it by tomorrow, so she will.'

Liam followed the younger man through the curtain as he was beckoned. 'Jesus, I was beginning to think I'd got the wrong place,' he began before a finger to the lips of his companion silenced him. He waited while a heavy door was unlocked and he was led into a small room beyond.

'Sorry about that,' said the man. 'Me Da only comes in a few hours a week. Just a bit of bad timing.'

'Ah.'

'Connor's the name. Take a seat. It'll be documents you're after?'

'Aye. So you're the forger then?' Liam asked.

Connor just smiled.

'I'll be needing a full set of travel docs,' Liam continued. 'Can you do anything with Spanish papers?'

'Now Mr. Flanagan didn't mention anything about Spain, so he didn't. Spain? Bit dodgy that. New security seals, do you see? Would anywhere else be doing you?'

'What else have you got?'

'Well now, there'd be the Republic. You could have a full script from there, so you could. Or there's Great Britain, of course, and the new Italian stuff's fine.'

Liam frowned and shook his head. 'Britain and the Republic are definitely out. Italy would be good if I could speak Italian, but I can't. It's got to be a Spanish speaking country.'

'Ah well now, if we're willing to broaden our horizons and go beyond Europe, there's always South America to be considering.'

'And you can do stuff from there?'

'To be sure, I can do anything you like. 'Tis just that European documents are better for world wide travel if that's the main point here.'

'No, not really.'

'Well, then, I'd be saying Argentina. It's a big Irish community they've got over there and you've got a bit of that swarthy look going on, so you have.'

'You think so?'

'Oh, aye, for sure you have.'

'Then Argentina it is. How much?'

'So you'll be wanting a passport at four thousand, a driving license at five hundred and another five for the D.N.I.'

'The what?'

'Government issued I.D. card, and very useful it is. Non-negotiable on the prices there. In this world you get what you pay for.'

'I've no problem with your prices,' Liam assured him. 'How long to prepare the docs?'

'Well I'll be taking the photos now, and then you'll be all set in three days.'

'Perfect. What about a name?'

'If you have any preferences, I'll be seeing what I can do,' Connor offered.

'No, not really. Just as long as it's not Maria.'

Connor slowly wrote Maria on a piece of paper and then drew a line through it. 'There, Maria has gone. Left the building, so she has.'

Liam smiled. Connor wasn't what he had expected, but Laa Laa had assured him he was the best and could be trusted completely. After the photographs were taken the two men shook hands and agreed on a time for three days hence before Connor showed him back into the shop.

'Goodbye, Mr. Foley,' Liam offered to Connor's father, who was still hard at work on the kettle.

'And a good day to you, young feller,' the old man replied. 'And don't you be forgetting that radio next time.'

Mrs. Quinn's Guesthouse with the welcoming notice of *Vacancy* provided what he needed as he walked down the street. A sweet old lady met his request for a room with a sea view that just happened to look out directly over Foley's shop. Laa Laa may have vouched for the man, but you could never be too careful. He used the cover story of being a journalist for the Irish Times and Mrs. Quinn was delighted to think he'd be writing an article about 'Our lovely little town'. Of course she understood his need for peace and quiet and he would not be disturbed. So began three days of boredom as he kept an eye on the shop. He'd stocked up on supplies from a little grocery store and now he just had to wait it out. Patience was yet another word that had acquired a chalk circle.

Several people came and went, but each looked to be innocently in need of electrical repair. An elderly lady walked out smiling with an ancient kettle clutched to her chest. 'That'll be Mrs. O'Shaughnessy then,' Liam reasoned. The following morning Mrs. O'Shaughnessy was back, unsmiling and still with the kettle. 'Maybe he'd better just sell her a new one,' Liam suggested to his bedroom wall.

After three days the vigil came to an end. He checked out, assuring Mrs. Quinn that the article had come along just fine, and headed back to the shop. Mr. Foley senior arrived at the same time.

'Another problem with the kettle?' Liam enquired.

'Ah, 'tis a relic, so it is,' Mr Foley confirmed.

There was no mention of a radio this time and Liam was shown directly through to the back. 'Any problems?' he asked.

'Nothing out of the ordinary,' Connor informed him. 'There was the one phone call, mind, but that happens every now and then, so it does.'

'Really?'

'Ah, to be sure. 'Twas a fella' with your accent wondering if I had a job on at the moment.'

'And?'

'We talked about knobs and dials on radios for a while.'

'Meaning?'

'Well, 'tis a code, like, and he'll be thinking there's an American couple here needing to get out of a nasty little tax problem.'

'So no one knows anything about me?' Liam pressed.

'Well I'd be having no business left now, would I, if I was to be telling the truth. So, Señor Agea, here's what you'll be needing.'

Liam inspected the contents of the envelope Connor passed to him. His photograph stared back at him from the passport of one José Luis Agea. The work was excellent and there was even an entry stamp from the Irish authorities. 'Thanks,' Liam said as he handed over the money and saw it thrown casually in a drawer. 'You're not going to count it?'

'Sure you don't look like a stupid man to me, so you don't, and, if you were to be underpaying me, then wouldn't you expect the authorities to find out some unfortunate gentleman from Argentina had his passport stolen?'

'I guess I would,' Liam grinned. 'Thanks Connor.'

'And 'tis very welcome you are. Adios señor.'

Liam took his leave, safe in the knowledge that Connor hadn't once asked for his real name. That was quite handy, and not just from a security point of view. There were occasions even Liam forgot his real name. Anyway, that was one more job done and now he had to go and scare some Lord's cousin's husband.

14

Jeffrey Hubert Coulson III

Liam glanced down to the fuel gauge and smiled. He was almost empty again and that would mean another refill. This was likely to cock up the ledger for those poor bean counters in Whitehall. Oh dear, what a shame. It was still quite a way to Connemara and he may well have to fill up again after that. 'Fuckin' gobshite accountants,' he grinned.

He located the address in the dossier with little trouble and the Ford Capri arrived in darkness, unobserved, on a small side street. The neighbourhood was quiet and secluded, with just one street lamp at the side of the road, but the fancy house was brightly lit and two cars stood on the drive. It appeared that both members of the household were at home, so Liam went back to the digs he had secured earlier and decided to wait.

The following morning he left the Capri some distance away, found a secluded vantage point, and watched. Around lunchtime a woman emerged, took one of the cars and drove away. He wasn't about to attempt anything in the middle of the day, but at least he knew which car belonged to the wife. He returned that night, but both cars were back on the drive. He decided to give it one more day.

On the third attempt the scene was much more promising. Just one car on the drive and most of the house was in darkness. A weak light came from a downstairs window, but that was all. Liam sat in his own car and considered the situation. It wasn't a sure thing. Maybe the husband had borrowed the wife's car. Maybe the wife had just nipped out and would be back in a few minutes. Still, it was his best chance so far and he decided to take it. He walked quietly to the house.

Garçon, said the ornate sign hanging from on the gatepost. What a bloody stupid name. Not nearly as stupid as that of the owner, though. Just what sort of moniker was Jeffrey fuckin' Hubert Coulson anyroad? To make matters worse, there was a "third" tagged on the end. Wanker.

Within a couple of minutes he was over the fence and moved silently to the rear of the house, checking for any visual signs of an alarm system. There were none. No small flashing lights, out of place cabling or anything to suggest security. He reached inside his jacket for his home made "key" then, on a whim, he tried the door first. Well, you never knew your luck. 'Jesus Christ,' he whispered under his breath when the door opened quietly at his touch. 'This is either a very safe neighbourhood of Jeffrey the fuckin' third is an idiot.'

Liam tip-toed silently into the kitchen, closing the door behind him and then pausing to check that he hadn't been heard. Nothing. The only sound was that of soft classical music coming from somewhere down a passageway to his left. He donned his ski-mask and made his way stealthily towards the music, and then the job was nearly over with as quickly as it had begun when he rounded the corner and came face to face with another masked intruder staring at him from the gloom. He stepped sharply backwards into a table, which rattled ever so slightly. He caught the table to silence it and, in the same moment, realised that the other intruder was his own reflection in a large hall mirror. Jesus Christ all fuckin' mighty. He held his breath, but the music didn't stop and there was no sound of movement from the room ahead. There was, however, a low growling noise coming from his rear.

Liam turned slowly to face a rather large Doberman. Shite. He stood his ground, stared the dog in the eyes and let out a long, low, almost silent whistle. It was an old gypsy trick. In seconds the growl changed to a soft whine, the dog's tongue lolled out and his short stump wagged.

'Shush, there's a good lad,' Liam whispered, as he dropped his jacket to the floor and bent to stroke the dog's head. He could just make out a nametag in the light that came from under the nearby door. 'You wait here, Chauncey, there's a good feller.' Chauncey rolled a couple of times before lying on his stomach with his head and paws on the jacket.

Liam moved to the door and pushed it slowly open. He was greeted by the sight of a fat, bald man in a silk kimono sitting on a sofa, his head tilted back as he stared at the ceiling. His legs were splayed out and, in between them, was a woman dressed in a black basque, French knickers, stockings and suspenders. Her face was buried in the fat man's lap, her head moving rhythmically up and down. Bollocks. Who'd gone out in the other car then? Ah well, he was here now.

'Ahem,' he coughed.

The fat man took a second to register his presence before gathering the kimono around him and shouting, 'Chauncey, Chauncey,' to no avail. The woman jumped to her feet, turned round and promptly fainted as Liam took a step backwards. It was hard to say who was the more shocked, the stocking-clad figure, at the sight of the masked intruder, or Liam, as he saw the moustache, tit-less body and a flaccid penis hanging from the French knickers.

'Jesus, now, will you look at that?' he said. 'I'm guessing that's not the wife.'

'Money, I have money, I have money,' the fat man was screaming. 'Take it. Take it all. Take this,' he added as he pulled an expensive gold watch from his wrist. 'Just don't hurt me.'

Liam stood for a second staring at a shiny watch, an unconscious transvestite, a fat man in a kimono and an array of dildos, the likes of which he'd never seen before. 'Well I never. Not in all me born days,' he mumbled.

'Wh…wh…what?' stuttered the fat man.

'Mr. The Third?' asked Liam, gathering his senses.

'What, who?'

'Jeffrey Hubert Coulson the fuckin' third?'

The man nodded his head, but seemed unable to form another word.

'Ah, 'tis good to be meetin' yer, so it is,' continued Liam, laying on the accent. 'I've been sent down here from Belfast. The boys say I've to ask yerself to kindly shut yer fuckin' mouth.'

Jeffery gulped and looked ready to pass out himself.

'Ah, no, don't you be fainting on me now. How would you be hearin' what it is I have ter say then? If you did that, I'd just be havin' to put a bullet in yer head, so I would. So, are yer still with me skin?'

Another nod and Liam continued. 'There now, that's a good feller isn't it? Me and you need to get along, you see, if you're gonna live, like. So, Jeffrey me old mate, it seems like you've been doing a bit of talkin' around town haven't ya? And, you've been talkin' about some friends of mine and they don't like it one little bit.

Well, when I say "friends", it's more like employers really and they gave me this job to do. Well, I say "job", but it's more like a contract kind of thing. I'm freelance, d'ya see, and I work as an enforcer. There, though, when I'm saying "enforcer", I'd be meaning more of a killer, like. Are you followin' me here Jeffrey?'

Again there was just a trembling nod.

'Ah, that's grand, so we're understanding each other nicely. And, me being freelance an' all, it's kind of up to me what I do with you, and those boys up in Belfast will pay me for me trouble, so they will. Mind, when I say "trouble", it's really no bother at all, you see. I kinda like it really, truth be told. Are you still with me Jeffrey?'

'Wh… wh… what have I s…s…said?' the man finally managed.

'Ah now, that's fine. A bit of conversation at last. And here was I thinking I was talkin' to meself. As for what you've said, I haven't got a clue mate. That's not my business, d'ya see? Just like it shouldn't be your business what anybody else is doing, do you get my drift?'

'I th…think so.'

'Oh, now, that seems like you're still not sure there.'

'No, I am, really I am,' Jeffrey said hurriedly. 'Listen, just go. I won't say anything about anyone, I promise, and I won't say anything about you. I haven't seen your face so there's no need to kill me.'

'Now you have a point there,' said Liam. 'This mask is a bit dramatic. Nearly shit meself earlier, so I did, when I saw me own reflection.' He began to lift the mask.

'No,' cried Jeffrey. 'No, please, I don't want to see you. I don't want to know.'

'But Jeffrey, old mate, this is the face that will be back to kill you if you keep talkin' like you've been talkin',' said Liam as he removed the mask. 'This face and this gun,' he said as he pulled the .38 from his pocket and aimed it. He would rather have threatened him with *The Killer*, but that was the Butcher of Belfast's knife. His face, he knew, didn't matter. The Butcher hadn't had any scars.

'No,' yelled Jeffrey again.

'Now you don't be frettin' there,' said Liam. 'I'm not gonna shoot you right now, not with you in that fancy dress of yours and your boyfriend all tarted up, like. No, I'll be back to shoot you later if the boys hear one more word. Actually, I say "the boys", but it could be anyone really, even the Provos. No more talking about the troubles or anything to do with the north. Then again, I say "the north" but it's probably best if you don't say anything about the south either. Because if you do, Jeffrey old son, it won't be one of those dildos goin' up yer arse, it'll be this gun. You'll be arse-shot, and that's a nasty way to die. Could take ten or twelve hours of agony. So, we'll be understanding each other then?'

Jeffrey gulped, nodded and hung his head just as a moan from the ground indicated that the transvestite was coming round.

'So I'll be off then,' said Liam. 'Say goodbye to your girlfriend for me and give my regards to your wife.'

As he walked from the room he heard the sound of tears from behind him and whimpering in front. 'Let's be having my jacket there, old feller,' he said as the dog stood to greet him. He patted him and then strode from the house and back to his car.

The next day he took a detour to Cork, delighting in another tank of petrol, and called in to see Laa Laa where he left his new travel documents. 'Don't want to cross a border with two sets of I.D,' he explained, and Laa Laa agreed to post them over to Montse. Then he headed home.

15

The Payday

'Oh, very good Liam, very good,' Turner smiled as he looked at the photographs of McMurphy. 'This is exactly what we need. He's obviously still in the game. It looks like all that training and planning paid off?'

'I just stuck to the timetable,' Liam lied.

'Excellent, dear boy, excellent.'

'So, does that mean that I can go and get him now?'

'I think it will be very soon,' Turner confirmed. 'You obviously did a good job on that other pesky fellow too. He's gone very quiet all of a sudden. I will need a full briefing on that as well, of course.'

'Found him, caught him, scared him, job done,' Liam announced.

'Pardon?'

'Honestly, Mr. T, a wee lass with a rolling pin could've done the job just as well. Jesus, what a desperate little poof the feller is.'

'Really? Well we're going to need to say more than that, Liam. Now we have a file on this fellow, we need to add anything interesting you might have discovered about his habits.'

'Oh, he has some bold and interesting habits all right,' Liam confirmed.

'There, you see, that will all be very useful. You'll be in the good books for this and that will all help towards your end goal.'

'Whatever you say, Mr. T, you're the boss. And you really think that end goal will be soon?'

'Moore is going to take a bit longer, but I think we're very close to McMurphy now. Early in the New Year I'd say.'

'So two months?'

'Maybe three or four.'

'Four more fuckin' months?'

'Now don't start, Liam. You're recent behaviour has been exemplary. Let's not spoil it. Besides, you've waited this long. What's a few more months?'

'But that's still only for one of 'em. What about Moore? He's the one I really want. McMurphy's just some tosspot money man who sat on a committee and signed a death warrant.' Liam lit a cigarette and inhaled angrily. 'Peter Moore's the one who ordered it just to get me to join the Provos and I still don't know fuckin' why. Come on, Mr. Turner, how much more fuckin' exemplary do I need to be before I can get the bastard?'

Turner closed his eyes and shook his head. There was no point trying to reason with the lad over this point. Besides, if the truth be told, he agreed with him. 'You may never know why son,' he said sadly.

'Yeah, I know. Fuck.'

'Now, would you like some news that may cheer you up?' Turner continued.

'Aye, that'd be good.'

'You remember those friends of yours over in America with that strange name?'

'The Druids? Aye, of course I remember.'

'Well,' said Turner, as he puffed on his pipe, 'I managed to secure finance for them for their termination of James Malcolm Brennan.'

Liam couldn't be absolutely sure, but it looked as if Turner had just puffed out his chest a bit. 'Really?' he asked. 'Jimmy Mal? How on earth did you manage that?'

'I have to admit that I'm a little proud of myself, actually, and I think this will tickle you.'

'Go on then, I'm all ears.'

'First I checked into the other two chaps who were killed in the car at the same time as Mr. Brennan and it transpired that one of them had reached our board room level.'

'What?'

'It means he was being sanctioned for termination. It seems he was a very nasty fellow and we really wanted him out of the way, but it was going to be quite an expensive operation. The third man was masquerading as a driver, but he was also on our schedule. Not as high up our list as the other chappie, but still of considerable interest. So, your friends, quite by chance, just happened to terminate two individuals before we had to issue an order. I also successfully argued that James Brennan himself was a previously sanctioned target and still officially on the table. That's when the accountants went to work.'

'And?'

'And your friends have ended up with thirty thousand dollars between them.'

'You are joking.'

'No, not at all, and this is the bit that will amuse you. I told them that there were four of the Druid boys. So, everything was factored in and it worked out at two-and-a-half thousand dollars per man per kill and that, apparently, is an absolute bargain. Your friends have saved Her Majesty a substantial amount of money and our accountant is a very happy man.'

Liam stared at his companion. 'That is so messed up I can't even get my head round it. Who would calculate the cost of bodies that way?'

'I quite agree, Liam, but the books balance and that is what matters.'

'Mr. T, you are a marvel.'

'I know,' said Turner, and this time there was no mistaking the pride in his voice.

16

The M...M...Meeting on the C...C...Costa B...B...Brava

'Montse, it's me. Put the gun away,' Liam shouted as he pulled up outside the farmhouse on a chilly day in late December. It was their regular joke now every time he arrived and she always laughed at him. On this occasion, however, she seemed a little distracted as she ran to meet him at the car.

'Is everything okay, love?' he asked after her kiss of greeting.

'I am not sure,' she told him as they went inside the kitchen. 'I had a strange phone call for you, Darren.'

'For me? Here? Who was it from?'

'Well, that is the problem. I am not sure. I wrote down everything that the man said, but he was so difficult to understand.'

'In what way?'

'He spoke in Spanish, but his words were very odd. He stopped and then he started again. He asked if I was M…M…M…Montse.'

'Laa Laa,' Darren exclaimed.

Montse furrowed her brow and then her face relaxed in a moment of realisation. 'Of course, it was the friend you told me about. Oh, how could I be so stupid? In English I would not have been so confused. In Spanish, well it made no sense. It was just as if he was saying "the the". That is what I heard. Oh, am I so relieved.'

Darren laughed. 'Yes, he's bad enough in English. I can't imagine what he would sound like in Spanish. Anyway, what did he say?'

'I wrote down what I could understand. There is a hotel and you are to meet him there. He will be at the bar at twelve o'clock every day for the next week. This is what I think he said.'

'Did he say it was urgent?'

'I don't think so. It sounded more like "might be important".'

'Okay, I'll take a trip tomorrow,' Darren decided.

The hotel in L'Estartit was easy to find and Liam spotted Laa Laa sitting alone at the bar. He crept up behind him, grabbed his shoulders and yelled, 'Gotcha.'

'F...F...F...F...F...Fuck m...m...m...me, B...B...B...B...Butch,' stammered Laa Laa, spinning round. 'You n...n...n...nearly g...gave me a f...f...f...friggin h...h...heart attack.'

'Didn't know you had a heart,' Liam grinned. 'Anyway, mate, how are you and what's this all about? Shall I get the beers in?'

'I'm d...d...d...doing p...p...p...p...p...p...pretty g...g...g...'

'Okay, hold it there mate. I'll assume you're doing pretty good and that you do want a beer. You just concentrate on the "what's this all about" bit.'

They took their drinks to a small table and Laa Laa began. 'Well, I th...th...th...think I'll c...c...c...call you L...L...L...Liam today.'

'Whoa, this must be serious.'

'I d...d...d...don't know for s...s...s...s...for a f..f...f...fact. I heard s...s...s...s...s...s...something.'

'About me?'

'Has t...t... to be.'

'Okay, you have my attention,' Liam told him.

'Y...y...y...y...you have a s...s...s...s...s...s...s...s.'

'Jesus Christ mate, a what?'

The letter S always presented Laa Laa with the greatest problem, and this time he gave up, pointing instead to Liam's cheek.

'My scar?'

'Y…y…yes. There is t…t…talk of a m…m…man with a s…s…s…s…s…'

'Scar.'

'Yes, a s…s…s…s…s…s…'

'Laa Laa, for Christ's sake, I've got it.'

'Ok…k…k…kay.   P…p…p…p…people   are s…s…s…s…s…s…s…'

'Saying?'

'No.   s…s…s…s…s…s,   oh   f…f…fuck   it, f…f…fright…t…tened of h…h…him.'

'Ah, scared.'

'Yes.   The   w…w…word   is   he's   a s…s…s…s…s…s…s…s…s'

'Psycho?'

'No, a s…s…s…s…s…s…s…'

'Sociopath?'

'No, a s…s…sp…sp…sp…sp…'

'Specialist?'

'S…s…spook,' Laa Laa finally managed with great effort, the word coming out in a spray of spit all over Liam's face.

'Shit man.'

'S…s…s…s…s…s…s…s…'

'Apology accepted,' Liam said as he wiped himself clean with a napkin. 'A spook, eh? What, like a ghost kind of thing? Well, I've had worse reputations, I guess. Who's saying it Laa Laa. Are they high up?'

'I th….th…think s…s…s…'

'The boys? The R.A?'

'I th…th…th…'

'Think so, yes I get it. Laa Laa, have you ever heard of a man called Peter Moore?'

This time Laa Laa just nodded.

'Is it him?'

'M…m…maybe.   And   th…th…they're l…l…l…looking for y…y…you.'

'Thanks, Laa Laa. This is very interesting. Has anyone ever mentioned any of my other names?'

'Not th…th…that I've h…h…heard.'

'So they don't know who I was then?'

'N…n…no.'

Liam sat quietly for a while considering the information. He could think of three times when his face had been seen by people he had left alive. There was a hotel receptionist from the Mad Dog job, two henchmen from a contract in Scotland and now a fat faggot from Connemara. He and Turner had discussed this a couple of times before and decided it was no bad thing if his appearance scared people, but if the boys were now actively looking for him, maybe he could use that to his advantage. Maybe it would finally get him to McMurphy and Moore before he became too hot.

He suggested another beer and returned from the bar with three. 'My girl will be joining us,' he explained. 'She had a bit of shopping to do in town, but then I thought it would be nice if you met.'

Montse arrived about five minutes later and Liam made the introductions.

'Hello and how very n..nice to meet you,' said Laa Laa. 'I thought you s…sounded lovely on the phone.'

'Jesus, mate, where did the stutter go?' asked Liam. 'You hardly missed a beat there.'

Laa Laa turned back to Liam. 'I f…f…f…find w…w…w…women easier to t…t…t…t…talk t…t…to f…f…f…face to f…f…face,' he explained.

'Well that would have been helpful to know sooner,' Liam said, the exasperation clear in his voice. 'Fuck me.'

17

The Beeline Plan

'So you will go first to Argentina?' asked Montse, her brow furrowed.

'It will be easier that way, and more confusing for anyone else trying to find me,' Darren explained. 'Laa Laa can sort out a visa so that José Luis can go to America. Tommy will meet you in New York and take you to Dinwiddie.'

'Din-que?'

'Don't worry about that. American words are even stranger than English ones.'

'You do not speak the same language?' asked Montse in concern. 'I only speak English. Will I have to learn American as well?'

'Oh Montse, you don't know how funny that is.'

'You are laughing at me now,' she pouted.

'No, lass, I'm not,' Darren assured her. 'The Americans do speak English, but there it's just that little bit different. Listen, you have nothing to worry about. You'll like Tommy and he will look after you. Now, you know the code words and what to do?'

'Yes, you will ring me and say you want some eggs over easy and that means I have to prepare. Then, in maybe one or two days, there will be another call and you will say "Beeline". I will be ready and I will wait for Vasi. He will take me to Laa Laa and Laa Laa will send me to Tommy and Tommy will take me to somewhere else.'

'Dinwiddie.'

'Yes, I have it.'

'Good girl.'

'And when will you get to this Dinnywinny place, Darren?'

'I guess a couple of days later, but that depends on Laa Laa too. Everyone knows the code words and what to do.'

'And when will you ring me? When will you ask for eggs and say "Beeline"?'

'I don't know, love. It could be a week, a month or a year. It depends on so many things. For now I need to make a call.'

Liam rang Turner every day when he was in Spain. It was part of his agreement to follow protocol, always be in touch and never go off script again. The call usually consisted of little more than Turner's "Hullo", Liam's

"Yerself" and then a general "everything's OK", but today he was going to suggest an early return for a cup of tea. It was their code for needing to talk and he knew Turner would be surprised to hear it. He placed his call to the switchboard and waited to be put through.

'Hullo,' came Turner's voice eventually.

'Yerself,' said Liam.

'Fancy a cup of tea?' said Turner. 'Soon as you like.'

'Sure,' Liam said. The man had stolen his line. 'I'm on my way.'

18

The Close of 1983

'I told you the New Year was likely, my boy,' Turner said over his tea and biscuits in Liam's drawing room. 'He's in the south now and it's perfect. You don't have long, but it shouldn't be too complicated. In and out, I should say, but we would like it bloody. Gates is on stand-by to get you there and back.'

'A one-day job? I guess that's the time and motion guys again. What if I don't want to do it in one day?'

'Liam, don't be childish. Yes it's a one-day job, just like with Larry O'Brien. I doubt you would want to stick around after the deed is done.'

'Mad Dog? Yeah, we all know how that turned out. Just as long as Gates is on the same schedule and doesn't leave me behind this time.'

'Really, my boy, I thought we were over that. Anyway, I had expected more enthusiasm. This is McMurphy.'

'Oh, Mr. Turner, I'm enthusiastic all right. In fact I can't fuckin' wait, but there's something I need to tell you too.'

'That sounds serious.'

Liam filled him in on Laa Laa's information and what seemed to be a hunt for the scarred man.

'So, he really said they are calling you a spook?' Turner asked.

'Eventually.'

'Sorry?'

'Never mind. Yes, that's what he told me. So it seems to me that I need to get Moore as well, and as soon as possible.'

'Hmm,' Turner considered. 'Yes, this is very interesting. You have the fear factor on your side now. Yes, indeed, it would make sense to strike while the iron is hot, so to speak.'

'So, you'll get onto it then?'

'Indeed, dear boy, I will see what I can do.'

19

Cigarettes and Whiskey

As Liam heard Turner's car heading out of the drive he reached for his bottle of whiskey. A little celebration was in order. It might not be Peter Moore just yet, but getting Martin McMurphy would make three out of four and it was a step in the right direction. 'Bloody, too.' Liam grinned at the thought. 'And you won't be far behind, Peter old son. I promise you that.' Jesus, he hadn't felt this good in months.

Then the grin left his face as he looked at his bottle of Jameson. It was nearly empty. A swift glance in the cupboard showed he was almost out of fags too. 'How come you've missed this then Mr. Turner?' he wondered aloud. Turner always seemed to know everything, including how well stocked his booze cabinet was. Ah well, a little fresh air would do him good and he quite enjoyed a trip out to Matlock and his favourite off-licence.

He took his regular route to the shop. It was against the advice, dished out by government experts, to always use different routes and different destinations. That was all well and good in the classroom, but Liam lived in the real world and the trouble with unfamiliar routes was that you never knew what to expect. On a well-worn path Liam knew exactly what should and, more importantly, shouldn't be there. It wasn't as if the bad guys didn't know about anti-surveillance measures too. Besides, many operatives taught to use different routes were dead. He was still alive.

Liam followed his own safety routine, checking the car for explosive devices and basically staying alert. The journey to Harding's off-licence wasn't long and there was nothing untoward on the street. He entered the shop and saw the thin proprietor at his ancient till. He was a strange old man, eccentric even, but he always had a supply of Jameson whiskey and Capstan cigarettes.

'Good afternoon Mr. O'Neil, and how are you today?' came the friendly greeting.

'I'm very well Mr. Harding, thanks, and how's yerself?'

'Can't complain, son, and no one would listen if I did,' said the old gentleman and Liam smiled. He said exactly the same thing every time. 'So what can I get for you today?'

'A bottle of Jameson and a carton of Capstan, please.'

'That'll be two hundred cigarettes, right?'

'Aye,' Liam confirmed with a grin. He'd lost count of the number of times he'd been in the shop and he always left with the same brand of whiskey and the same number and brand of cigarettes. Even when he called in for change to make phone calls, he still bought the usual supplies. Maybe that was why he liked the old guy so much. There wasn't a lot in Liam's life that could be counted on, but Leslie Harding was about as reliable as you could get.

'Now, Capstan, Capstan, where are they?' he was mumbling to himself as he searched along the shelf. They were there, right in front of him where they always were, but Liam didn't point them out. This was just part of the routine. Next would come the pen and paper while he added up the bill, which always came to the same figure, then Liam would send his regards to Shelagh, Mr. Harding's wife, and then Mr. Harding would tell him to drive safely.

Liam paid over the requested money with a patient smile. 'Please give my regards to Shelagh,' he said.

'Ah, that reminds me,' said Leslie. 'We were just talking about you yesterday.'

'You were?' asked Liam in surprise. This was new.

'Yes, do you know anyone else round here that's from your part of the world?'

'Why do you ask?' said Liam, his suspicions immediately aroused.

'Well, a man called into the shop you see, and he had exactly the same accent as you,' smiled Leslie. 'So I was telling Shelagh and she said, 'Well that's unusual for this part of the world,' and I said, 'Well, yes it is.' Then Shelagh said that maybe he was from your part of the world and I should ask you. So – that's what I did.'

Liam swallowed hard, 'Did he ask anything about me personally?'

'Oh goodness me no. I'm not even sure he knows you. It was just his accent that started us wondering. That and the fact that he also buys Jameson.'

'What's he look like, this feller? Can you describe him Mr. Harding?'

'Well, he was an older gentleman; somewhere around my age I should guess.'

Liam relaxed a little. This didn't sound like anything to bother about. 'No, doesn't sound like anyone I know.'

'Well, as I was saying to Shelagh, Ireland is a big place, but she said that it's not as big as England, and I said I wasn't so sure about that, not when you take off Scotland and Wales, that is, but she said there's a lot more people live here than live in Ireland. "You've only got to look at London," she said and I had to admit she had a point there. Anyway, we were just wondering that's all. Sounds like nothing but a coincidence, then.'

'Sounds like.'

'Well, you drive safely, Mr. O'Neil.'

'I will. Thanks Mr. Harding,' said Liam as the door bell chimed behind him and he saw Leslie's smile disappear to be replaced by a look of shock. He spun round and faced two men in balaclavas. 'Shite,' he thought. 'The boys have found me.'

'Don't anybody move, this is a robbery,' one of the men yelled as he levelled a gun directly at Liam.

'Oh Jesus Christ, thank the Lord for that,' gulped Liam as he stared down the barrels of the sawn off shotgun. If they had been the Provos he'd be facing an AK, not an old scattergun, and he'd already be a dead man.

One of the men remained guarding the door whilst his accomplice strode quickly to the counter. 'Gimme yer money, all of it ya old twat,' he hissed in a strong Yorkshire accent.

Leslie froze as he stood at the counter, unable to utter a single word.

'Ah said gimme it, d'ya 'ear mi?' snarled the Yorkshireman.

Still the shopkeeper said nothing.

The robber's patience quickly wore thin and he drew back his fist to hit the old man. With the speed of a pouncing cat Liam sprang and grabbed the man's arm, threw a couple of fast punches and had the assailant on the floor in seconds. The next thing he heard was a loud boom, his vision clouded and he promptly passed out. Later he was vaguely aware of sirens before he descended into blackness once more.

20

Whitworth Hospital

Turner sat in the chair, his feet on the coffee table and head tilted backwards, gently snoring away as the patient began coming round.

'Fuck me,' whispered Liam in a dry and raspy voice. 'Oh Jesus Christ, that really fuckin' hurts.'

Turner was alert in an instant. 'Ah, there you are my old chum. You really had me worried you know. Thought you were a gonner. Tell me, how do you feel lad?' he asked as he yawned and began rubbing the sleep from his eyes.

'Shite man, I feel like I've been run over by a bleedin' steam engine. What happened?'

'Can't you remember old boy?'

'I can remember seeing a sawn-off but, after that, not so much.'

'Well, I have to say old fellow, from the report I received it seems that you are a bit of a daredevil; a regular hero, don't you know.'

'A what?' asked Liam in a daze.

'A hero, old bean. Seems that you not only prevented a robbery, but you also protected one of Her Majesty's citizens from a beating and possibly worse. I'm seriously considering putting you forward for a gallantry award,' joked Turner.

Liam shook his head as he tried to remember. 'Yes, there were two of 'em, I think. Mr. Harding's okay?'

'Yes, he's fine Liam. What a charming man. We had to have a little word with him, of course. Make sure he didn't go saying anything to the press and we got him out of the police station as soon as we could. I don't think he really understood the situation, but we've managed to keep your name out of things. I've always been concerned about your insistence on going to the same place all the time, you know.'

'There was no one watching me, I'm sure of it,' said Liam as his mind began to clear a little.

'No, it doesn't look like anything other than a robbery and you were just in the wrong place at the wrong time. The shopkeeper did mention another man with an Irish accent, but we couldn't find any link.'

'Oh yeah, there was something. I just… I can't remember. I… oh shite,' groaned Liam as pain shot through his side. 'What happened to me?'

'Your hipbone was shattered by the gun blast and you took a nasty bang to the head when you fell. It's kept you out of things for a while. Lots of monitoring and all that. They wouldn't let me in to see you until today. You get some more rest and we'll talk later.'

Liam was quickly back in the land of oblivion and the next time he woke his mind was clearer. Turner was asleep in the chair again and he shouted to bring him round. 'Oi, you still here then?'

Turner jumped and took a second to gather his thoughts. 'It would appear so, wouldn't it?' he said finally through a yawn.

'What day is it?' Liam asked urgently.

'Ah, I thought we'd come to that. It's Friday Liam, and, yes, you did miss the McMurphy job.'

'Fuck,' Liam spat as he instinctively moved to sit upright before a shooting pain dragged him down again. 'Shit, oh fuck, ow, shiting bollocks. Jesus Christ. Oh, fuck me.'

Turner remained silent as Liam took deep breaths to dull the pain and gather himself. 'Sorry, Mr. T,' he managed finally through gasps of air. 'That was some bad language there.'

'Special dispensation today, lad,' Turner assured him. 'I imagine I might use the odd profanity myself if I was in that much pain.'

'Fuck the pain,' Liam gasped. 'What about McMurphy?'

'We sent in another operative, but he was unprepared and, I'm afraid, we lost him.'

'Lost who? McMurphy or the operative?'

'Both. We have a dead agent and McMurphy lives to see another day.'

Liam closed his eyes and sighed. 'I'm sorry about the agent, Mr. Turner, but that means McMurphy's still mine, right? When do I get him?'

'Liam, have you any idea how long it will take you to recover from this attack? You have a shattered thigh bone that required major surgery, dear boy. You will be out of action for months.'

'No fuckin' way. I was so fuckin' close. I'll be back on the job before you know it.'

'Well, that's another thing. There might not be any jobs for some time, Liam.'

'What?'

'We believe the robbery was pure happenstance and we think the Irishman who called in the off-licence was merely a tourist. He didn't ask about you, after all. However, when you put it together with that intelligence you gathered about the phantom with the crescent shaped scar... well, it may be one coincidence too many and we can't take the chance. Liam, you must brace yourself for some bad news, but you may be out of the game altogether.'

Pain shot through Liam once more as he sat bolt upright, but he ignored it. 'No – fuckin' – way!' he shouted with such force that a nurse came running into the room in panic. 'Fuck off,' he yelled at her, and immediately regretted it, but she had gone before he had time to apologise.

'Liam, you really must calm yourself,' Turner said hurriedly. 'Nothing is sure right now, but we have to be cautious. At the very least you need some serious convalescence and that is being organised as we speak. Please, dear boy, you have to be realistic. We'll have you out of here as soon as we can, but you need to be a good patient.'

'Patient? A good fuckin' patient? I'd rather be an assassin.'

'Yes, well, we can't always have what we want, can we?'

'Oh can't we? You just wait, Mr. Turner. I'll show you.'

'I'm sure you will, dear boy. I'm sure you will.'

Liam had been in hospital for a week and was as bored as he could ever remember, but his wound was healing, the pain lessened daily and he was moving around on crutches. He had been allowed to call Montse, and Turner was trying to arrange for her to visit, though it turned out she had no travel documents. That was something Liam had never considered and he admonished himself for the oversight that would have put a big dent in his Beeline plan. An alternative strategy was looking more and more necessary and he kept his mind active by planning how he could get McMurphy and Moore himself and then fuck off to America with Montse. For that, though, she needed a passport and Liam allowed himself a small smile. The

British authorities were liaising with the Spanish to rush that through for her, which was a nice little twist of fate.

'How awfully decent of them,' he commented to Turner on his latest visit.

'We do like to look after our operatives, you know,' Turner had informed him. 'So, how are you today, my boy?'

'Well, apart form a shotgun hole in my leg and bed sores on me arse, I'm just peachy.'

'If you insist on sarcasm I won't give you the good news.'

'What news?' Liam was immediately alert.

'You leave hospital tomorrow and we have a private nurse waiting for you at home.'

'Really?'

'Yes, Liam, I thought that might make you smile. It made me smile too,' Turner offered with what looked like a wink. How odd.

21

The Nursemaid

Late the following afternoon he was in an ambulance that pulled up the drive of the old manor house. An orderly was pushing him down the ramp in a wheelchair when he noticed a man wearing what looked like an apron and waving to him from his front step. His own arm raised automatically to return the wave, then dropped in alarm as he heard a shrill voice ring out.

'Yoohoo, hello, Mr O'Neil love. Yoohoo.'

Liam turned to the ambulance man in panic, but he was concentrating intently on the wheelchair brake and offered no eye contact.

'I've got him my darling,' the man in the apron cooed as he rushed forward. 'Now don't you worry my love, you come with me. I'm here to help you. You just relax and leave everything to me.'

'Who the fuck are you?' Liam managed. 'Look mate I think you've made some sort of mistake. Turner said he'd arranged a nurse for me.'

'Ooh, I am your nurse silly. My name's Robert and I'm to do absolutely everything for you. We need you to get well and get all those big muscles nice and strong again, don't we?'

Liam gulped. Was this a bleedin' joke? He looked again for help to the ambulance guy, but he was already jumping back into his vehicle. The engine started and it was off down the drive at speed. 'Er, now look here, Rob, I'm fine. I'll not be needing you, I reckon.'

'Oh you are being a little silly, aren't you sweetie? And please do call me Robert or Bobby. Rob sounds so common, don't you think? Come on now. Mr. Turner did say you could be quite a handful.' A little girl giggle followed. 'Oh dearie me indeed. Did I really just say that? A *handful*. Oh how could I?'

Liam just stared. Bollocks.

He was being wheeled into the house and then he felt himself lifted by surprisingly strong arms. In just a few minutes Robert had him out of the chair, up the stairs and sitting on his bed. He'd had no option but to lean on his nurse for support but, as Robert started to undress him, Liam decided it was time he did have an option.

'I can manage,' he said hurriedly.

'If you're sure, dear,' Robert said sweetly. 'Would we like a nice cup of cocoa to help us sleep?'

'I'd rather have a whiskey,' Liam said. 'There should be some in the cabinet downstairs.'

'Ooh, aren't we a naughty boy then? No alcohol for you until we've finished with all those wonderful little tablets. I'll make the cocoa,' Robert said as he bustled from the room.

Fuckin' cocoa? He hadn't drunk cocoa since he was a child and his Ma made it for him. Still, at least Robert had left him alone. He fumbled to change into the pyjamas that were lying, freshly laundered, on the bed. It wasn't easy and Liam wondered why on earth it should be that one limb out of action seemed to make the others less effective too. His hands trembled as he rushed to do up the buttons before the other man returned.

Robert reappeared, steaming mug in hand, just as Liam was wincing as he tried to lift his injured leg into the bed.

'There, there, don't be a little silly,' said the nurse as he deposited the cocoa on the bedside table. 'Here we go, one, two, three and oopsy daisy.'

Before he knew it, Robert had the injured leg safely in bed and Liam hadn't felt a thing. 'Now, let's get you tucked in all nice and cosy,' he offered as he arranged the bedclothes.

Liam tried to do it himself, but Robert had taken control and he felt completely helpless. He took his tablets, "like a good boy", dutifully drank his cocoa under the nurse's watchful eye and felt himself drifting to sleep. He struggled to stay alert, wanting to see Robert leave the room, but the journey had taken its toll and he was far from fit. He did indeed feel all nice and cosy. His last thought, as sleep overtook him, was that he might need to pop out and buy some more Jameson. He seemed to remember that he was nearly out.

The next morning he opened his eyes to a bright, wintry sun and struggled for a few seconds to realise where he was. He had memories of a strange dream of some effeminate man putting him to bed and he shook himself to remove the images. Then the bedroom door opened and in walked his worst nightmare.

'Time for your dressings changing dearie,' sang out Robert in a cheerful voice.

Liam cringed and pulled the bedclothes tightly to his chest.

'Oh come on now, don't be a baby. You let Bobby take a little peep.' The bedding was off and his pyjama bottoms down before he knew what was happening and there was nothing he could do about it. At least he'd had the good sense to leave his underwear on, but he still turned his head away while Robert did what was necessary and rambled on about not wanting any infections. If he hadn't been feeling so vulnerable and so bleedin' uncomfortable, he would have laughed when he heard the nurse say, 'clinical cleanliness'. Oh, the irony.

'There, now, all done and we're nice and clean again, aren't we,' Bobby said with a smile. 'Now, time for our tablets.'

'Well "we" don't really want "our" tablets,' said Liam, wondering why everything had to be plural. 'I had enough of the bleedin' things in hospital.'

'Now don't be such a silly. Doctor knows best, you know, and these antibiotics will stop any nasty infections. Just two more days and you'll have finished the course. Then you can have a drink. Mr. Turner has sent over some whiskey and cigarettes for you.'

Well, he was thankful for small mercies, but two more days. He screwed up his eyes as Bobby put the pills to his lips. Jesus Christ, had he died and gone to Hell? Was this God's revenge? He swallowed his tablets and leaned back with a sigh.

'That's a good boy,' Bobby hummed, 'and, as a special treat, you can have a visitor today.'

'Who? Not one of your bleedin' mates, is it?'

'Oh no, silly, it's your friend, Mr. Turner. He'll be round at midday.'

'That'll be nice. I'll be needin' a bleedin' word with him.'

At one minute before twelve a car pulled up and Liam could hear a high pitched giggle and a deeper, more cultured voice in conversation downstairs, though he couldn't make out what they were saying. A few minutes later his nurse led his boss into the room.

'Thanks, Rob, you can leave us now,' Liam instructed.

'Robert or Bobby,' the nurse reminded him before closing the door on his way out.

'Hello old chum,' said Turner. 'So, tell me, how are you feeling today?'

'How am I feeling?' Liam snapped. 'How the Hell do you think I'm feeling? I've been shot to shit and now I'm forced to share the house with… with him.'

'Him?' quizzed Turner, a small smile playing on his lips. 'I'm not sure I know what you mean. Are you suggesting there is a problem? I was informed that Robert is an excellent nurse. Hasn't he been looking after you?'

'Oh aye, he's been looking after me all right. But the big problem is that *he* is a *him*, and not a *her*. I daren't bleedin' sleep last night with him hovering about the place all the time. I'm absolutely knackered man.'

'Well, I'm a little confused by that,' Turner told him, his smile still in place. 'If I'm being honest with you, Liam old boy, I can't see the difference. A nurse is just that, a nurse. The sex shouldn't have any bearing on the matter. As for not sleeping, Robert informs me that you slept very well last night. He came in to check on you several times.'

'He bleedin' what?'

'He's a nurse, Liam. That's his job.'

'Listen, Mr. Turner, I can see you're enjoying this but I don't want some bloke wondering round my bedroom while I'm lying here all helpless, like.'

'But that's why he's here, Liam, because you are helpless. We have to consider your security as well as your health and I doubt a female nurse would have been up to both jobs.'

'What the Hell are you on about, Mr. T? He couldn't protect me. If someone broke in here he'd go all "Gone with the Wind" swoon on me and I'd be a dead man. So I might as well have a woman. At least then I'd have something to look at. Blonde, brunette, I don't care. Just anything but him.'

'Oh, Liam, you really shouldn't go jumping to conclusions. Robert is not only an excellent nurse but he even did a spot of instructing at Hereford.'

'Instructing? Instructing in what? Needlework?'

'Unarmed combat, dear boy, your very own speciality.'

'You have got to be joking,' Liam said. 'He's a bleedin' shirt lifter.'

'A what lifter?'

'Shirt. You know, he's bent, a poof, a queer.'

'Are you trying to suggest that he is homosexual, Liam?'

'Aye. He's as bent as a bleedin' nine-bob-note.'

'Well it may interest you to know that he has seen action several times. Many missions require a good medical practitioner, but also one who can take care of himself. I had to go to quite a lot of trouble to secure him for this duty, and his regular crew were not happy about that at all.'

'They weren't?'

'Oh no. His commander is a fellow a lot like you, actually, and he didn't want me stealing him away. He said to me, "He may be a poofter, but he's our poofter." So, you see, you really are quite lucky to have him. I'm sure that Robert would be much happier back in his regiment, but at least he is carrying off his duties with good grace. I suggest you take a leaf out of his book.'

'Well, that's interesting,' Liam conceded, 'but he still makes me nervous. What if he tries anything in the night, like?'

'You have nothing to worry about, Liam. Robert has a long term partner and he has already told me that you are not his type.'

'I'm not?' Liam asked with a long, relieved whistle.

'No, so does that make you feel better?'

'Yes, it does, at least... well... yes... but, what's wrong with me?'

'Oh, Liam, really,' said Turner with an exasperated sigh.

The Englishman left a few minutes later and then the nurse appeared carrying a tray of lunch with a packet of Capstan full strength next to it.

'Thank you Rob, er, Bobby,' Liam said.

'You're very welcome, sweetie,' said Robert with a smile.

Over the next forty-eight hours Liam became increasingly bored. He was moving about as much as possible on his crutches and he had some magazines and a book, but he had never been a reader. At least in hospital there had been plenty of activity and things to look at. The only breaks in the monotony here were Robert's visits with food and medical attention and Liam found he was beginning to look forward to them. He'd decided to be blunt and just ask Rob straight out if he was safe.

'Don't you worry yourself, I can look after you,' Robert had assured him.

'No, I didn't mean that. I meant here, me with you, is it safe? Am I safe – with you?'

'Oh do relax, you silly man. I have a boyfriend called David and he's an absolute love. I have no interest in anyone else. Besides, you're far too butch for me.'

Liam cringed at the "butch" reference, but said nothing.

'If you still don't believe me, I'll bring David to meet you one day,' Robert continued.

'No, mate, that's fine,' Liam assured him. 'One of you is quite enough.'

'Well, we'll see when you're stronger. Talking of which, how are we feeling today?'

'Bored out of "our" mind.'

'Good,' said Robert, ignoring the sarcasm.

'What's good about it?'

'Well, we've finished our course of antibiotics and we've had less and less pain killers. That means we're becoming stronger and more alert. Now, if we're up to it, how about a little trip downstairs to watch the telly?'

'Hey, Rob, that'd be great.'

'Please don't call me Rob. It's just so tacky,' Robert said with a pained expression.

'Tell you what,' Liam offered, 'I'll call you Bobby if you'll stop with all this we and us crap. There is no "we". Got it?'

'Now that's such a shame, sweetie,' Robert said with a smile. 'And I was just going to suggest that we had a little drinkie of the good stuff when we got downstairs as well.'

'Really?' Liam grinned. 'You know, Bobby, you're not so bad after all.'

The trip downstairs was difficult, but Robert handled him skilfully and the shot of Jameson that greeted him made the discomfort worthwhile. Bobby turned down the offer to join him in a whiskey, claiming it was "too harsh", but agreed to a small gin and tonic after dinner. He also declined a Capstan cigarette, declaring them "common and stinky", but pulled out his own pack of Silk Cut which, apparently, were more refined. They watched television in the evening and then Bobby bustled round the kitchen singing to himself.

Each day the trips up and down stairs became a little easier and Bobby began some gentle physiotherapy. Turner visited in the middle of one session and smiled as he saw Liam with his hands on Robert's shoulders while the nurse helped him flex his leg. When they were done, Bobby offered to make them some tea and left them to talk.

'Any news on McMur....' Liam began, but Turner gave him the "shush" signal.

'Not authorised,' he mouthed, indicating the kitchen where Bobby could be heard humming to himself.

'But we trust him,' Liam whispered in surprise.

'Indeed,' Turner assured him quietly, 'but it's all about specifics, clearance levels, need to know and all that. We should talk in general terms for now. So,' he continued, his voice at a more normal level, 'how is the leg?'

'It's coming on fine, Mr. T. I'll be back at work in no time.'

'Patience, dear boy, patience. You are doing well, but it's going to be months before you're fully fit.'

'Months?' Liam coughed. 'I can't wait months.'

'It will take as long as it will take, my boy. It's not as if you're going back to work in an office, is it? We require a much greater level of fitness from you than from ordinary men. I'll be by to see you as often as I can, but with you out of action I'm spending quite a bit of time away.'

'Away where?'

'Now, now, Liam, you know that is classified.'

Bobby knocked at the door and offered to replenish their tea.

'Yes, please, Robert' Turner said, 'and how is our patient doing?'

'He's coming along nicely, sir, but it will be months before he is fully fit.'

'Fuck,' said Liam.

'Language,' said Turner and Bobby in unison.

22

Months Later

Montse had made a few visits and Bobby had moved out, though he still called in to check on him. Liam was fully mobile but his leg remained a bit stiff. 'I'm so fuckin' bored,' he whispered to David over dinner one night. Bobby had taken to inviting him round for a meal on a weekly basis and Liam had become friendly with the couple. David was, indeed, the love that Bobby had suggested and he wasn't averse to the odd bit of swearing as long as it was out of earshot of his partner.

'Bobby says you have an evaluation this week,' David began. 'Any chance they'll reinstate you now? It's been a bloody long time.'

'David, really, you know we're not supposed to talk about that,' Bobby scolded.

'Oh do be quiet, you silly old queen; I'm not asking for any details. I just think he's looking pretty fit these days, if you know what I mean,' David said with a wink.

'Don't start, boys,' Liam warned. He had become used to their joke flirting and, what had once made him uncomfortable, was now just good fun. 'Anyway, wish me luck on Friday. Do you think I'll pass the physical, Bobby?'

'I think they'll put you back on regular training now,' his nurse suggested.

'Jesus, I hope so.'

Liam presented himself for evaluation at nine o'clock on Friday morning. The process took all day but he was finally passed fit for training and Turner was there to congratulate him. The next week he reported to barracks and began a strict regimen in the pleasant summer weather. He worked hard and felt his strength and general fitness improving by the day until he could take up some of his old combat training duties, return to Derbyshire for a break and even see if he could fit in a quick trip to Spain. As autumn arrived Turner assured him he was now back on active service and could expect a call any time.

It was the middle of the night as he lay in his bed in the Derbyshire manor house dreaming of Spain. The hum of crickets was a pleasing sound on a mountainside where he was relaxing with Montse. Then the sound of crickets grew louder and Montse had to shout at him to be heard above their noise. 'Wake,' she was screaming at him. 'You must wake up.'

He sat bolt upright in panic, taking a second to realise that the crickets of his dream were, in reality, the buzzing of his security alarm. 'Jesus fuckin' Christ,' he cursed as he grabbed his .38 and cautiously looked out into the hallway. He saw nothing and made his way carefully down the stairs, gun at the ready and aimed in all directions. He reached the darkened drawing room and took a quick look inside before leaping through the door and immediately falling to the floor, pistol still outstretched. Finally he was able to see his monitors and then he rose and stared in disbelief. Out on the drive, with his fingers in his ears, stood Turner.

Liam was at the door in seconds. 'What the fuck?' he yelled as he flung it wide.

'Drive, Liam,' said Tuner, 'we need to take one.'

'What?'

'Now. Alarm off and in the car.'

'I'm not dressed.'

'Now lad.'

Liam fumbled with the alarm, reset it, stuck his feet in some boots near the door and stumbled out into the night. 'What time is it?'

'2am, Liam. Let's go.'

They jumped in the silver Mercedes and Turner was heading to the road before Liam had even settled in the passenger seat.

'Christ, Mr. Turner, what is this?'

'Put that away and I'll tell you.'

Liam followed Turner's gaze to his lap. 'Fuck man, I told you I wasn't dressed,' Liam stammered as he fumbled to push his manhood out of sight through the gaping fly hole of his pyjama bottoms. 'Christ, this must be serious.'

'Have you seen the news?'

'I saw the ten o'clock, why?'

'No, it's since then. I've been trying to raise you on the phone, Liam, but it was constantly engaged. I came round here and hammered on the door, but you didn't answer. My only option was to trigger the alarm.'

'For fuck's sake, Mr. Turner, what is going on?'

'We have a problem.'

'That much I could've guessed. What the Hell is it?'

'A P.I.R.A. active service unit was arrested in Scotland. The unit consisted of four men and it seems they were planning a renewed bombing campaign here on the mainland,' Turner explained.

'And? I could've read that in the bleedin' morning paper. There's no need to come rushin' over to tell me. Not at this bloody time. They've been arrested, so what the Hell do you expect me to do about it?'

'Oh, there's nothing you could do about the arrest.'

'Then what the fuck?'

'Liam, I am ignoring your language due to the unusual hour, but you must let me finish.'

'Well get to the fuckin' point then.'

Turner swung the car off the main road and Liam had only a second to wonder where they were going before the other man's words had his full attention. 'One of the arrested men had an address on him, Liam. Your address. He also had a full wiring diagram of your security system.'

'What? Fuck me. Oh fuck me. How the…? Oh, fuck.'

'Precisely, Liam, and we've no idea how he got it or where he got it from but, right now, you need to leave.'

The rest of the drive passed in grim silence and Liam had no idea where he was as the car finally pulled up to the gates of a secluded bungalow. Turner activated a mechanism, the gates swung open, and they drove down to the door.

'Welcome to Chez Anthony,' Turner announced. 'You'll be safe here.'

'This is your house?' Liam didn't know what was more surprising; the fact that Turner had just told him his Christian name or that he was at his private home.

'It's one of them. Let's get you inside.'

Turner led the way and Liam followed, one hand holding his pyjama jacket round him against the chill of the night while the other held onto his bottoms and tried to keep his dignity intact. They walked through the kitchen and into a lounge where Liam stopped short at the sight of dozens of fighting knives, pistols and even assault rifles hanging from the walls. 'Expecting trouble, are we?' he asked.

'Oh goodness me no. I'm very well protected here. Safe as houses, you might say. This is just my personal collection.'

Liam removed an automatic pistol from the wall and whispered, 'Hmm, Beretta - 93 R eh?'

'Very good old boy, you do know your firearms don't you?'

'Aye Mr. Turner that I do, but I'm just wonderin' to meself; if you're only a bit of a collector, how come this one's cleaned, oiled, loaded and ready to go?'

'Not only that one. They're all loaded, every one,' Turner informed him. 'Just because a fellow has round the clock security on the outside of his house, doesn't mean he can't be overly cautious inside you know.'

Liam smiled. 'Jesus, I'd hate to be a bleedin' burglar breakin' into your house mate.'

'Yes quite, they would get rather a nasty shock wouldn't they? Now, would you like a nice cup of tea or do you want to go straight to bed?'

'I'm not sure I'd sleep right now,' Liam decided. 'Maybe a cup of tea and you can tell me a bit more about what's going on.'

'I don't know any more than I've already told you, dear boy,' said Turner as he went into the kitchen and put the kettle on. 'Hopefully we will find out more tomorrow. For now we just needed to get you out quickly. It's frightfully unorthodox bringing you here, but it seemed the safest option under the circumstances. There is security watching your house and there was a back up team making sure that we weren't followed.'

'This is freakin' me out a bit,' Liam confessed.

'Hardly surprising. I was very worried when I couldn't raise you on the phone, old chap.'

'The phone hasn't rung all night and I'm sure I didn't leave it off the hook.'

'Well, there's nothing we can do about it right now,' Turner said as he passed the tea. 'Let's see what tomorrow brings and figure out how much of a liability this makes you.'

'Liability? You reckon this is all my fault then?'

'Actually, no, I don't see how it could be. I think the problem is far more serious than your usual transgressions. Tell me, Liam, what do you call a mole in Ireland?'

'A mole? What, a traitor like?'

'Indeed, and I think we might have one buried deep inside the service somewhere.'

'Fuck me.'

'Liam, really, not in my own home.'

'Sorry, but what does all this mean, for me that is?'

Turner paused for a second and Liam sensed he was considering what to say. In the end he just offered, 'Let's talk tomorrow, my boy. It's late and we don't have all the facts. Finish your tea and then I'll show you to your room.'

'I don't believe you don't know anything at all,' Liam said as he drained his tea. 'This is more than just unorthodox, I'd say, bringing me to your own home - Anthony.'

Turner winced but did not comment on the use of his given name. Instead he let out a long sigh and looked sadly at the younger man. 'It could be the end,' he said finally. 'At the very least you will have to be taken off the active service list for a while.'

'Off active service? Fuck me, I've only just got back on.'

'Liam, please.'

'Please, what? Please don't swear? Please be a good boy? Please play the game? Mr. Turner, I've done nothin' but play the fuckin' game all fuckin year. This is not my fault. Christ, what do you expect me to say? I was this fuckin' close to gettin' another of the Committee men when I got fuckin' shot. That wasn't my fault. You said yourself that there was nothing to suggest it was anything but a robbery gone wrong. Then you set me up with a fuckin' poof under my own roof and still I behave like a good boy. OK, he turned out to be a nice guy, but still. Then I get myself fit, pass every little test your stupid government throws at me and you tell me to expect the call any time, and then some guy shows up in Scotland with my address and that's it? Game over? Stand down yet again? No fuckin' way. Mr. Turner. No fuckin' way.'

'Liam, go to your room.'

'What?'

'Now, Liam,' said Turner, his voice calm but his eyes angry. 'I will simply not tolerate this over my own kitchen table. We will talk tomorrow. You're down that corridor, second on the left, and it's past your bed time.'

Liam just stared at him for a moment. 'Ah, what the fuck,' he spat before turning on his heels and marching off in the direction of the indicated bedroom.

The phone rang early next morning and Liam groaned as he came round after so little sleep.

'Hullo?' he heard as Turner, sounding awake and alert, answered the call. There was a pause and then the one-sided conversation continued in bursts.

'Yes, quite, old boy.'

'Absolutely.'

'Yes, I think he'll be happy enough with that.'

'On that point, William, I entirely concur.'

'No, indeed.'

'Yes, definitely, that would be the best plan. We could even… Yes, yes, exactly old boy. That's just what I was thinking.'

'Oh yes, like a baby. I'd better put the kettle on for him.'

'Yes, indeed I will. Bye for now William.'

Liam heard footsteps head into the kitchen followed by the sound of water filling a kettle. He jumped from bed and into the en suite bathroom, making use of the toiletries he found there. He threw his pyjamas on the floor and jumped in the shower. It was a powerful affair and he would have loved to spend several minutes luxuriating under the steaming jets, but he thought he'd better make this quick. He reached for a towel, dried himself off and then looked for his pyjamas again, but they had gone. Instead, on a small stool in the corner, lay a neat pile of clothes. Oh fuck. He picked up a flannel shirt, a pair of corduroy trousers and a woollen cardigan and closed his eyes in dismay. The pants were at least two sizes too big, though there was a belt provided. Shite. He'd been sleeping in Anthony Turner's bed and now he had to wear his clothes. This really wasn't cool. Still, he didn't seem to have much choice.

'Toast and jam?' Turner offered as he walked into the kitchen.

'Aye, that'd be fine thanks,' Liam accepted as he hoisted up the sagging trousers and sat at the table.

'Sorry I didn't have anything in your size, but you'll be back in your own clothes soon.'

'I will?'

'Yes, we have good news,' Turner told him.

'About my house?'

'Quite. Well it's more of a good news, bad news thing really. No, in truth, I suppose it's really only bad news, but we can make it good news.'

'Mr T, what the Hell are you goin' on about?' Liam pressed.

'Well, dear boy, your telephone line has definitely been tampered with, but we didn't find any nasty little bugs. So we think that someone was preparing to put surveillance into your house, so, that's the bad news bit. Someone is onto you, do you see, which is more bad news.'

'And the good news?'

'They clearly didn't finish the job so it's safe for you to go back home, pack a few things and take one of your little trips to Spain while all this blows over. You haven't been to Spain for a long time, have you?'

'No, and I'd love to go, but if they have my address here, might they have Montse's too?'

'Possibly, but what good would that do them? They obviously want to listen in on operational discussions. I doubt they'd be interested in your bedroom antics, Liam.'

'True, but when you say, "blow over", Mr. T, what do you mean? Blow over like it's all okay and I can get back to work, or blow over like it's all over, full stop?'

'That remains to be seen, dear boy, but for now you just need to go away for a while and I need to go to HQ and fill out a lot of paperwork. This might prove a little costly to sort out.'

'So, yet again, I'm not cost efficient,' Liam sighed.

'Well, you have been in convalescence for months and then retraining. These things aren't cheap. But that's some good news, do you see? That money wouldn't have been authorised if you weren't still useful. Now, I'll take you back home to pack and then you can leave everything else to me. We just have to wait for the new car and then you can go whenever you like.'

'New car?'

'Yes, our technician found one or two things he didn't like with your old one. Nothing serious, but best to be on the safe side, eh?'

Liam shuddered. Car problems, as in bomb problems, were always uppermost in his mind. 'Thanks, Mr. T,' he said.

They had their breakfast and then Turner took him home.

23

The Fruit Trees - Undecorated

Liam had decided on a different route for safety and he left the ferry in Calais to begin the long drive through France to Spain. His new car was exactly the same as the old Jag, but this one was finished in metallic silver instead of blue.

'I wonder if Turner's family has a Jaguar dealership?' he thought as he drove south down the N20. He made it as far as Perpignan before tiredness got the better of him. He knew he didn't have that much farther to drive, but by now he really needed to sleep. *Hotel Crêpe Suzette*, read the illuminated sign, so he pulled into the car park, booked a single room for one night and slept.

The following morning, as he crossed the border into Spain at La Jonquera, he sang out loud, 'Ah yes, Jesus Christ, it feels so friggin' good to be back home in Catalunya again.' Just a few hours later he pulled on the handbrake, blew the horn and killed the engine as he sat smiling to himself outside an old farmhouse. Then his smile disappeared as the front door cracked a little, the double barrels of a shotgun slowly poked through the gap and the shattering blast above his head almost deafened him.

'Qui es?' a voice shouted.

'Jesus Christ woman, it's me. Put that bleedin' old blunderbuss down will yer?' he yelled back as he lifted both hands gingerly from behind the Jag and waved.

A head appeared round the door before it was flung wide and Montse came dashing out. 'Oh Darren, I'm so sorry,' she called as she ran to him.

'What the Hell are you doin' woman? It's me.'

'I thought it was a stranger. I did not recognise the car.'

'It's a Jaguar, it's right hand drive, it has English plates. Who else could it be?'

'Darren, I do not know about these things. I only know that you drive a blue car. That car isn't blue.'

'So you shoot at anyone who doesn't drive a blue car?'

'Oh Darren, don't be silly. Anyway I did not shoot at you, I shot over your head. If I had shot at you, your body would now be decorating these lovely fruit trees.' She pointed to the orchard around her and Darren smiled. The autumn lemons glistened in the weak sun and the beauty calmed him, as it always did. More beautiful than that, though, was the woman in front of him now, absentmindedly pushing a strand of hair behind her ear.

'Ah, lass, I've missed you, gun and all. Come here and give me a kiss,' he said as he pulled her into his arms.

The embrace was the longest they had shared in many months. Montse had visited England twice as soon as she had her travel documents, but she had been uncomfortable under the watchful eye of Bobby, and Liam's injured leg had ruled out any real intimacy. When she finally moved from his arms, she glanced down.

'Your leg, it is all better now?'

'Aye lass, one hundred percent and ready for action,' he said with a wink. 'I think I should freshen up first, though. I've been driving a long time.'

'I will make a quick coffee,' she offered as she ran to the house.

As they sat at the kitchen table, Montse was admonishing him for not letting her know he was coming.

'I tried ringing yesterday, but there was no answer,' he told her. 'I didn't expect you to be out mid-week.'

'Ah, but I have to work a few extra days now. It has not been cheap coming to see you in England.'

Darren smiled at her. He had once suggested that he made enough money to look after her so that she didn't have to work, but she had been immediately offended and insisted his money was for their beeline plan. 'I will give up my job when you give up yours,' she had told him, so that ended that conversation.

'Have you been thinking about America again?' he asked her now.

'Oh, yes, Darren, I think about it often, but I do not believe it will ever happen. Always you tell me it will be soon, but then there is still something else you must do first.'

Darren nodded sadly. 'Aye, lass, you're right there,' he admitted, 'but this time I really think it's almost over. They've stood me down again.'

'Stood you down? This I do not understand.'

'No, it's our stupid language. Let's just say I think they are getting ready to end my contract. That means they have broken their word. That means I don't have to keep mine and that means I can finish the job myself and then we can leave. I just have to stay away for a few more weeks to see what happens.'

'A few weeks? Do you mean you can stay with me for a few weeks?'

'Aye, if you'll have me. I should go to see Rosa and the boys too.'

'Oh, but of course, yes,' Montse nearly squealed in her excitement. 'Let us go and see Mamma Rosa and then we could maybe have a little holiday?'

'A holiday?'

'Yes, there is a beautiful place I have not visited for many years. It is called Cadaqués and it is not very far. Could we, Darren? Please?'

'Yes, love, I think we could,' he agreed. 'So, you've missed me then?'

'I missed you very much.'

'Ah, 'tis only natural. You are a girl, after all.'

'Oh Darren,' Montse giggled as she gave him a playful slap, 'but you are right that we must go to see Mamma Rosa first. I think she will hit you harder than that. She is always complaining that you have been away for too long.'

Darren winced at the thought of a good, hard slap from Rosa and laughed. 'Mamma and the boys can wait,' he said as his glance lingered on the pretty face in front of him and then slowly lowered to her chest.

Montse smiled sweetly and reached out to take his hand as they rose from the table and headed to the stairs, stopping short at the bottom step as the door crashed open and her brothers burst in.

'Señor Darren,' exclaimed Alex. 'Welcome back.'

Darren gave Montse a "this will have to wait" look and a grin before going to greet the brothers.

'We knew it must be you,' said Esteban. 'No one else would arrive here in a Jaguar.'

Darren raised his eyebrows at Montse in a "told you so" fashion and then sat back down at the table. He was gratified that the lads' resentment of him had gone and they now accepted him as a friend, but he wished that friendship could have waited for an hour or so on this occasion. Still, there was always this evening.

'So, how are you boys?' he asked.

They chatted away in clearly accented Español. This was, indeed, a compliment to Darren. The brothers were Catalan through and through and had used only that language when they first encountered him, soundly marking him a stranger. With greater acceptance they had moved to a language he could understand and the fact that he did not use any Castillano pleased them.

'*Th*ervesa,' they would laugh, mimicking the short-tongued Spanish that every non-native speaker automatically adopted in the belief it would make them sound fluent. 'Bar*th*elona,' they would spit. 'Why do the idiots from Madrid decide how we should pronounce our own capital city? It's BarSSSSelona, Barcelona, simple.'

Darren laughed along with them. He knew all about pride in nationality and, as with the Basques and their Euskara, he admired them for it. The trouble was, Català and Euskara were difficult languages and he had picked up only a few words in all his time there. Español was their common tongue.

Soon the alcohol came out and the afternoon quickly disappeared into night. Montse eventually went to bed and was asleep by the time Darren finally made it, swaying, up the stairs. He looked at her fondly, stumbled and landed awkwardly down beside her. 'Wouldn't have been much use to you tonight anyway, love,' he belched before falling into a drunken sleep.

He woke next morning to a mushy head and an empty pillow next to him. He went groggily downstairs in search of his woman and a good, strong cup of coffee. Montse was preparing breakfast and she greeted him with a swift, 'Sit, eat and then we go.'

'Now?'

'Yes, my brothers are having their friends round and we will have no privacy. At least Rosa will give us a room and see that we are not disturbed.'

'OK,' he agreed.

Esteban stumbled into the kitchen and yelled, 'Coffee,' at his sister.

'Just this one,' she said, 'and then you can make your own. We are leaving.'

'You are going to your Basque friends?'

'Yes,' Darren confirmed.

'I see them sometimes in La Seu,' Esteban said, 'and they mention you, but they never ask a direct question. They are very secretive. I think they could be E.T.A.'

When Darren just looked at him but made no reply, Esteban continued quickly. 'Yes, you are quite right, forgive me. That was a stupid thing to say, it's just…'

'Just what?' Darren prompted.

'La Seu. It is a small town, big gossip and it could be nothing, but yesterday there were four Guardia Civil Toyotas parked just off the Cami. Maybe your friends should know.'

'I'll tell them,' Darren nodded. 'Thanks Esteban.'

'Maybe you should take the van, too,' added Alex as he wobbled downstairs to join them. 'Your car it is very, how would you say, distinctive?'

Less than an hour later, Darren and Montse were blending in nicely as they drove along in the brothers' van.

They went as far as they could up the dirt track to the camp before abandoning the vehicle and continuing on foot, making themselves visible and waiting for someone to meet them.

'Meester Bootch,' came the expected squeal after only a few minutes. Darren ran to the approaching jeep, stood patiently to receive his slap and scolding from Rosa and then helped Montse into the vehicle. They were at the old farmhouse in no time.

Rosa insisted on feeding them immediately, despite Darren's protestations that they weren't really hungry, and then demanded to know everything that had happened to him over the past months. She knew of the leg injury but was pressing him for details. Was he sure it was just a coincidence, was he really still safe in that God forsaken country, could he still trust the people he worked for and, most importantly, when was he going to come home and stay with them for good?

Darren struggled to find suitable answers. He couldn't lie to Rosa, she would see straight through that, but he wasn't honestly sure of the truth. 'Mamma,' he said finally, 'I think everything has been a coincidence and there is still one man I trust, but I can't wait much longer for answers.'

'You have said that before,' Rosa scolded him. 'Last time you left us, almost a year ago, you said it was nearly over and still you are no further with your quest. There are still two men left, yes?'

'Aye, Mamma, that's right. I was very close to one and then I got shot.'

'Pah, then it is not a coincidence, this shooting. We all love you here and you must be very careful, my son.'

'I will, Mamma, I promise,' said Darren as he swallowed hard to remove the lump from his throat. He was thankful to hear an approaching vehicle and the arrival of the ever-exuberant Vassi saved him from further motherly interrogation. Instead he was engulfed in a bear hug and released only when Vassi noticed Montse and swept her off her feet in a brotherly embrace.

'I have missed you,' he finally announced.

'I've missed you too, you hooligan,' Darren laughed. 'Where are the others?'

'My company is not good enough for you?' Vassi huffed.

'Listen, all this hugging is exhausting and I'd rather get it all over with in one go. My head is still banging from too much rum last night.'

'Then you need the dog hair,' Vassi announced as he produced another bottle. 'You too, señorita?' he enquired. 'How is your head?'

'I am fine,' Montse assured him. 'I will help Mamma prepare dinner and leave you to your man things.'

'She is a very good girl,' Vassi whispered as he poured the rum. 'As for the others, some will be along later. Hector and Sixtro, they are away for a few days on the coast.'

'On holiday?'

'Mr. Butch, of course not. We do not take holidays. They have gone to meet one of our suppliers.'

'Arms?'

'Yes, my brother. Kadar, the Libyan. You know of him, no?'

'Can't say I do,' said Darren, shaking his head.

'Well he is a very big dealer in Europe and has supplied E.T.A. for years. The I.R.A. too, I think.'

'No, I've never heard of him, but when I was R.A. I was just a soldier. Never got involved in any shipping or dealing.'

'Oh well, no matter, but that's where Hector and Sixtro are. They will be gone a few days more, I think. Holidays? Pah, they had better not take any holidays.'

'I am taking Montse to somewhere called Cadaqués for a few days. Do you know it?'

'But of course. My uncle's house is practically next-door in Llançà. I know all of the Costa Brava well, but Cadaqués is very special.' Vassi lowered his voice before adding, 'Very romantic.'

Darren grinned. 'Hope so, and maybe we should get off tomorrow. It could be weeks before I go back to England so it would make sense to have some days now and then come back when all the boys are here.'

'Excellent plan, my friend,' said Vassi as he poured another rum.

'Oh, before I forget. A contact told me that there were Guardia Civil in La Seu yesterday. More than usual. Is there a reason?'

'Not that I know about,' Vassi considered. 'That is interesting information. I will pass it on. Roberto, José and Valentino leave for a different job in the morning. They may need to change their route.'

As if on cue, Rosa's sons arrived then and Darren and Montse went through the bear hug treatment again. Dinner was served, the alcohol flowed, Montse eventually went to bed and Darren was drunk by the time he joined her in the early hours. 'Tomorrow night,' he whispered. 'I promise you.'

24

Cadaqués

There had been a quick detour back to swap the van for the Jag before heading to the coast. The sun was shining but the wind was fierce as they pulled up outside the Llané Petit Hotel. Waves crashed on the rocks below and Darren stopped to admire the stunning view. 'Wow,' was all he could manage.

'You like it?' asked Montse.

'Wow,' he said again.

'Corner sea view, sea view or garden view?' asked the receptionist when they went to check in.

Liam glanced at Montse and asked, 'A garden view? Is he joking?'

'Corner sea view with a terrace please,' Montse told the man. 'I am here to show him the sights.'

It didn't take long to unpack and then they sat sipping coffee on the terrace. For several minutes they simply looked at the incredible scene below them and didn't speak. Darren lit a cigarette and inhaled deeply. 'Wow,' he said again. ''Tis a fine view all right.'

'I told you so,' Montse agreed.

'So, when will you be showing me those sights then?'

'What do you mean? Look at that. What more could you ask for?'

'Maybe I had some other sights in mind,' he suggested as he leaned forward and slid the top of her blouse down her shoulder.

Montse slapped his hand away. 'Oh no,' she scolded. 'Last night I waited for you. The night before I waited for you. Tonight you will wait for me. Tonight you will take me to the lovely restaurant downstairs. You will buy me a wonderful dinner and a fine wine. Do I not deserve this?'

'Aye lass, you do, but there's nothing wrong with a little appetiser before dinner, is there?'

'Yes, Darren, there is. When we first met, you had been blown up in a bus and I had to heal you. Then we were arrested. Then you take me to live with terrorists and then I have to go to England because you have been shot. I do not think this is normal, and tonight I would like to be normal.'

Darren stubbed out his cigarette and reached immediately for another to give himself time to think.

Whoa, talk about being put in his place. She was completely right, of course, and he was suddenly struck by the thought that he really didn't deserve this beautiful creature in front of him. In fact, he didn't deserve any happiness at all, but she did.

'Montse, my love,' he began as he laid his hand on hers, 'you are anything but normal, but tonight I promise you everything you want. I owe you my life in more ways than one and I will make it up to you.'

'There is nothing to make up, Darren. I just want a nice time in a hotel. That is all.'

'I know, love, and I'm sorry. It's just that it's a long time since I took a real holiday and I can't remember the last time I was in a hotel…' He stopped short as the image of Gates lining up his sniper rifle while he sharpened *The Killer* jumped into his mind. 'Well, no, I can remember, but the time before that was…' A Waterford hotel came into his head then with one of the Belfast Committee men, Larry-Mad Dog-O'Brien, dying in the pool of blood where Liam had left him before jumping out of the window at the start of a chase through Ireland that left his best friend dead in the grounds of a residential country club. 'Let's just say, I don't really do hotels,' he finished lamely.

'Tonight you do,' said Montse, 'and now I am going for a long soak in that wonderful bathroom.'

She emerged an hour later in only a bath towel and pretended not to notice he was there as she moved slowly around the room. Darren gritted his teeth and grinned. She was teasing him and he deserved it. He left her to it and went for his own bath. He presented himself later in the smart trousers and shirt that Rosa had forced on him before they left. He'd thought she was crazy, but now he thanked her with all his heart as he looked at the sight in front of him. 'Holy shite,' he whispered.

'Do I look all right?' asked Montse as she turned to him in a long, figure-hugging dress, her thick hair falling gently over one shoulder.

'Wow,' he said for the umpteenth time that day.

Darren felt uncomfortable the second he walked into the restaurant. It was quiet and refined and he was suddenly longing for a pie and chips in a Little Chef. Montse put her hand on his arm and smiled at him in support as they were led to their table.

He reached to pull out his chair, but the waiter beat him to it. There was a napkin in a glass and Darren talked silently to himself as he took his seat. 'OK, me lad, you'll not be sticking this down the front of your shirt. 'Tis for your knee now.' He reached to take it, but again the waiter was ahead of him and spread it across his lap. He looked across at Montse who seemed to be handling this quite well and knew that she should let the waiter do everything for her, but he also noticed the way her cheeks were sucked in. The little minx was trying not to laugh.

Darren consulted the menu and played it safe by ordering soup and steak. When the wine list arrived, Montse rescued him by asking for the house red. He tried to think, but couldn't remember ever drinking wine before in his life.

'No beer or whiskey?' he whispered across the table.

'Maybe later,' she suggested in a hushed tone.

The restaurant was over half full and, as he looked around, he saw several lips moving but he couldn't hear any conversation. 'It's very quiet in here,' he mouthed, and Montse nodded before coughing slightly to cover the small laugh that nearly escaped her.

The wine arrived and Darren had already decided that he would do nothing until he saw Montse do it first. The man showed him a bottle, which had a very pretty label he had to admit, and when he noticed Montse nod, he nodded too. The waiter poured about an eighth of an inch into the huge glass in front of him and then stood back. Was this all he was getting? He'd wait for Montse, that was best. Only Montse didn't seem to be getting any at all.

'Would sir like to test?' the waiter said finally.

Oh shit. He raised the glass and took a tiny sip. It tasted strange, but he assumed it was supposed to taste that way so he just placed the glass down and nodded once more. The waiter poured again and now Montse received some too. There was still only about two inches each, though.

When they were alone again Darren whispered, 'How come they give us such bloody great glasses if they're not gonna fill 'em up?'

'Something to do with breathing,' Montse whispered back. 'I'm not really sure.'

'Breathing?'

'I think so.'

'OK, if you say so, but it seems such a waste of space.'

Montse nodded, though she was biting hard on her bottom lip. She raised her hand to cover her mouth and Darren could see from the slight shake of her shoulders that she was silently laughing. He had to agree, it was quite funny. He raised his glass as a distraction and offered, 'Salut', one of the few Catalan words he had acquired.

'Salut,' she giggled back at him, raising her drink in return. As their glasses touched, the clink sounded far too loud and seemed to echo round the room.

'Oh shite,' said Darren, and then immediately coughed to cover up while Montse's attempt to swallow a giggle ended in a loud hiccup.

Thankfully their soup arrived at that moment and they both concentrated intently upon it, eating and drinking to keep their mouths occupied. The trouble was, the more they tried not to laugh the more they wanted to. What had started out as something mildly amusing now seemed hilarious and when, during the main course, a piece of wonderfully succulent steak fell from Darren's fork into his wine glass, the cause was lost. Montse's eyes were streaming and Darren let forth a huge belly laugh.

The waiter was with them in a second, offering a fresh glass and apologising as if the whole thing was his fault. Darren waved him away, unable to speak, but Montse managed to suggest a new bottle of wine to take to their room instead. They left the restaurant as quietly as they could and tried not to look at any of the other diners. By the time they were back in their room they could hold it no longer and they dissolved in helpless laughter.

'I'm sorry, lass,' Darren managed when he finally regained control of his breathing. 'I really didn't mean to embarrass you like that. You all dressed up and me behaving like a complete idiot.'

'Oh Darren, don't be silly,' Montse assured him. 'It was wonderful. I haven't laughed like that in a very long time.'

'Nor me,' Darren agreed, 'but you said you wanted a normal night. I don't think that counted as normal.'

'No, not really,' Montse confirmed and that brought forth a new set of giggles until they were finally all laughed out.

Darren looked at his girl where she had fallen back on the bed, her dress riding up her thigh and her hair wonderfully dishevelled over her beautiful face. He leaned over to kiss her and this time there was no attempt to stop him as he slid the dress down over her shoulders. He took his time removing the rest of her clothing, but soon they were naked in bed together. Montse rolled into his arms.

'Ah, lass,' Darren began, when a loud pounding on the door stopped him mid stride. 'What the fuck? Go away!' he yelled.

'Butch, my brother, are you there?' came the voice from outside.

'You have got to be shittin' me,' Darren growled as he jumped from the bed, stormed to the door and flung it open. 'What the fuck do you want?' he spat at the eye-patched face that greeted him.

Vassi rushed into the room. 'We need you, brother. Hector has been arrested. The Mossos d'Esquadra have him down in L'Escala.'

'Oh fuck. Why?'

'They caught him with The Libyan. Tomorrow the Guardia Civil will take him and then he'll be gone, locked away for years. We… oh, pardon me señorita,' he said as he belatedly noticed Montse in the bed, the covers pulled up to her chin. 'I, we, oh, I came to ask for your help, Butch, and that you should bring a weapon. I just…well…I didn't mean that one,' he said as his gaze dropped from Darren's face.

'Oh, shite,' said Darren, grabbing a towel to cover his nakedness and the fact that the shocking news hadn't completely deflated him yet. 'Don't get any ideas. That wasn't meant for a maricón like you.'

'I hope not, my brother,' Vassi grinned, though he was immediately serious again. 'So?'

'There's no one else?'

'Sixtro is outside waiting. Hector is locked up, Roberto, José and Valentino are too far away and I do not trust our young recruits yet for this kind of job.'

Darren looked across at Montse. 'Just go,' she said. 'I'll be waiting.'

'Give me five minutes and I'll see you downstairs,' he told Vassi. The man left and Darren rushed to Montse's side. 'I'm so sorry, lass,' he began, but she silenced him with her finger to his lips.

'Go,' she said. 'You have five minutes.'

Darren ran out of the hotel, but it was Butch who jumped into the waiting BMW saloon. 'Nice car,' he commented.

'Thank you,' said Sixtro from behind the wheel. 'It's an M5.'

'What's an M...?' Butch began, but Sixtro already had his foot down and was accelerating away, throwing the other men back in their seats.

'An M5 is fast,' Vassi informed him unnecessarily.

25

L'Escala

The three men sat in the car as they stared at the building. 'You sure that's where they're holding him?' asked Butch.

Sixtro nodded. 'Yes. I was late for the meeting and I arrived just in time to see the Mossos arrest him. I followed them here.'

'What happened to The Libyan?' asked Vassi.

'I have no idea. I saw only Hector as they threw him into the van.'

'Right then, what's the plan lads?' Butch asked.

'Why, to break him out and take him back home to La Seu of course,' Vassi informed him. 'What else is there to do?'

'OK, so how many men in there, do you reckon?'

Sixtro considered the question for a few moments before replying. 'There will be lots of them right now, but when the shift changes around midnight there should only be around three or four troopers left on duty.'

'How do you know that?' asked Butch.

'Because, my brother, that's all it takes to man a station late at night.'

'Right, so what have we got?'

Vassi threw a couple of woollen masks over into the front seats. 'We have these and these too,' he replied as he passed each man a short stock AK.

'Hmm,' said Butch thoughtfully as he poked two fingers through the eyeholes of the knitted ski mask and inspected it. 'What, no E.T.A. white hoods and berets this time? How come we've got these black things?'

'I'd have thought that was obvious,' Vassi grinned. 'We want the cops to assume that the T.L.L. have broken him out of jail, not E.T.A.'

'The T.L.L.? Who's that?'

'Terra Lliure.'

'Never heard of 'em. Who are they?'

'T.L.L. are the Catalan version of E.T.A. They want a free Catalunya, just like we want a free Basque country.'

'So, they're a separatist group then? How come I've never heard of them?'

'That's because all they do is talk a little treason, get drunk, and go home.'

'Oh, so we're supposed to be three Catalan terrorists then are we?'

'Exactly. Then they will spend their time hunting the T.L.L. down and search only for Catalan boys, not for us,' said Vassi with a grin.

'OK, I get that as a plan,' Butch agreed, 'but I see a little problem.'

'What's that?'

'Does anyone actually speak any Català?'

'I have one phrase,' offered Sixtro.

'Well, come on then man, let's have it,' demanded Vassi.

'Que m'ho podria escriure, si us plau?' said Sixtro slowly.

'Que m'ho podria escriure, si us plau? - hmm - Que m'ho podria escriure, si us plau?,' repeated Vassi slowly. 'Sounds impressive. What does it mean?'

'Please write that down.'

'Please write that down? What bleedin' good is that?' snapped Butch.

'Well, when storming a police station and breaking out a prisoner, not that much I guess,' admitted Sixtro with a frown.

Vassi glared at his Basque colleague and slowly shook his head. 'But Montse is Catalana,' he said, turning his attention to Butch. 'You must have picked up something from her.'

Liam thought for a moment. 'Not much. We use English and Spanish. I've picked up the odd word, but I can't see much use for please, thank you and good health in this situation, though. Can you?'

'Not much,' admitted Vassi. 'Anything else?'

'Oh yes, "Sit down, shut up and keep still". Montse is always yelling that at her brothers, and I know the word for keys, too, as long as a car key is the same as a jail cell key. Then there's in, out, bits like that, but not much else.'

'Well, that's better than nothing,' Sixtro said.

Vassi agreed. 'You're on crowd control, Butch, while I do the breakout. Besides, these guns should do most of the talking for us.'

'OK.'

Under the dim illumination of the weak street lamps the three sat waiting in the car for the best moment to make their assault. Midnight came and went with no shift change and Vassi glared at Sixtro, but said nothing. There had to be a change soon and they just had to wait it out, but it was stretching their nerves and there was a growing tension in the vehicle.

'What was that?' said Sixtro suddenly, his head going from side to side.

The other two men strained their eyes. 'I can't see anything,' Vassi said finally.

'Me neither,' Butch agreed.

'Nor me,' said Sixtro, 'but can't you smell something?'

'No' said Butch and Vassi in unison.

'You will,' Sixtro promised, just as the vile smell of a fart assaulted their nostrils.

'Oh Jesus Christ man,' gulped Butch between mock vomiting sounds, 'just what the fuck have you been eating?'

'Animal,' said Vassi as he wound down the window. 'Have you got something up there dying, man?'

'Sorry,' Sixtro laughed. 'Couldn't help it, and... Hey, now I really do see something.'

A jeep pulled up to the station and two men jumped out and headed into the building. A few minutes later, several others came out and drove away.

'I make that two in, six out,' said Butch.

'Yes, and figure two more doing a cross over shift and I think we've halved the odds,' Vassi agreed. 'Time to go.'

'Good luck boys,' said Sixtro. 'I'll be waiting.'

Butch and Vassi walked briskly to the front door and pulled on their ski masks. With the AKs dangling at their sides they walked calmly into the building, noting just three officers at their desks. Two looked to be in their thirties while the third didn't look old enough to be out of school. One of the older Mossos lifted his head slightly, about to ask how he could help, but the words stalled in his throat as he saw the ski masks.

'Sit down, shut up and keep still,' yelled one of the intruders in Català.

Three troopers stared in silence. They were already sitting down, but the order had clearly confused the younger officer who stood for a second, just so that he could sit down again. This wasn't supposed to happen in their little town on a quiet Tuesday night.

'Keys,' snapped Butch.

'Keys,' followed by something Butch couldn't understand, came from one of the trooper's mouths. Shit. If only he knew more of the language.

'Keys please,' he tried as he aimed his AK. It was all he could do.

The second older officer opened a drawer, said something unintelligible and threw a large bunch of keys over the desk.

'Thank you,' said Butch. Maybe all that was needed were a few good manners.

Vassi grabbed the keys and ran through to the back. Butch kept his gun trained on the troopers and watched them closely. The two older men seemed calm, but the young officer looked terrified. One of the men said something so Butch just yelled 'Shut up,' again, and that did the trick. 'Come on Vassi,' he said under his breath. 'What's taking you so long?'

Finally Vassi and a very dejected looking Hector emerged from the back. Vassi had obviously warned him not to say anything, so Hector looked at the ground and fingered his half ear in embarrassment.

'Up,' ordered Butch. Nothing happened. 'Up, please,' he tried, and the two older officers stood, but the young lad remained frozen at his desk. Shit. 'Look, you stupid idiot, don't you understand your native tongue?' Butch tried in Spanish. 'If you force me to speak this language any longer, I will not be happy.'

The tactic worked wonders as the young officer finally rose. Vassi aimed his gun and the three troopers walked towards the back.

'In, please,' Butch ordered in Català once more, as he motioned to the open cell with his AK. They did as ordered and Vassi locked them inside.

'Keep quiet,' said Butch, 'and thank you.'

He followed Vassi and Hector out of the station and Sixtro had the BMW turning over just a few yards away. Before they could reach it, a green and white Toyota Jeep came cruising round the corner.

'Shit, Guardia Civil,' shouted Hector.

It hardly took any Sherlock Holmes type detective skills on the part of the patrol to decide that the scene, clearly visible in the streetlight, of three men, two of them in ski masks, heading towards a powerful, revving car outside a police station was probably just a little bit suspicious. Their guns were out in an instant and Hector ducked the first bullets as he ran for the back of the car. Butch was behind him, jumping in the motor and immediately firing from the window while Vassi raked the Toyota with automatic gunfire as he made his sprint for the front passenger door.

'Go, mate, fuckin' go,' yelled Butch once they were all inside and Sixtro floored the accelerator, screeching away like a scalded cat. The Toyota was disabled, with steam spewing from its engine, but an officer was still firing and hit the driver's door as they passed and shards of glass flew through the interior. Sixtro swerved momentarily, hit the throttle once more and then they were gone.

'Jesus,' screamed Vassi, 'what bad timing. Everyone OK?'

They were hurtling along, Sixtro expertly handling the winding roads at speed, as Butch and Hector checked themselves for damage and came up clean. 'All OK, they confirmed.'

'I may neej a bish of ashenshion,' came the garbled answer from Sixtro.

'Holy fuckin' Christ,' yelled Butch as he leaned over from the back. 'They've shot Sixtro in the cheek.'

'I'm OK foh now,' he insisted.

'No, pull over and let me drive,' said Vassi.

'I am shosh in je sheek, noj in je head. Ju can't jrive jish car.'

'He's right,' Hector said. 'You're a good soldier, Vassi, but you're a useless driver. Not that I'm close to Sixtro's standard either. How about you Butch?'

'Not for something like this. If Sixtro's OK, let him get us well away and then we'll find another car.'

Sixtro nodded briefly and spat two teeth on the floor as he continued to drive. There was no one behind them, but he didn't slow down until he had taken enough twists and turns to be sure they couldn't be followed and they entered the small seaside town of Roses. Finally Sixtro slowed and pulled the battered, bullet ridden BMW into a car park. He was out in an instant, his hand to his face but showing no other signs of discomfort, and he disappeared into the night.

'How bad did his face look?' Vassi asked. 'I couldn't see from my side.'

'Pretty bad,' Butch confirmed.

'We'll have to get straight back to the camp for some treatment, then.'

'I don't know. I don't think Sixtro can go much longer and that means one of us off-road driving at night and then a hike through the mountains.'

'So what do you suggest?' asked Hector.

'How about heading to Cadaqués?'

'Wha...what?' stammered Vassi. 'There's one road in and one road out. We'd be trapped.'

'I'm not so sure. Look, we lost them so they are going to try to look for us in the most logical places first.'

'And Cadaqués would be completely illogical,' Hector butted in. 'I like it, but who do we know there?'

'Mister Butch has a love nest,' Vassi informed him.

'What?'

'I'll tell you later. Here comes Sixtro.'

A late model Ford Cortina pulled up next to them. There was a quick explanation of the plan and Vassi was finally allowed to drive the Ford. Butch and Hector jumped in with him and Sixtro followed behind in the BMW until they reached the far side of town and a small side street. The bullet-ridden car was abandoned and Sixtro thankfully took a back seat in the Ford.

'Can I pash out now?' he asked.

Vassi stuck to the speed limit and they made their way to Cadaqués in the innocuous looking car, eventually arriving at the hotel.

'You take Sixtro up to Montse,' said Butch, handing Vassi his room key plus the first aid kit from the boot of the Jag,' and try not to be seen going through reception. Me and Hector will dump the car and see you up there.'

Butch jumped in the Jag and Hector followed in the Ford until they found a suitable dumping ground on the outskirts of Portbau, just before the French border. They were back at the hotel while it was still dark and made it upstairs unseen. Butch knocked quietly on the door.

'Darren, I am so relieved,' cried Montse as she flung her arms round him.

'I'm sorry, love,' he told her quietly. 'I'll make this up to you. How is our patient?'

'I've done what I can, but I think you should take him back to Rosa as soon as possible. All I had was the first aid kit. I've given him some painkillers and he's sleeping now, but it is a nasty wound. I wonder where the bullet went?'

'Lodged somewhere in the car, I guess,' said Darren.

'It probably just missed me,' said Vassi.

'Yes, I guess we were lucky really.'

'So what do we do now?' asked Hector.

'Well we have the room for three more days,' Darren said, 'and that should be long enough to let the heat die down. It's going to be tricky keeping you all out of sight, but we'll manage somehow.'

Montse displayed unexpected acting skills over the next days. She giggled coyly to the staff who delivered room service, poking her head shyly round the door and explaining how hungry her new husband was. She sweetly declined house keeping and just swapped a few towels without letting the maid in. The Do Not Disturb sign was employed most of the time and the "newly weds" made one more visit to the restaurant for the sake of appearances, but departed early, whispering to each other. The staff smiled fondly as they left the honeymooners alone.

On check out day she charmed the receptionist and kept him busy while three strange men walked from the building. In one close shave in the car park, where Sixtro's scarf covered face was noted, she commented on what a butcher the dentist was. Finally, with five of them crammed in the Jag, she fell asleep from exhaustion.

'She is a marvel,' Vassi whispered to Darren. 'You are a lucky man, my brother.'

'I know it,' Darren agreed.

Eventually they arrived back at the camp and Montse thankfully relinquished her duties. She had managed to keep Sixtro's cheek free from infection, but it wasn't healing well. Rosa took control and roughly stitched the wound, making Sixtro cry out, but she just told him off for being a baby.

Darren fingered the large crescent scar on his own cheek as he remembered how Rosa had stitched that for him too. No, the woman wasn't gentle, but she got the job done and never made a fuss. He watched her now, and then looked across at the others in the room. They were all tired. Three nights of sharing a small hotel room had starved them all of sleep and Vassi sat rubbing his good eye while adjusting the patch over the other. Hector was turning his head from side to side to ease out an aching neck while he absently stroked half an ear. Sixtro made one last yelp as Rosa put the final stitch in his lip and suddenly Darren was laughing out loud.

'Whash up wi' ju?' Sixtro mumbled.

'Oh man,' Darren managed through his laughter. 'Look at yourselves. You're like three monkeys.'

'What?' asked Vassi.

Darren tried to control his breathing as he put his hands to his ears, then his eyes and then his mouth. 'You know, like the proverb, hear no evil, see no evil, speak no evil.'

'I still don't get it,' said Vassi

'I think he means los tres monos sabios,' explained Hector. 'I do not think that is very funny.'

'I think it's hilarious,' said Darren.

'Well, I remind you, that is three *wise* monkeys. And you should not joke at our misfortunes.'

A strange noise filled the room then and they all looked across at Rosa who was bent double. 'Three wise monkeys,' she cackled. 'Oh, Meester Bootch, that is excellent.'

'No it ishn't,' huffed Sixtro, 'and I neej a jrink.'

Bedtime came early for the exhausted band of warriors and everyone rose late the next morning. Darren and Montse were sitting on the porch, wrapped warmly in thick jackets but enjoying the weak sun and fresh October air, when Rosa came rushing from the house carrying a small transistor radio and babbling at the top of her voice.

'Mamma, calm down,' said Darren as he jumped to his feet in alarm. 'Whatever is the matter? I can't understand a word you're saying.'

'It is your lady, the iron one. They have blown her up.'

'What? Who's blown who up?'

'The Irishmen, Meester Bootch, they have put a big bomb in a hotel, near the sea I think. It is your Prime Minister. They have blown her up.'

'You are fuckin' joking. Are you sure? Is she dead?'

'I don't know. Some persons are dead, yes, but I don't know about her.'

'It's definitely the R.A?'

'They say so, yes. This is bad, no?'

'Well I'm sure the R.A. will be very happy, but, for the rest of us, I'd say all Hell is about to break loose. I need to call Turner.'

There were no phones at camp, but Rosa hooked him up to the radio and Darren searched his brain to remember the old codes he had been taught. Finally he made it through to some exchange or other, somewhere in London, gave a code word and, after what seemed like an eternity, heard, 'Hullo, Liam my boy, is that you?'

'Mr. Turner, thank Christ. Is it true?'

'Yes Liam, it's bad here. The PM's OK, but all leave is cancelled, as they say. How soon can you come back.'

'You need me? I'm back on active service?'

'It's all hands on deck, Liam.'

'I'm on my way.'

His goodbyes were a hurried affair. He lingered with Montse the longest, but then he had to leave her too.

'We will look after her, Butch,' Vassi assured him. 'She is family now.'

26

The Brighton Aftermath

'No paperwork, no bloody expenses sheets, nothing?' Liam asked as he sat across from Turner in a small office at headquarters.

'No one cares about those little niceties right now. This has forced our hand.'

'Well, if there hadn't been so many restrictions to start with, maybe this would never have happened.'

'You could be right, my boy, but we'll never know for sure.'

'How could they be so bloody stupid? They had to know what this would mean.'

'I assume, Liam, they thought they would kill the Prime Minister and be victorious. Did you see what Sinn Fein said in their statement?'

'No, what?'

Turner selected a paper from his desk and read, "Today, we were unlucky, but remember, we only have to be lucky once – you will have to be lucky always."

Liam let out a long, low, whistle. 'So the gauntlet's down, then. Listen, I've no real love for the woman but, Jesus Christ, what were they thinking?'

'She's not that bad, you know.'

'Ah, it's the way she speaks. It's so snotty, like. Gates told me she was electrocuted, or something, and that's why she talks like that.'

'What on earth are you on about, dear boy?'

'Gates. He said she'd had electrocution and it had affected her speech. Honest, that's what he told me.'

Turner shook his head slowly and let out a small laugh. 'Sergeant Gates is a fine soldier, Liam, but he's not the most educated man I've ever met. Elocution. She had elocution lessons.'

'Ah.'

'Anyway, back to the matter in hand. There will be many men lying low right now, but they can't stay hidden for long. As soon as we find them, they will become legitimate targets.'

'Moore and McMurphy?' Liam asked hopefully.

'Indeed, dear boy. Keep yourself ready. A week, a month, two months, who knows, but it will be soon now.'

'I can't wait.'

'Well, keep your nose clean and stick to the new protocols.'

'Aye, so run that by me again, Mr. T.'

'You are to move back to the manor house and I will make regular visits, but we will never discuss any specifics while I am there. If there was an attempt to bug your house once, it could easily happen again. So, we don't want to be too clever and pretend that nothing goes on there. That would only let them know that we know, so to speak. We just keep it short, sweet and very professional'

'I get it. So, general stuff only and you'll let me know where to meet for the detailed briefings.'

'Exactly, my boy. Exactly.'

27

Derbyshire, 1985

Just before dawn in the half-light of day he rubbed a small circle of condensation from the ice-cold windowpane. 'Only the needy and the greedy are out today Liam me lad,' he whispered quietly as he stood shivering. Gazing out over the bleak landscape he took a deep, satisfying drag from one of his favourite fags, Capstan full strength. 'Ah Jesus, what a miserable cold, grey day,' he sighed as he continued to stare out at the light rain drizzling slowly down onto the mist-covered fields surrounding the old Derbyshire manor house. Everything was quiet.

Draining the remains of a strong black coffee, he struggled to counter the pounding effects of last night's bottle of Jameson as he took his place at the old desk and started his daily ritual of stripping and thoroughly cleaning today's weapon of choice. Closing his eyes he picked up the piece and engaged the safety. He removed the mag and cocking handle, continued with the butt and grip, then finally the retracting bolt head assembly and recoil spring.

Only when the HK MP5 was broken down into all its parts did he open his eyes to inspect every single component. He then cleaned and oiled each piece individually. 'Clinical cleanliness always, Liam,' he repeated to himself as he sat in the eerie grey glow coming from the bank of security monitors. He was about to close his eyes once more to rebuild the MP5 when something caught his attention and a glance at the monitors confirmed the movement. A car was approaching. Springing from his seat he watched a silver Mercedes saloon car making its way down the long drive. Finally it arrived and parked next to his Jaguar, directly opposite his front door.

The bell rang twice. Checking the monitors for any further movement Liam, a 9mm pistol in his right hand, cautiously eased open the door with his left. The visitor stood and nodded. Neither man uttered a word of greeting as Turner entered and strolled across to the drawing room. Liam secured the front door again before following and eventually taking his seat behind the antique mahogany desk. In total silence Turner took the seat opposite then, opening his briefcase, he slid a large envelope in the direction of Liam who grabbed it, tore it open and pulled out the sheaf of printed documents.

Page after page he studied the contents of times, dates and locations. Finally he arrived at the collection of images; cars, houses and offices along with their associated blueprints. Then he saw a photograph with the face of his new target. 'Jesus, Mary and Joseph,' Liam thought. 'I'd happily hit this bastard for free.'

Showing no emotion at the picture of a man he recognised only too well, he looked directly at Turner asking, 'Same money?'

'Yes, of course old chap, the same money as always,' nodded Turner. 'However, this one will carry a bit of a bonus. It cannot appear to be an accident, I'm afraid. It has to be a very public affair.'

'Why in public?' Liam asked, his fingers tracing the line of the old crescent shaped scar on his cheek.

'Orders,' Turner replied. 'You have all the information you need. The transfer of funds will be made when the work has been completed and the termination is confirmed.' Turner stood and waited for the briefest of moments, should there be any further questions. There were none. He turned and left without uttering another word.

Locking the door once more Liam watched as the Mercedes exited the driveway and then he returned to the drawing room where he studied the security monitors. Nothing. Once again all was quiet, just as it should be.

He looked down at the paperwork on the desk and grinned. It had been difficult to remain calm when Turner had handed him the dossier, but he had managed it. His house had been tested regularly for transmitting devices and none had been found, but it was all about being on the safe side these days. No names were to be spoken out loud. Instead Liam read silently to himself. "T-order. Martin McMurphy." The "in public" bit was unexpected, but he assumed that was because McMurphy was a money man. Turner had said they couldn't go right to the top of the political chain, but they wanted to make an example of the Committee men who had helped finance things.

'Their latest campaign will have taken a lot of planning, and that means a lot of money,' he'd said. 'We can't let them think they can try this again.'

Liam read the dossier from cover to cover, smiling when he came to the part about Garvary. Some of the information was from his own surveillance work. It looked as if Martin had been avoiding the area since the Brighton bomb, but had now been spotted there again. 'Seems like a good place to start,' he decided.

28

Back in the North

Liam took the Larne ferry again and went to hire a car. 'Do you have a Ford Capri?' he asked, remembering the large hatchback.

'Ah, it's a good car is that,' said the lad on the desk. 'Plenty of room in the back.'

'Aye, got to fit all me fishin' tackle in,' smiled Liam as he took the keys.

What with bird watching and now fishing, he was turning into a regular outdoors type. Shame he didn't actually have any fishing gear. Still, there were other uses for all that space.

***

Martin McMurphy wiped the egg yolk from his plate and smacked his lips. 'Fiona, you're a fine cook girl,' he said.

'Are you sure you can't be staying for one more cup of tea?' she pouted as the man rose to leave.

'No time, not these days lass. You know how things are.'

'I don't want to know.'

'That's best,' Martin agreed. 'I might see you this evening, but we've got a lot on today and it could drag on into tomorrow.' He walked from the cottage to his car and was soon heading out of Garvary down a small country lane in the direction of the main Derry road. As he neared the junction he was forced to brake hard. A car was parked facing him with its bonnet up, blocking the road, and a figure was bent over the engine. Shite, not today. There was never anyone on this road, that's why he used it. Why today, of all days? Impatiently he blew the horn, but nothing happened. He tried again and then rolled down the window. 'Get that fuckin' thing out of the way,' he yelled.

The man turned. 'It won't start,' he said. 'Just died on me, so it did.'

'Useless bastard,' hissed Martin under his breath. This would make him late, and he didn't want to be late. 'What's wrong with it?' he shouted.

'It's broken,' said the man.

'Broken how?' Was this man a retard or what?

'Could be it's fucked.'

Oh well that was nice and technical then. Martin jumped from his vehicle. Looked like he'd have to start the car himself or push it in the ditch. 'Let's have a look, you bleedin' bert,' he offered.

'Maybe it just needs a boost,' said the man, a strange, vacant look on his face. 'I've got some jumping leads in the back.'

'Jumping leads is it?' Jesus, was this guy some sort of spastic idiot? 'Aye, go and get your "jumping" leads and I'll give you a boost.'

Martin watched the man limp behind the car and, when he didn't come back after about a minute, called out, 'You got 'em yet?' Fuckin' useless retard, he added under his breath.

There was some sort of muffled reply that he couldn't work out so he stomped round to the rear of the offending car – and then he froze. The vacant, idiotic expression had gone and Martin now faced a cold, hard stare and a pistol. 'What the fuck? Hey, now, don't go doing anything stupid, son. Do you know who you're messin' with?'

'Do you?'

Martin looked at the face in front of him and, for the first time, noticed the crescent shaped scar on his cheek and alarm bells started to ring. There had been stories going round last year about a guy with a scar like that who had taken out some of the boys, but he'd forgotten all about it.

'Hey listen,' he said. 'Whatever this is, we can talk about it.'

'Shut the fuck up,' said scar-face before unexpectedly sliding the gun back in his pocket.

McMurphy was caught off guard for a second, but then he seized his opportunity and lunged at the man. All he got for his efforts was a fist in the face and everything went black.

Liam jumped into the Escort and drove it off the road into a large bushy area, quickly covering it with a pile of freshly cut leafy branches. 'And there's some I prepared earlier,' he laughed. It wouldn't stay hidden for long, but it should be long enough. He went back to the Capri and checked that his captive was still out cold. He piled him into the large, body-sized, hatchback and quickly secured him with tape and rope. 'Got ya Martin, you fuckin' murderin' bastard,' he spat.

He drove rapidly to the main road, but was soon off down another side lane heading for an abandoned farm he knew from his childhood holidays. The place was in ruins, yet the old five bar gate was still in place. He pushed it on its rusty hinges, took the car through, and then conscientiously closed it again. His Ma and his aunt would have slapped him if he had left a gate open.

He bumped up the disused track to a dilapidated cow shed and checked around. The crumbling walls and overgrown grass gave him plenty of cover and he was happy that he would not be disturbed. He opened the boot and a semi-conscious form moaned at him. Liam reached down and shook him.

'What, nothin' to say for yerself then Martin?' he asked as he pulled him roughly from the car and yanked the tape from his mouth. 'On yer fuckin' knees, you bastard.'

'Who the fuck are you?' asked Martin, his voice hoarse.

'Funny, and there was I thinking you were starting to recognise me back there.'

'The scar,' croaked McMurphy. 'I've heard stories.'

'Ah yes, I've heard some of those stories meself, but it's not the scar you should be recognising.'

'H…have we met before?' Martin asked him.

'No, we've never met, which is strange really when you come to think of it. Now why would you be wanting to murder the Ma of a man you've never met?'

McMurphy's eyes shot left and right. 'I don't…I can't… I honestly don't have any idea what you're talkin' about.'

'No, and I'm believin' you. Kind of makes it worse.'

'What the fuck? Listen, just tell me what the Hell this is all about, will ya?'

'Mary Jeanette McCann,' said Liam. 'You signed an order to have her killed, so you did.'

McMurphy's brows furrowed. There was something familiar about the name, but he couldn't quite place it. 'McCann? I don't know. There's somethin'. Fuck, man, I've signed loads of papers.'

'Keep diggin', Martin old mate, 'cause you're just makin' that hole bigger and bigger,' Liam told him as he pulled the .22 from his pocket and rolled it in his palm.

'Listen, just tell me what this is all about,' Martin pleaded, his eyes fixed on the gun.

'Well Mary McCann had a son called Darren, you see. Do you remember now?'

'Darren? Darren McCann? I don't… oh wait. Didn't he…wasn't he the But…'

'Butcher of Belfast. Aye, that's right,' Liam cut in.

'Yeah, right, the Butcher of Belfast. Oh, he was a legend. Died in the H-Blocks years back.'

'Aye, so I heard.'

McMurphy's eyes were widening as he spoke. 'What's that got to do with this? For Christ's sake man, what's goin' on?'

'Oh, aye, forgotten to introduce myself, haven't I? Thing is, I've had a lot of names. Seems I'm even some sort of scarred phantom now. Hard to keep track, like, but one thing never changes, Martin old son, and that's the name of me Ma. A good catholic woman, she was, called Mary Jeanette McCann and you had her killed.'

McMurphy swallowed hard as he tried to take all this in. 'You mean, you're…'

'Aye, it is a bit complicated, like, but I'm sure you can figure it out now. See youse Committee fellas had me Ma killed just so I would join the R.A. Never could figure out why that was and, of course, I didn't know it back then so

I worked for you – became the Butcher. Then I met someone who told me the truth, and Darren McCann died that day. The name's Liam now, if you're interested, but, hey, you can call me Scar Face. I think there's a joke in there somewhere.'

'I can't believe it,' stammered Martin.

'Well I'd give it a try if I were you, 'cause it's the truth like. Of course, it's all secret, but I'm sure I can trust you to keep that secret, can't I Martin?'

'What, er, yes…'

'Oh, I'm pretty sure you'll not be tellin' a soul,' Liam said as he pointed the gun at the man's face. Strange to think he had once told Tommy over in New York that a .22 wasn't any good. It was actually the perfect weapon for today's little job.

Martin felt the gravel cutting into his knees as he began to squirm, trying to loose his bonds, but he knew it was no use. His time on earth was at an end and he looked up at his captor. 'Are you going to make this quick?'

'Depends. What can you tell me about me Ma?'

'I…oh fuck… I don't know,' Martin mumbled. 'I do remember that Moore wanted her dead to get you in, but I honestly don't know why. We didn't question Peter, you know. He was always the boss. Even Mad Dog…' his voice trailed off.

'Aye, it was me as did for Mad Dog,' Liam confirmed.

Martin nodded. 'Aye, well, even him. We all did what Moore said.'

'I believe you, so now I'll be taking you home.'

'Home?'

'Aye, Martin lad. You've one more job to do back in Derry and, just to say thanks like, I will make this quick.'

Martin McMurphy hung his head and started to pray. Liam gave him a few moments to say what was needed and then put one shot in the back of his head. There was hardly a sound and he looked at the weapon in appreciation. 'Nice little pop gun,' he said to himself. 'Should have told Tommy to hold onto his.'

So, McMurphy was dead. He wished he could feel something, but he didn't. Since the day he'd realised that Moore, not Mad Dog, was the real reason that his Ma was dead, he'd known that only the death of Moore could bring him peace. The others had to go because they had signed the death warrant but, like McMurphy had said, they signed a lot of papers. How fucked up was that?

Now he had a job to do and he pulled out *The Killer*. It was hard work carving into a body and he was sweating by the time he had finished. He left just the face untouched so that the body could be recognised. The dry old straw on the cow shed floor soaked up most of the mess and he didn't bother about leaving the evidence of murder there. Shite, he was planning to leave a lot more evidence soon.

He rolled the body onto the heavy duty plastic he had brought with him and lugged it into the back of the Capri. He didn't want to make any mess for the car hire company and this was where he didn't want to leave any evidence. He still had quite a way to go and quite a while to wait until nightfall and he just hoped the body didn't start to smell before then.

29

Derry

The drive from the cow shed to Derry could have been a short one, but Liam was forced to take a circuitous route to avoid any checkpoints. Eventually he made it through the city walls into Bogside and drove slowly along Westland Street until he came close to the Free Derry Corner and could clearly see the square where the white monument stood out against the darker buildings. There were plenty of people around and he decided he would have to wait until the small hours before he could be sure to be unobserved. Eventually, around 3am, he felt it was safe to move.

He left the engine quietly ticking over as he dragged the body from the boot and over a fence, finally placing it against the monument in a seated position. It was perfect. He retraced his steps and was almost back at the car when he stopped dead in his tracks.

'And a very good evening to you sir,' mumbled the dishevelled, drunken old man who came tottering towards him.

Liam ignored him, kept his head down and continued on to his car.

'Hey son, you there. Why I don't believe it. Is that you yerself there laddie?' the man slurred, rocking and swaying unsteadily, his bewildered and bloodshot eyes constantly roaming back and forth between Liam and the car.

'Fuck off, you're pissed you dirty old fucker,' snapped Liam.

'I am. Yes indeed, that I am, but I'm not drunk enough to forget an old mucka now, am I son?' he slurred.

'I've already told you. Now fuck off, before I fuck you off for good,' snapped Liam as he levelled the .22 at the man's head.

'Oh Jesus Christ, all right then son, there's no need to get all snappy with me you know. To be sure I was only being friendly, just saying hello I was, that's all. I don't mean no harm to you son,' replied the drunk between hiccups.

Liam jumped in the car and drove slowly away. 'Fuck, fuck, fuck,' he cursed. 'Just who the fuck was that old bastard anyhow?' He was racking his memory, desperately trying to place the man's face. 'I fuckin' swear to God I've never laid eyes on that old feller in my life,' he spat out of the window. 'One thing is for sure, though, he fuckin' well knew me. Shite, I gotta get out of here - and now.'

Still driving at a steady pace he began heading out of the city. He took a roundabout route again but kept a basically eastern heading. Four o'clock, he saw as he glanced down at his watch. 'Jesus Christ man, you're gonna get pulled for sure driving round here like a bleedin' spanner at this time in the morning,' he admonished himself. He needed to park up somewhere and hide, until daylight at least.

30

6.30 in the morning: Free Derry Corner

Meanwhile, back in Derry, a crowd had begun gathering at Free Derry Corner, and it was growing larger by the minute. Every face was staring in horror at the remains of the horrendously mutilated body propped against the wall. The man's corpse was naked, his throat had been cut and the poor bloke's tongue was poking through the gaping slit, giving it a grotesque appearance. I.N.L.A. and the word *Traitor* had been carved deep into his chest and stomach.

People gasped in disbelief. The locals here were used to death, but this was something completely new. No one could remember anyone ever being cut up like this poor feller had been. Women were quietly weeping or openly sobbing when someone in the crowd thought he recognised the man. 'Oh Jesus Christ no, that looks like Martin McMurphy. I'm sure it is,' a voice whispered. The whole crowd fell suddenly silent until one man, in a low, trembling voice said, 'Jesus, the provos aren't gonna take this lying down.'

Everyone knew that such a bloody and depraved act would call for serious reprisals, guaranteeing the restart of the violent and bloody feud between the two rival groups. After an atrocity like this, the future looked grim for the entire province. Very grim indeed.

Two men stood at the rear of the crowd. To them Martin McMurphy had been well liked and a brother in arms. After the initial shock of seeing his badly disfigured body they had only one thing on their minds – revenge. Their tears would have to wait.

The older man, Kelly, leaned closer to his young companion and whispered, 'Those fuckin' murderin' commie bastards.'

'I've told you before mate, they're not communists, they're Marxist Leninists,' corrected Kennedy.

'Marxist Leninists? Communists? What the fuck is the difference man? You bleedin' bert. The I.N.L.A. are all bleedin' commies, and they're gonna fuckin' well pay for this,' snapped Kelly.

'So, looks like we'll be heading over to Belfast then does it?' asked the younger man.

'Well, we'll not be off to bleedin' Moscow now will we lad? 'Course we're off to bleedin' Belfast. We'll get as many of those bastards as we can, trap 'em like. They'll all be sitting up in the Divis Flats laughing' an' gettin' pissed, and that's where we'll do 'em - all of 'em.'

As the men were talking they became aware of something strange in the air. At first it was just a slight smell, but then it became a really bad smell, and the odour silenced them as effectively as any slap in the face. Kelly sniffed a little longer, wrinkled his nose and then spun round to stare in disgust.

'Jesus Christ, Keeper, get back from me man,' he ordered. 'Go on, move you foul old git.'

Keeper didn't seem to be aware that anyone was speaking to him as he rocked slightly on his feet and contemplated the scene. 'I wonder if the lad saw what happened to this poor feller?' he said.

Kennedy grabbed a pen from his pocket and, poking the old man in the chest, pushed him back. 'You deaf are ya? Ya dirty old fucker, now stand over there. Keep away.'

Despite taking a step or two backwards the old man kept on rambling. 'I'll be betting he did see something, you know. Must've done really.'

Kennedy raised his fist, but Kelly caught it in mid air. 'Hold on a second son, listen to what he's saying. He may know something.' He smiled at the old man and in a gentle tone asked him, 'Now Keeper, me old mate, tell me, who is this lad you're talkin' about then?'

'The lad, the wee boy - you know laddie,' he mumbled.

'Are you saying that someone saw this happen? Tell me who was it man?'

'Aye,' he yawned, 'tis a fine soft mornin' don't you think sonny?'

'Fuck the morning, who are you talking about man?'

Keeper screwed up his face. He didn't like being questioned, not this early in the day anyhow. 'Aw fuck off, the pair o' ya. Ya little gobshites. Leave me alone, I'm doing no harm,' he hissed at the two men.

'You wait here,' Kelly ordered Kennedy, 'and don't let him leave.'

Kelly disappeared for a few minutes only. 'Has he said anything else lad?' he asked on his return.

'Oh aye he's not stopped, but Christ only knows what about. The pissed up old sod's rambling. Look man, he's just an old drunkard. He doesn't even know where he is, never mind know what the Hell he's talking about.'

'We'll see lad, we'll see.'

Two other men arrived and Kelly nodded in Keeper's direction. Instantly the old man was hooded, his arms were tied behind his back and he was promptly dragged away towards a car. Young Kennedy's face dropped as he realised the car they were heading for was his.

'Take him over to the factory lad, we'll soon find out what he knows,' ordered Kelly.

'What? In my car? Oh come on man you can't be fuckin' serious. I've only just had the seats reupholstered in crushed velvet. Ya know they're black and white, in 2-Tone style. He'll filthy it up, the dirty, stokey, stinking old bastard.'

Kelly pushed his face aggressively toward the younger man. 'To the fuckin' factory I said. Now. And, yes, he goes in your fuckin' car. Do you hear me laddie?'

Kennedy nodded. He had no choice. 'Aye sir, that's grand. Suckin' diesel I am, that's for bleedin' sure.' He walked forlornly away towards his car, muttering as he went. 'Dirty stinkin' old bastard. If he pisses on my seats I'll shoot the old fucker meself, I swear to God I will.'

Keeper had already made himself comfortable on the back seat and didn't seem at all concerned by the bag over his head. The stench was overpowering. Kennedy wound down the windows, gagged a few times and ordered the old man to keep still.

'Aye sonny, now don't you go worrying your head about that. I'll not be making any mess. This is a very comfy car you have here. Now tell me, yours is it son?'

Kennedy didn't answer, wincing instead as he noted the old feller's pee stained trousers. He turned to the wheel, gagged again and then drove away.

31

Just past the Gasworks, At The Factory

When the hood was removed Keeper blinked his eyes rapidly until they regained focus and he found himself sitting in an old chair. He was in the middle of what looked like a disused meat warehouse. He could see Kennedy off to his left and a table on which he could make out a hammer and some chisels, a few hand tools he didn't recognise, and an electric drill. That was interesting.

A man he'd never seen before grabbed him by the shoulders and snapped a single question at him. 'Who did you see last night old man?'

Keeper blinked his eyes several times again. 'So, are you going to torture me son?' he smiled.

'Listen. Just answer me. Who did you see?'

'Well, now, let's be thinking. I'm not too sure, you see, so I don't…' He was interrupted by the slamming of a door and another unknown face appeared.

'I'll take over,' said the new guy. 'Now then old feller, tell me, who was it you saw?'

'Well, it's like I was saying to the other feller, I don't really…' The door banged again as Kelly marched into the room.

'Leave it lads, I'll see to this,' he ordered. 'You two guard the door. Kennedy, stay by me. Now,' he began, pushing his face into the old man's and immediately regretting it. He stood back to take a breath of fresh air, though the stink was quickly pervading the whole area and nothing was that fresh anymore. 'Who did you see old timer?' he tried again from a safe distance.

'Well,' replied Keeper, 'As I was about to tell yer man here, I didn't really…' He paused in expectation of another interruption, but it looked like this was it. 'Oh fuck it lads, it was the young feller I saw. That's all it was.'

'Which young feller? What's his name?'

'Now then boys, you look here. I wouldn't want to go getting anyone in trouble you know,' whispered Keeper.

'Don't worry you won't. Now can you tell me who it was you saw last night?'

'Aye laddie. Of course I can tell you. D'ya think I'm simple or what?'

'Well who the fuck?' snapped Kelly, but quickly softened his voice. 'I mean, will you tell me then? It'll go no further and no one'll get into trouble. So, will you tell me who it was you saw last night, please?'

'Aye lad, I'm sure I will, but it's as I already asked yer man over there sonny. Are ya gonna torture me then, or what?'

'No, no old timer, of course we're not going to torture you.'

'Oh,' sighed Keeper, 'and here's meself thinking that I'd be in for a bit of a torture session. So tell me young feller, why aren't ya then?'

'Why aren't we what?'

'Gonna torture me, like. You've got plenty of tools, seems to me.'

'That's for other matters,' Kelly explained patiently. 'Look, there's no need for torture. We're only here for a little chat, that's all. Do you understand?'

'Oh, so it's kinda like we're all friends here in this room then, is it?'

'Yes that's right, it is. Now can tell me who you saw?'

'I don't suppose you'd be having a spare smoke on you lads, would you?' Keeper asked, scanning their faces hopefully.

'Yes, of course. Kennedy give the man a cigarette.'

Kennedy slowly pulled a new pack from his pocket and held it out for the old man to take one.

'Ah, thank you son, thank you kindly. It's very good of you, you know,' said Keeper, licking his fingers before running them across the pack and selecting a cigarette.

Kennedy stared down in disgust at the remaining fags, which were now coated in the old man's drool. 'Here, keep the pack,' he cringed, thrusting it towards the man.

'Oh, that's very kind of you son and, would you look, the boy's an aristocrat. Kensitas, I like them.' Keeper smiled to himself. That little trick of licking his fingers always worked.

'Now, you've got your smoke, so tell me who it was you saw?' Kelly tried again.

'When?'

'When? Last bleedin' night, that's when. Who was it man?' said Kelly raising his voice in frustration.

Keeper stared and nodded slightly. 'Oh so it's last night you'll be wanting to know about then is it laddie? Hmm, now, I don't suppose you'd be having a wee drop of the good stuff there to help me old memory along, now have you boys?'

This time Kennedy didn't need asking, he just pulled a pint bottle from his pocket, broke the seal and handed it to the old man.

'Thank you son. Keeps an old feller like me cosy you see,' he smiled as he took a deep swig. 'Mmm, lovely stuff, warms me old bones,' he grinned, smacking his lips and handing the bottle back towards the nice lad.

'Keep it,' said Kennedy.

'Well, thank you again young man. You're a very generous young feller aren't you?'

'Now then, old timer, you've got your smokes and you've had your drink. So tell me, who the fuck did you see?' Kelly repeated. 'To be clear, that's last night we're talking about.'

'Ah, right you are. Now then lads, let me see if I can remember for you. Oh aye, I've got it. It was young Dazzer I saw. Saw him as clear as I see you lot now,' Keeper explained as he reached for another drink.

Kelly grabbed his hand. 'No more just yet Pop. Who is Dazzer?'

'Dazzer, you know, Dazzer. Dazzer from Belfast. Good lad is Dazzer. Was always good to me, he was. But do you know something, boys? Last night, why the little fucker only went and threatened to shoot me. Had a gun and everything, so he had. Seemed mighty unfriendly, it did.'

'What is his name, this feller Dazzer?' asked Kelly slowly.

'I told you, Dazzer. Dazzer from Belfast.'

Kelly sighed. 'Tell you what, Keeper, you go ahead and have another drink. I know you said he's called Dazzer, but let's see if you can remember his full name for me will you? If you can I've got a big bottle of whiskey in the car.'

Keeper smacked his lips and grinned. 'And can I have it then son?'

'Aye, you can have it, but only if you can remember his real name. You can have another pack of fags too.'

'What? More smokes, just for me? I have to say son, you're a nice friendly bunch of fellers you lot, aren't you? Now then - let me see, Dazzer's real name - hmm.' Keeper stroked his chin as he thought and absent-mindedly lifted himself slightly from the chair and let out a low fart.

'Oh Christ,' said Kennedy, stumbling backwards.

'Sorry lads, but 'tis me guts, you see. They've been a bit bad recently, like. Don't think I've been eating enough. Hard to think on an empty stomach, so it is.'

'I'll go,' said Kennedy, rushing to leave the stink.

'So I'll just be waiting here for me breakfast then, will I lads?'

Groans echoed through the room and Kelly suggested they all take a little break, as he too escaped to the fresh air outside.

'Who the fuck is that?' asked one of the guys guarding the door.

'Just one of the local drunks,' Kelly explained, lighting a cigarette and inhaling the wonderful, pungent smoke to clear his nostrils.

'Are we supposed to wait on him hand and foot, then?'

'Aye, for now, until we figure out if he really knows anything.'

Around half an hour later Kennedy returned carrying several greasy paper bags. 'Here,' he said, chucking one of them in Keeper's direction.

The old man tore open the package and smiled at the delicious smell. 'Mmm bacon, that's me favourite you know boys,' he told them, then creased his brow. 'What, no eggs?'

'No eggs? No fucking eggs? Why you ungrateful old….' Kennedy snapped.

'Leave it lad. Let's just all have a bite to eat, then we'll finish up,' said Kelly.

The group of interrogators sat as far as possible from the old guy while they ate their breakfast. 'How'd the old stoke get that name anyhow? I've never heard of anyone with a name like Keeper,' asked one.

'Don't know for sure,' replied Kelly, 'but some say it's been shortened from "keep away", 'cos that's all anyone says to him when he gets too close. Keep Away.'

'Aye, that sounds about right,' nodded Kennedy. 'You should smell inside o' me bleedin' motor. It stinks to high Heaven of the dirty old bastard.'

32

Breakfast's Over

'Right then, Keeper, let's start again shall we?' Kelly asked. 'What's this Dazzer really called?'

'Well son, I've had a little think for you and I remember now.'

'So?'

'So, what?'

'So, what is it then? What's his fucking name, man? Jesus Christ, you've got our fags, you've got our whiskey and now you've had yer bleedin' breakfast bought. So, tell me now, WHAT THE FUCK IS HIS NAME?'

'Hey, there's no need to go shouting at me son, I am doing my best for you, you know.'

'I know, I know you are,' sighed Kelly, trying to keep his temper in check. 'Come on now Pops, what is he really called this Dazzer of yours? What's his full name?'

'Well if that's all you wanted to know - why didn't you ask in the first place?'

Kelly breathed in as he slowly counted to ten and said nothing.

'Right then son, let me see,' Keeper began. 'Oh aye, Dazzer. Lovely young lad, he was. Always gave me the time of day, so he did. I knew his Da, back in the day, when I was all respectable, like. 'Course, he died when Dazzer was only a nipper. Car crash I think it was. Aye, a terrible business all round. Mr. Nolan was really broken up about it as I recall.'

'Nolan? Willy Nolan?'

'Aye, that's the feller. You're better with names than I am, that's for sure.'

'How do you know Mr. Nolan?'

'Ah, son, I knew everyone back then you see. I used to be somebody, so I did. Aye, but things change. Found my wife in bed with another feller and it sort of sent me a little bit mad. At least, that's what folks tell me - that I'm mad, like. So that's why I remember Dazzer, you see. He was always nice to me, he was. 'Course, he didn't have that big scar back then, but it was Dazzer all right. I'm not so good with names, but I never forget a face.'

'Scar?'

'Aye, right on the side of his face. Just like the moon at night it was.'

Kelly took a deep breath and leaned in, ignoring the smell. 'Tell me his name, Keeper, and tell me now.'

'Jesus Christ, you Derry boys know fuck all, do ya? Well, Dazzer, 'tis a nickname for Darren, like,' beamed Keeper. 'See, I knew it would come to me.'

'Darren who?'

'McCann, Darren McCann,' said the old man, dropping his voice to a superstitious whisper before adding, 'You know, the Butcher of Belfast.'

'Holy fuckin' Christ,' breathed Kelly. 'It can't be.'

'Isn't he…' Kennedy began, but his superior glared at him to shut him up.

'Give him that other bottle and get him out of here,' Kelly ordered. 'I have to make a call.'

A phone rang in Belfast and was answered by a man with a broad County Armagh accent. Kelly explained what had happened.

'Must've been a ghost, then,' said the voice on the end of the phone. 'The Butcher's dead and gone. Is this witness of yours reliable?'

'Is he hell,' said Kelly. 'The man's always pissed and I wouldn't have believed him, except…'

'Go on,' prompted Mr. County Armagh.

'He mentioned that Willy Nolan had known this guy's father and he said the man he saw last night, this Dazzer, had a big scar on his face.'

'A crescent shaped scar?'

'Well, he said like the moon, but I think that's what he meant.'

'Jesus. Well, if the guy's a drunk he's probably wrong, but I'd better pass this upstairs just in case. Good work Kelly.'

'Aye.'

***

Liam had been driving east, his eyes scanning everything, everywhere, both in front and behind, for any hint of trouble. The roads were quiet and, for the moment, he seemed to be safe. He wanted to blend in with the other cars, but there wasn't really that much traffic available for blending. Inhaling deeply on his cigarette he tried to calm himself, but he couldn't shake the growing sense of fear. 'Jesus man, you're gonna get pulled by the peelers or shot by the bleedin' boys.' He flicked his tab end through the window, then immediately lit another. 'Fuck, fuck, fuck,' he cursed, as a small sign came into view – *The Ponderosa*.

A pub car park. It was hardly perfect, but it would have to do. He pulled into the yard, killed the engine and the Capri rolled to a stop alongside five other cars that looked like they might have been there all night. He tried for a couple of hours' rest, though there was no chance of real sleep.

Around six-thirty, just as McMurphy's body was being discovered, the darkness was fading and a bit of traffic was building up on the roads. It was time to go and he mentally prepared himself for the long, nerve-racking drive on small roads out of Derry to Larne. That would still only put him about half-an-hour away from Belfast, but it should be far enough.

It was a hard, concentrated journey, but he made it and was finally on board the ferry and heading home.

33

Family Ties

The old manor house had never seemed so welcoming. He placed a call to Turner, announcing he was home but saying nothing more. He kept his voice light and cheerful, but he knew Turner would detect his tiredness. He always did. Strangely, when Turner breezily suggested calling round for a cup of tea the next day, Liam thought he heard something strange in his voice as well. He was too exhausted to think about that now, though, so he went to bed. He slept fitfully and woke next morning with vague memories of a dream about an old drunk from his childhood. Keeper, that was his name. Jesus he hadn't seen the guy in, what, must be twenty years at least. Surely he couldn't have recognised him after all this time – could he?

Turner arrived on time, as always, and they had the required cup of tea. This was their new routine of keeping things normal on the surface. They spoke briefly about the weather and then Turner suggested a drive. The car was considered a safe place to talk, but today both men seemed reluctant and the journey passed in awkward silence. After the short drive they arrived at a small complex of office buildings that had become one of their regular meeting places. Turner arranged more tea and then the conversation finally began.

'There's something wrong, isn't there?' Liam asked.

'Well, my boy, we may have a little problem, but let's deal with the good news first, shall we?'

'OK.'

'That was absolutely excellent work with McMurphy. I admit that, when the order first came down that it should be a public affair, I had my doubts you could pull it off.'

'You and me both, Mr. T.'

'Well, quite. I mean how were you supposed to deal with a high profile fellow like that in public and live to tell the tale? It was sheer genius, my boy. Genius. I assume the termination was carried out away from the scene, leaving just the final display to be public?'

Liam nodded. 'Aye. It was all I could think of.'

'Well, it was brilliant, though I must admit to being rather shocked by the state of the body. Did you have to carve him up like that? His throat, his tongue? I mean, it was all rather gruesome. Truly the stuff of nightmares.'

'You said you needed to make a statement.'

'Oh indeed, dear boy, indeed, and that little touch with carving I.N.L.A on him was inspired.'

'Should have put the Provos' backs up, that's for sure,' Liam agreed. 'Wouldn't surprise me if they're already busy up in Belfast taking some of those commie bastards out right now.'

'Oh, we are already hearing rumblings,' Turner confirmed, 'and we're happy to leave them to it. Yes, it was a magnificent touch, but it was all so bloodthirsty. It does make me wonder how you sleep at night.'

'I don't.'

'What?'

'Sleep well.'

'Yes, well, that's hardly surprising. You do look rather tired, my boy, and I wonder if there is something on your mind. Beyond carving men up and leaving them on public monuments, that is.'

Liam pursed his lips and ran his finger along the scar on his cheek. 'Something happened,' he said finally.

'Were you recognised?'

'How did you know?'

'No, Liam, you first. Tell me what happened.'

'It was this old drunk. He was the only one around and he saw me just after I'd done with the body.'

'Did he see you with the body?'

'No, I'm sure he didn't. He was too far gone, but he came up to me and said "Hey, is that really you?" or something like that. I couldn't place him at first, and I didn't hang around to ask, but I've got him now. He was just this sad old drunk when I was a kid, but he was a nice old feller and I took pity on him. He always said I looked like me Da, and that was grand. I can't really remember me Da, so it was just kind of nice, like, that he would say that.'

'He mentioned your father?'

'No, not then. That only came to me this morning. I guess that's how he still knew me.'

'Did he mention William Nolan?'

'What? No. All that happened was he looked as if he recognised me and I got outta there as quickly as I could. What the fuck is this, Mr. Turner?'

'Something I can't put down to coincidence this time, Liam. Yesterday evening, probably just as you were leaving Ireland, I was tipped off that someone was asking questions about your father and William Nolan.'

'What the fuck's me Da got to do with anything?'

'He went to school with Mr. Nolan, you know, and Peter Moore.'

'Aye, you told me that ages ago, but you said it didn't mean anything.'

'No, as far as I could tell it didn't, but now I'm wondering if I might have missed something. I investigated your past, Liam, long before I recruited you, and your family came up clean. As far as I could tell they went out of their way to be neutral and stay out of any politics.'

'Aye, me Ma always told me to stay out of the troubles and I always did, until the murdering bastards had her killed, that is.'

'Yes, we know all that, but there has to be something more to this. Now listen, Liam, you have been questioned several times about William Nolan and you have always said that you only knew him vaguely. I have to ask you again, and this is really important dear boy, how well did you really know him?'

'Fuck,' spat Liam as he put his hand to his head and frowned in concentration.

'I have to know lad,' Turner pressed.

Liam pursed his lips together and sighed. Willy was one of the good guys and he had always managed to avoid speaking about him, but now he knew he had no choice. 'All I know,' he said finally, 'was that me Ma hated him. He lived down the street from us when I was growing up and she would never let me have anything to do with him. Then, when I was about twelve or so, he moved away and I didn't see him for years. It was only when I joined the R.A. that I ran into him again and he sort of took me under his wing. He was like a father to me, so he was. I never saw him involved in anything, Mr. Turner, and that's the truth, but I know he had a lot of respect from the boys. He was always someone you could go to if you needed anything and one time, when I was really in the shit, he got me out of Ireland and into Spain. He saved my life that day, but I haven't seen him since. And that's it. That's all I know.'

'Yes, well, that sounds about right,' Turner said thoughtfully. 'Mr. Nolan has always been clever enough to keep himself clean and we have never been able to link him to anything nasty. Honestly, we believe he pulls a lot of strings, but he's not someone we could ever target. Still, this latest development is very interesting and I will have to investigate further.'

'You'll let me know what you find?' Liam asked.

'Yes, my boy, I will.'

34

The Phone Call

Liam waited as patiently as he could, but it was a week before the phone rang and Turner suggested a cup of tea. Liam drove to the pre-arranged rendezvous, yet another small hut in the middle of bleedin' nowhere, and was immediately aware that his handler was distracted. He took longer than usual to light his pipe and turned the selection of a biscuit into an unnecessarily drawn out affair.

'What have you got to tell me?' Liam finally pushed when he could take the silence no longer. 'There's obviously something up.'

'Liam, my boy, I am ashamed,' Turner began. 'I am known for my thorough work and always digging until I've uncovered all the information that is there to be found.'

'You don't have to tell me that. I've seen it for meself many times. You're a marvel.'

'Well, that's kind of you Liam, but this time I didn't dig deeply enough when I was looking into your background.'

'So there is something about Willy Nolan and me Da, then? Christ, Mr. Turner, don't tell me that he was R.A. after all.'

'No, I am absolutely sure that he wasn't. However, his connection to Willy Nolan was stronger than I had realised. Did you know that he was your mothers' cousin?'

'What? No, it can't be. Me Ma hated him.'

'Did she ever tell you why?'

'Not really. He was a connected man and she hated all the R.A. so I put it down to that. She did seem to hate him more than most, though. Her cousin? Really? Jesus, Mr. Turner, that doesn't make a lot of sense. I mean, I'd have known. Even if she didn't tell me, why didn't he?'

'Well, now, I don't think the family connection is all that important. It was one of those second cousin jobbies, possibly with a "once removed" thrown in, and I have always been a little confused by family trees. I am an only child, do you see? My mother was an only child and my father was an orphan and…'

'This is fascinating, Mr. Turner, and I'd love to spend some time and get to know you better, but not right now.'

'No, you're quite right, my boy. I am procrastinating and putting off telling you the truth.'

'So for fuck's sake, just tell me then.'

Turner glanced sadly over the rim of his teacup and made no attempt to criticise Liam's language. Instead he took a deep breath and said, 'William Nolan killed your father.'

'What? How? No, it was a car crash.' Liam slammed his cup down on the table and the liquid sloshed onto his hand, but he didn't notice. 'Me Ma always told me he was drunk and crashed his car. Oh Fuck me, Mr. Turner, what in Christ's name are you saying?'

'I believe your father probably was drunk, lad. That's certainly what the official report said. Blood analysis, and all that, but he was not the one driving the car. That was Mr. Nolan, who was equally drunk.'

' So why…?'

Turner raised his hand. 'It really does look like an accident, Liam, but that's not the point. Mr. Nolan was highly connected, even as a young man, and his involvement was covered up. The police report made no mention of it and I didn't dig deeply enough to find it until now. I am truly sorry, my boy.'

'Holy Mother of God, I don't know what to say.'

'No. Quite. In all honesty I can't see that it necessarily has anything to do with anything. Your mother may not have known, though her hatred for Mr. Nolan suggests that she did. If she decided to protect you from the truth, then I don't think you should hold that against her.'

'No, no, she was always trying to keep me out of the troubles. I can understand why she didn't tell me.'

'Indeed, and Mr. Nolan was hardly likely to tell you himself, so there really is no great implication in the grand scheme of things. Yet….'

'I… I don't understand all this,' Liam butted in. 'I mean, this is earth shattering, like, but…what the fuck does it mean?'

'I'm not absolutely sure, Liam. The only thing I know for certain is that someone else is looking into it too. I don't know who that someone is, which is deeply worrying, and I don't know why, but I can make an educated guess. It has to mean someone is onto you, Liam. At least, somebody has come to believe that Darren McCann is not dead.'

'Fuck me, what do I…? I mean, I don't… Jesus, I'm sorry for all the language, like, but fuck me.'

'I quite agree, which is why I have done something that I would never have thought possible. I have broken protocol.'

'You're shittin' me. How? What the Hell have you done?'

'I have kept this information to myself. So far, only I know about the connection between Nolan and your father and only I know that someone else has been looking into it. When this comes out, then your contract with Her Majesty's government will be over.'

'No fu…'

'It's obvious, my boy,' Turner interrupted. 'Liam O'Neil is only useful as long as The Butcher of Belfast is dead.'

Liam stared at his empty teacup and took long, deep breaths. He had to try to hold himself together, but this was terrible news. 'What about Moore?' he asked eventually. 'Will I still get a crack at him?'

'Well, that's the big question, isn't it?' Turner admitted. 'The job is on the table and has a green light for when the time is right. I just don't know when that time will be and how much time we have.'

'Fuck.'

'Liam, I will do all in my power to expedite matters, but nothing is going to happen overnight. Right now I think you could do to go away for a while until we are sure your cover isn't blown. Or, at least, that the top brass don't know that there's a chance it might be.'

'Spain?'

'It seems the obvious choice, but please be extra conscientious about reporting in. I would suggest the good old fashioned radio for a while rather than the switchboard.'

'OK, Mr. Turner. Will do. I guess there's nothing more to say for now, except…'

'Except what?'

'All this with me Da and Willy Nolan. Was there anything else? I mean, was there anything to suggest Willy was involved with me Ma's murder?'

'No, Liam, there wasn't but, if I were you, I might be a little suspicious.'

'Aye.'

35

A Dead Man Calling

The journey to Spain was such a familiar one by now that Liam put himself on auto-pilot and let his mind wander. He could rationalise the situation with Willy and his father's death. He didn't like it, but he could see how it had happened and why he had never been told. What he couldn't deal with was the possibility that Willy had anything to do with his mother. In his heart he couldn't believe it, but he had to be sure and there was only one way to find out.

He planned as he drove and knew that it was an immense gamble. He had to trust in two things; that the document he had from an electrical repair shop was really as good as it looked and that a man he had always trusted was as honourable as he believed.

Liam arrived at the small farm in Catalunya, Darren spent a couple of days in Montse's calming presence, José Luis Agea left for Ireland on the second evening and Butch was in Crossmaglen just before daylight broke the following morning. He parked his car opposite a slight gap in the tree line before diving headlong into the bush and disappearing from view.

Concealed by the dense, thick foliage he cautiously made his way forward. A shiver ran down his spine as he crept along. If he was caught sneaking about here, in Cross, by the Provos they'd shoot him on sight, no questions, no explanations, no second chances. He'd be a dead man for sure. Slowly he zigzagged his way in the direction of the old farmhouse, pausing every few yards to hold his breath and strain his ears. He could smell last night's smoke from the chimney but heard nothing to give concern.

Eventually he arrived at the edge of the woodlands and stood perfectly still as he watched and waited for any sign of movement. Everything was quiet. He checked his watch and tutted. If the guards were still sleeping they would certainly be in trouble for it later. One last check and then he sprinted over to the house and pressed himself into the shadows against the wall. Still nothing.

He made his way to the front door with gentle, even paced footfalls, the gravel underfoot quietly crunching at his tread. Every now and then he ducked low, but still there was no one to be seen. Finally he reached his goal and gently turned the handle. The door opened with a slight creak and he was inside. The last time he'd been at this house was back in eighty-one when he had been warmly welcomed and fed, but he didn't expect that kind of treatment this time.

The place was deathly quiet, the only sound coming from an old brass faced grandfather clock as it ticked loudly away. Liam took a deep breath before creeping carefully up the wide, carpeted staircase, timing his steps to the sound of the clock. He arrived at the landing and saw two bedroom doors standing ajar. A quick peak through each showed that they were empty, leaving a third closed door at the end of the corridor. He pushed gently and it opened to reveal a sole occupant in bed, snoring softly. Tiptoeing to a seat in a shadowy corner, he sat and waited.

Willy rolled over in a deep sleep, the picture of oblivion, and still Liam waited. Then a shrill sound assaulted his ears and Willy jumped to silence the alarm, yawning as he glanced to the weak morning light coming through the window. He stretched slowly and looked as though he would settle down again, but the next moment he was alert.

'Good morning Mr. Nolan,' came the low, deep whisper.

'What? Who?' Willy mumbled as he rubbed the sleep from his eyes. 'What the Hell?'

'Mate, you need to give yer boys a bleedin' slap. Anyone could walk in here. You could get your throat cut in the middle of the night you know,' whispered Liam as he pressed the release button on *The Killer*.

'What the …?'

'Where's Mary at?' Liam interrupted.

'What?'

'I asked, where's Mary. You goin' deaf or what?'

'Mary? She's down in Cork at her sister's place. Look, who the hell are you and what do you want?' Willy threw back the covers and reached to his bedside drawer.

'You'll not be needin' a gun just yet,' said Liam as he stood from the shadows, folding the blade and pocketing it once more. 'Jesus, don't you recognise me man? I've not been gone *that* long - have I?'

Willy stared at the intruder as his eyes focused and Liam saw the recognition cross his face. 'So it's true,' he said finally.

'Aye, it's true Willy. What's up? Seen a ghost?'

'Jesus Christ, we all thought you were dead. Where the hell've you been son?'

'Son is it? Strange you should say that, since I've been nobody's son for years. That's why I'm here, mate. I want some answers.'

'Butch, this is insanity. Do you know how quickly I could have someone in here to take you out?'

'But you won't, will you? Not if you're the same man I knew before.'

'Christ, son, that depends on what you're going to do. I saw that knife in your hand just then.'

'Aye, but it's back in me pocket again. All I want is to talk, Willy, and the knife'll stay where it is for now if I get the answers I'm lookin' for. You want to put some clothes on there? It's a bit distracting, like, dealing with a man in his underwear.'

Willy looked down at himself, belatedly aware of his semi-nakedness, and reached for last night's garments. Liam dragged the chair from the corner and positioned it opposite the man who was now sitting, haphazardly clothed, on the edge of his bed.

'That's better,' said Liam, taking a seat. 'So, mate, did you kill me Da, then, or what?'

Willy blinked rapidly before letting out a long sigh. 'Who told you?'

'You know,' said Liam, his voice low and controlled, 'on a one to ten of bloody stupid questions, that's way up there. What the fuck does it matter who told me? I'll just be taking that as a "yes", will I?'

Again Willy sighed. 'It was an accident, Butch, and one I've regretted all my life. I thought the world of your Da.'

'Aye, that's what I figured from what I heard. It's a shame you weren't man enough to admit to it, like, but that wouldn't have brought me Da back. That's why I'm here to talk instead of carve you up into little pieces.'

'So, you want to talk about your Da? That's why you're here?' Willy asked, the confusion clear on his face. 'You do know what you're risking just by being in the country, don't you?'

'Well, that depends on what you'll be doin' when I'm gone, but we'll come to that later. For now I just wanted an admission from your own lips about me Da, and then I want to talk about me Ma?'

'Your Ma? I can't tell you anything about your Ma. We only spoke once after the crash. She refused to even look at me, let alone speak to me. I tried and I tried, but she totally cut me off, wouldn't even acknowledge that I existed.'

'Was that because she knew what you'd done?'

'Aye, Butch, she knew,' said Willy, and the sadness in his voice was evident. 'She cursed me for his death and she cursed me for a coward and she was right, but things were different back then. I couldn't be going down for an accident that couldn't be put right, no matter how much I prayed for it.'

'You prayed?' Liam let out a small snort of disgust. 'You killed me Da and then you prayed. That make you feel better, did it?'

'No, Butch, it didn't. I've never forgiven myself and I couldn't ask God to forgive me either. Declan was a good friend all through school. Everyone liked him. When we grew up I joined the cause, but he would never come along. That's what we were talking about that night and we had a few too many and, well, he'd had more than me so I said I'd drive and...' His voice trailed off as he looked at the man opposite him. 'What do you want me to say, Butch?' he asked finally.

'Why didn't you tell me?'

'How could I? If your Mammy hadn't said anything then she obviously didn't want you to know.'

'Aye, I can see that. It's what I figured,' Liam agreed. 'But now I do know.'

'Yes, son, and I'm relieved, honest I am. I've lived with the guilt all my life and I've always wanted to tell you how sorry I am. You've got to believe me, Butch.'

'I do believe you,' Liam confirmed, and it was true. The sadness and sincerity in the man's voice were obvious. 'But that makes me wonder, like, was I second prize?'

'What? What the Hell are you talking about?'

'How many times did you try to get me to join the cause, eh?' asked Liam, his voice now rising a little as his anger threatened to break through. 'Was it because you couldn't get me Da?'

'What are you…? Oh, no, Butch, Lord help me, that can't really be what you think.'

'Willy, I don't know what to think. These last few years I've been pondering, like. What the fuck was it that made me so important? Why were you so desperate for me to join the R.A?' Liam rose to his feet and began to pace the room.

'Oh lad, that was for your own good,' Willy said, nervously eying the man who strode around his bedroom. 'I felt so guilty over Declan and I couldn't be letting you down as well.'

'You fuckin' what?' Liam spat as he turned on him, his control fading fast. 'You thought you could make up for killing me Da by getting me to join the Provos. Tell me, Willy, how the fuck would that have helped?'

'Butch, no, you've got it all wrong lad,' Willy said hurriedly. 'Back then, when you were growing up, it was obvious that the way you were heading you were going to get yourself killed, either on a bloody stupid motorbike or in a pub fight, that much was sure. And, though your Mammy hated it, I knew that if I could only get you to join the cause I could look after you. That's why I was so desperate to get you in. I knew you'd be far safer fighting the Brits than you'd ever be on the sharp end of a broken beer bottle.'

Liam narrowed his eyes and stared at the man sitting pathetically on the edge of his bed. He said nothing, but his hand went to his pocket where he slowly fingered *The Killer.*

'It's true lad, think about it,' Willy continued rapidly. 'That motorbike crew you were running with, how many of them are still alive? And, as for the pub fights - Jesus. If you'd been killed fighting a pub full of bloody drunkards, I'd never have forgiven myself. I felt I owed this to your Da, can't you see that? I can't count the number of times I ordered your recruitment, but stubborn as you are, you always refused.'

'But you got me in the end, though, didn't you?' Liam hissed, the knife now in the palm of his hand.

'What? No. I mean, yes you joined up, but that was only when your Ma was killed and none of us saw that coming.' Willy hunched backwards on the bed as Liam advanced on him menacingly, the knife flicking open.

'Didn't you?' asked Liam through gritted teeth. 'That was a surprise, was it?'

'O… of course it was,' Willy stammered, shrinking further from the knife. 'That was the Shankill boys. They're nothing to do with us. How the Hell could we know?'

Liam stood back as he checked his anger once more, breathing deeply and allowing a small smile to play on his lips. 'You know, Willy, I've been believin' you and I still want to believe you about me Da. Trouble is, now I know you're lying.'

'What? No, I'm…'

'It wasn't the Shankill Butchers who murdered me Ma, and you know it.'

'No, I… It was them… It…'

'No, Willy, it wasn't.'

'How…?'

'The name Jonny O'Leary mean anything to you, does it?'

Willy swallowed hard and lowered his eyes. Liam stared at him, his breath coming in slow, deep grunts as he waited for an answer. He wanted so badly to believe that this man hadn't had anything to do with his mother's murder, but the silence now made him think otherwise.

'I didn't find out until it was too late,' Willy said finally, his voice barely more than a whisper.

'Go on,' urged Liam.

'It was Moore, Peter Moore. He never liked you, you know.'

'Feeling's mutual, mate. Keep going.'

'I'd told Moore that I wanted you in the R.A. and sent him to recruit you, but you weren't having any of it. I don't know how many times he tried but, well, he's not a man who likes to fail. That's why he's so good. He always gets the job done but, I swear, I didn't know how far he was willing to go.'

'You swear?'

'Yes, Butch. He came up with the plan to have your Ma killed and it was done before I knew anything about it. Jesus, even I believed it was the Shankill Butchers.'

'So when did you find out it was Jonny O'Leary?'

'Oh, I don't know Butch. It was months later, maybe even a year. Larry O'Brien just mentioned it one day, all casual like, as if he thought I already knew. Moore had got all the committee to sanction it, so he thought I'd sanctioned it too.'

'You didn't tell me.'

'Jesus Christ, son, how could I? The damage was done. All the praying on earth couldn't bring your Da back, and telling you about your Ma wouldn't have brought her back either. By then you were well and truly in the fold and already turning into one of our best assets. What good would it have done if I'd told you?'

'What good?' Liam hissed. 'What fucking good? Well I can tell you what fucking harm it did.'

'Aye, I see that now.'

'You do, do you? Well that's just fine, Willy. That's just grand, so it is. And, of course, Peter Moore just gets to keep going about his business as if nothing had happened.'

'We had words.'

'Words, is it? Oh that makes me feel so much fucking better. Did you tell him he'd been a naughty boy, like?'

'Butch, listen to me. Peter Moore is a powerful man and he did a job I asked him to do. I didn't ask him to do it the way he did, but there wasn't a lot I could say. He's not afraid of anything, you know. I think that's when I realised what a psycho he really is. I mean, they say the man doesn't even feel pain. I've hardly spoken to him since, and, as for the other committee men – well, they're all dead.'

'So I've heard.'

Willy finally stood from the bed and moved towards the man who had once been his protégé. He reached out to place a hand on his shoulder and, when the lad didn't move, he squeezed gently and looked into his eyes. 'Darren,' he said, 'this is a bad state of affairs. Until last week, just after McMurphy was killed, I really believed you were dead. Everyone did. Christ, everyone still does. This rumour about a scarred phantom or spook being the Butcher of Belfast reborn – well it was just too incredible. Now, though…'

'Now what, Willy?'

'You know what I have to do, Butch. There are two guards outside. One call from me and it's over for you.'

'Are those the same guards who were asleep and just let me walk in here?'

Willy let out a small laugh. 'Aye, you've got a point there, lad. That's something I shall have to remedy. Seriously, though, what else do you expect me to do?'

'I expect you to give me twenty-four hours. I reckon you owe me that for me Ma and Da.'

Willy dropped his hand slowly from Liam's shoulder and studied the face in front of him. The deep, crescent shaped scar on his cheek and the smaller one on his lip gave him a lop-sided appearance, so unlike the young man he remembered. But it was other things that made the real difference. The pain in his eyes and the general weariness had aged him. This was a man who had seen too much.

'I reckon you're right,' he agreed. 'Twenty-four hours it is, but if you are ever seen here again there will be nothing I can do for you.'

'I know it.'

'That twenty-four hours had better start right now, son,' Willy said as he extended his arms.

Liam paused, but then joined in a brief shoulder hug. 'And you'll keep the dogs off?'

Willy reached for his radio and keyed the mike. It crackled briefly before 'Sir?' came faintly across the airwaves. 'You awake now, are you?' growled Willy.

'Sir?' came the disembodied voice again.

'I want both of you round back in the wood shed right now. I'm out of logs.'

'Yes sir.'

Willy moved to the window and watched as two burly guards hurried to the rear of the house, one of them still fastening his pants as he went. 'They'll get what's coming to them tomorrow,' he told Liam. 'Now go, Butch, and I never want to see you again.'

'Bye Willy.'

'Good luck, son.'

36
Twenty-Four Hours Later

José Luis Agea had left Ireland without raising an eyebrow at the border and Darren was heading back to Montse just as a phone call was placed in Crossmaglen.

'So it really is him?' came the strong County Armagh accent. 'I'll get right on it sir.'

Willy hung up the phone and stared at it. The lad was long gone and he figured they were even now. Confession was good for the soul, so they said, but he wasn't sure that was true. His gaze stayed on the phone for several minutes until his hand reached out and he placed another call.

'Yes?' said the English voice.

'Renegade,' Willy announced.

'OK, I'm ready.'

***

Back in Spain Liam was in regular radio contact with Turner and, with each day that passed, he became more and more uneasy. If Turner found out about his unauthorised visit to Willy it could present big problems. Even the stalwart Englishman would be unable to cover for him then. In fact there was no "if" about it. The real question was "when?" and he was running out of time.

Finally, about a week after his trip to Crossmaglen, Turner gave the coded message he'd been waiting for. 'I've got to go, lass,' he told Montse as he came off the radio.

'Right now?'

'Yes, and I think you should prepare yourself for a call about eggs pretty soon.'

'Really? It has been so long since we made the Beeline plan that I didn't think it would ever happen. Are you sure?'

'No, not one hundred percent, but I think it is very likely.'

'I am glad' she told him, though tears came to her eyes.

'Don't cry, Montse. Please don't cry love. This is what we've been waiting for.'

'I know,' she said quietly, swallowing hard to contain her emotion. 'Please be careful, Darren.'

'I will.'

She flung her arms round him then and he held her tightly until he was forced to break the embrace. 'I really have to go Montse.'

She smiled at him bravely. 'So maybe the next time I see you we will be in Dinnywinny?'

'Yes, in Dinnywinny,' he confirmed before heading smartly to the door. He needed to go now before she made him cry too.

37

The Last Man Standing

'I could kiss you, Mr. Turner,' Liam announced over his tea.

'I'd rather you didn't, old boy. Most unseemly.'

'Well, you're a marvel, so you are. How did you pull this off?'

'I really can't take much credit, Liam. I think this scarred spectre that everyone is so terrified of has done the trick. That's how the top brass see it, anyway. Personally I think it is more to do with a reincarnated Butcher.'

'And the top brass don't know anything about that?'

'No, I am still the only one who is aware the connection has been made. Once this job is over and you have returned, I will "find out" about it then.'

'So there's nothing new to report there?' asked Liam hopefully.

'Well, I'm not really sure. When my contact first tipped me off, it seemed as if it was all just a possibility. Someone had guessed that Darren McCann might still be alive.'

'And now?'

'They seem more certain. I don't know why or how.'

Liam drained his tea as a way to avoid responding. He could hardly tell him that the "how" was because Darren McCann had been in Willy Nolan's bedroom.

'Anyway, what matters is that Mr. Moore has either decided for himself that he must leave Ireland and go to America, or someone has ordered him to leave,' Turner continued. 'That's why we finally got the green light for the job. If we don't take him out now, we might lose him for ever.'

'At last.'

'Quite. That condemned building was rather fortuitous though.'

'Lucky for us, eh?' Liam smiled as he glanced back at the file on his knee. The luxury apartment complex where Peter Moore had lived for years had suddenly developed an unidentified problem and the building was being evacuated. Moore was to be among the last to leave and that meant, on the date specified in the dossier, there would be hardly anyone else around. Probably no one.

'I'm not sure I believe in luck,' said Turner. 'Honestly, my boy, it's a bit too good to be true and it makes me nervous. I have half a mind to call it off.'

'No fuckin' way,' Liam yelled as he jumped from his seat.

Turner didn't flinch. 'I expected that reaction, Liam, and you will note that I only said half a mind. It really is now or never so I know we can't miss this opportunity. Still, there should be one extra page in that dossier.'

'What's that then?'

'You will have back up.'

'Fuck off,' Liam spat at him. 'Moore is mine, and mine alone. You've always promised me that. I'm not having anyone else along and that's final.'

'Sergeant Gates has already agreed to the mission. In fact he volunteered.'

'You have got to be shittin' me, Mr. Turner. No way, never, ain't gonna happen.'

'Liam, for goodness sake sit down and listen lad. Jumping around and foul language will get us nowhere. You need to let me explain.'

Liam stared at him, further profanities forming on his lips, but he thought better of it. Turner was in one of his unflappable moods and that meant he would say what he had to say regardless of any protestations. 'Get it over with then,' he said sulkily as he threw himself back down in the chair.

'Right, that's better,' said Turner, puffing on his pipe. 'Now this has to be a helicopter jobbie, as you have seen from the file. It's not quite in and out, because we are not one hundred percent sure of Mr. Moore's full schedule for that evening, so there could be some waiting around. Besides, I thought you might want to take your time with this one.'

Turner waited for Liam's nod before continuing. 'Any helicopter operation requires the pilot and an armed guard. That is regular protocol. Are we agreed so far?'

'Aye.'

'So that armed man might as well be someone you are familiar with and who can provide back up if it is required.'

'But…'

'No, Liam, let me finish. I said "if" required. Sergeant Gates will be on the lookout for any bodyguards, but he is not detailed to follow you into the building. That is your job and yours alone. However, since we don't have a defined timeline, it is entirely possible that the helicopter would have to be recalled and we both know how you would feel about that, right?'

'Aye, that's right enough.'

'If that happens I do not want you on the ground alone again. It is simply too dangerous now that it is almost sure you have been identified. Where could you go for help this time? You would never make it out of the north and you know it.'

'You might have a point,' Liam agreed unenthusiastically.

'Therefore, Sergeant Gates will be along just in case anything goes wrong. He has no part in the mission and he does not even know the significance of the target. He is purely for back up and, under the circumstances, I consider him the best man for the job. There is to be no further discussion here, Liam. I have made my decision and it is final. Now, more tea?'

Liam sat for a moment considering the situation while Turner refilled his cup. The plan made sense and there was no valid argument against it. In truth he also thought the fortuitous condemning of Moore's building was too good to be true and that's why he was considering that it might be time for the Beeline operation. If Turner was wrong, if someone else in authority did know that the Butcher had been identified, it could be that he wasn't expected back from this mission. Did the British government want rid of him? It was a possibility he had to consider.

Gates could well be useful and he could be trusted, but he would also be an obstacle to a disappearing act if it came to it. Still, that wasn't insurmountable and, if having the sergeant along made the difference between getting Moore or missing him, he could live with it.

'Okay, I agree,' he said at last.

'Good,' said Turner. 'Now go home and get some sleep. You have just two days and then you're off. This is what you have wanted all along, dear boy, but you will need to be extra careful. I don't like the bad feeling that I have and I won't rest until you are safely back home.'

Liam could hardly meet the older man's eyes as they stood to shake hands. It was quite possible that he would be heading to a new home and this could be the last time he would be sharing tea and biscuits with this strange English gentleman he had come to view as a true friend. It was a sad thought and he had to make an effort to sound casual as he offered, 'I'll be fine, Mr. T.'

'See you soon Liam.'

'Aye.'

'Oh, one more thing,' Turner said, stopping him at the door, 'I might have a way to garner more intelligence on Nolan and any connection to your mother.'

'Really?'

'Yes. I am making no promises, but I shall pursue it while you're away.'

'I'm sure there'll be nothing to find, Mr. Turner.'

'No, you're probably right, but it doesn't hurt to try.'

38

Bangor, just off Belfast Road - Peter's Flat

Liam and Gates had greeted each other amicably enough at the chopper, but the din of the rotors limited any conversation during the flight and both seemed happy enough with that. Liam, particularly, was lost in his own thoughts, recalling the phone calls he had made the previous evening requesting eggs over easy. All messages had been received and his little troop was on stand-by waiting for the Beeline go signal or the instruction to stand down.

When the helicopter landed the two men found a car waiting and they set out on the short drive.

'I'm not sure how long this will take,' Liam said.

'I don't want any details,' Gates snapped. 'Not authorised.'

The silence that followed was awkward. 'You ever get that flat in Spain you were talking about?' Liam asked in an attempt at conversation.

'Yes.'

'So, you must have found some work, then?'

'Yes.'

'Well now, sure that's a wee bit of good news, isn't it?'

'Yes.'

And that was it. The silence returned until they arrived at their destination. Gates secreted the car and found himself a hidden position as Liam grabbed his backpack and set off into the darkness. He felt his pulse racing as the adrenalin pumped and he made a conscious effort to control his breathing, but it was difficult. This was Moore. This was the bastard he'd been after for four years. 'This is for you, Ma,' he whispered.

He quickly arrived at the tall building and gazed to the top. It was an old tea warehouse that had been converted, with terraces the only external modern addition. 'Shite, that's a bleedin' long way up, so it is,' he muttered in the cold February night air. He noted two weak lights at either side of the building, probably from stairwells, but there were no apartments lit. Perfect.

He climbed onto the first floor terrace, with the aid of a cast iron drain pipe, then continued up, level by level, until he arrived at the fifth floor and the apartment identified as Peter Moore's. He had a long gash in his jeans and the damaged skin round his ankles, from the burns he'd sustained in the bus bombing, felt tight and uncomfortable, but he had made it and he was ready.

Digging into his backpack he found a long, thin piece of aluminium. This was his "key", fondly named Mable, which he had fabricated from memory after seeing Tommy use one in the Bronx. It was simple but effective and the patio door was soon opening to his touch. This was when he had to hope that Turner's information was accurate as he navigated the apartment from the floor plan in his head, reached the alarm panel and entered four digits. Turner had been so apologetic that he hadn't been able to ascertain Moore's private code, 'but the manufacturer's override should suffice, dear boy,' he'd told him. When the alarm beeped twice as it deactivated and no bells rang, Liam smiled. 'It sufficed. Thanks Mr. T,' he whispered as he re-set it.

He took a quick tour of the place via torchlight to confirm that it really was empty and noticed several large boxes in the hallway, packed and ready for the removal men who were due to collect them the following morning. Again, this was just what Turner's dossier had said. The only unknown factor was when Moore would return this evening. The file suggested that it wouldn't be before midnight, but could be any time after that.

As he moved to the bedroom, something glinted in the dim glow from his torch and Liam let out a low whistle as he saw a samurai sword on the wall. A desk drawer he opened out of curiosity produced a .45 auto with three clips and a tall cupboard housed a double barrel sawn off shotgun. No doubt Moore would also be carrying a weapon on his person.

'Anyone would think you were expecting company, Peter me old mate,' he said with a humourless chuckle. The bedside table rendered a further firearm and Liam moved everything he found to the bottom of the wardrobe and covered the stash with a blanket.

He fingered the .38 in his pocket, but tonight wouldn't be about guns for him. The trusty Killer was honed to perfection and his tool roll contained a claw hammer, chisels, rope, screwdrivers and a dozen or so six inch nails. He went back into the living room and looked at two heavy old radiators above the solid wooden floor and grinned. It was just as Turner had said. He tied a short length of rope to each radiator and hid the ends from view. Then he undressed, down to his Y-fronts, took a seat in the darkness of the bedroom and waited. It was just before midnight.

The Killer was in his palm and he played with the blade, extending it and retracting it to a slow rhythm as he waited patiently in the gloom. Fifteen minutes passed and he thought he heard a faint sound, but Moore did not materialise. Half an hour later the loud hoot of an owl outside the window startled him, but there was still no Moore and still he waited. At a little after one there was a definite noise from not too far away. Liam took a deep breath and braced himself. Then he heard a key in the lock.

A door opened and closed and a light went on at the far side of the apartment. Beeps came from the alarm as it was deactivated again and then there was a loud thud as something heavy was thrown on a table. 'Fuckin' Proddy bastards,' he heard.

There were footfalls in his direction and then another door opened followed by the sound of a man taking a piss. 'That's a good strong stream you've got there, Peter,' Liam thought to himself. 'Glad to know you're in good health.' The toilet flushed and then the footsteps came again, heading to the bedroom. A silhouette appeared in the doorway and, a moment later, the room was flooded with light.

'Hello Peter,' said Liam, the .38 in his hand.

Moore stared at the near naked man in his bedroom. 'Who the fuck are you?' he spat.

'Don't you know me then?'

Moore squinted for a second. 'Aye, I know you all right, you treacherous bastard. Heard you were back from the dead.'

'So you've been expecting my visit then?'

'Honestly, I didn't think you'd be stupid enough. You have to know I have security,' Moore said as he pressed a button by the door.

'And you have to know I'd have dealt with them already,' Liam lied, silently thanking Turner for his insistence on back up and hoping Gates would do whatever was necessary.

'I doubt it, sonny,' Moore smirked, making Liam's heart miss a beat. The smile was short-lived, though, and Moore was glancing back at the intercom switch. 'Where the fuck are they?' he hissed.

'Couldn't tell you, Peter. Maybe they're sleeping, like. Anyway it'll be cosier just the two of us, don't ya think?'

'What, you some kind of bum boy here to take my arse then?' asked Moore, the grin returning to his face. He certainly didn't seem afraid; Liam had to give him that.

'Don't let the outfit fool you,' Liam smiled. 'It's not your arse I'm after, Peter old mate. All I want is a nice, friendly chat about me Ma. Remember her, do you?'

Moore was somewhere in his fifties and a little overweight, but his speed surprised Liam as he lunged towards him. Still, Liam was quicker and the .38 smashed into the older man's face, knocking him off balance and allowing for another whack to the side of the head, which laid him out cold. Liam had him stripped of his clothes, dragged through to the living room and tied to the radiators before he came round.

As Peter's consciousness returned he was aware of his arms stretched out to the side and his feet tied together so that his body formed a crucifix. 'I'll kill you for this,' he hissed.

'Don't think so, mate. I reckon I'll be just fine, but I'm pretty sure you're fucked,' Liam laughed as he smashed the claw hammer down on a kneecap and heard the satisfying sound of bones smashing. Moore's body jerked in reaction as he tried to sit and he let out a small grunt, but it wasn't the scream Liam had hoped for. 'Fuck me, so it's true then? I'd heard you didn't feel pain like the rest of us.'

Moore didn't say a word, but his mouth formed a psychotic grin on his mongoloid features.

'Now that's a shame then, but it just means I'll have to try that bit harder, won't I?' hissed Liam as the claw hammer repeated its business on the other knee.

The grunt was louder this time and the grin faded a little from the bound man's face, but still he didn't cry out.

'I'm impressed,' Liam admitted, and it was true, 'but you see, me Ma wasn't like you. She was just a normal woman and she could feel pain. Her legs and arms were smashed too, Peter. She was beaten to a pulp and it was all because of you, you evil, murdering, son of a bitch.'

He brought the hammer down again, twice in quick succession on each collarbone. The grin was still there, but the grunt of his captive had turned to a much deeper groan this time. 'Getting through to you now, am I?' Liam hissed, but the man had passed out.

Fuck me, this was some tough bastard, Liam decided as he slapped the man on the face to bring him round. Larry O'Brien was the one who had gained the nickname of Mad Dog, but he had cried out like a little girl when he was bound and beaten. Moore was the true mad man; that was for sure. Maybe he couldn't feel pain or maybe he was just psychotic. Either way, this was going to be tougher than he'd imagined.

As the man came round again Liam was gratified to hear a low moan as his senses kicked in. 'So, it does hurt a bit, doesn't it?' he whispered, his lips at the man's ear. 'Why did you do it, Peter? Why did you order me Ma's death like that?'

'You know why,' came the halting reply through broken teeth.

'Just so I would join the R.A. right? Just so you wouldn't have failed at your job? Well that's pathetic, you twisted, sadistic maniac.'

'You're pathetic,' Moore croaked. 'I never thought you were worth the effort.'

'So why, for fuck's sake? Why couldn't you just leave me alone? What had me Ma ever done to anyone?'

'Just a – casualty – of – war,' Moore managed as he raised his head an inch from the floor and spat a bloody mouthful of saliva in his captor's face. 'She – didn't – matter.'

Liam jumped to his feet, wiping the blood from his cheek and savagely kicking the prone body beneath him. 'Didn't matter?' he yelled. 'Didn't fuckin' matter? She mattered to me, you fuckin' cunt. She fuckin' mattered to me.'

Liam knew he was losing control. He wanted to enjoy this; to drag it out and make the man suffer just as his Ma must have suffered, but this wasn't working out as he had planned. The man would be dead soon, no question, but that wasn't enough.

He grabbed for his tool roll and pulled out the nails, dropping to his knees again. His eyes were blurred and he shook his head to refocus before raising his hammer and driving a nail through first one foot and then the next.

'Jesus Christ,' came something approaching a squeal from the prone body.

'Aye, that's what you'll be looking like, sure enough,' Liam snarled as he turned his attention to the man's hands.

He secured one hand to the hard wooden floor with a nail and then stretched out the other arm, delighting in the sound of broken, crunching collarbone, before driving a nail through the second palm as well. 'You want the crown of thorns too, do you?' he snarled down into the man's face.

Moore's face was white, his eyes bulging, but still the demented grin was in place. Liam rose with a deep sigh. 'I need a piss,' he announced lightly. 'You wait there for me, mate, and don't move. No need to worry. I won't be long.'

Alone for a couple of minutes, Moore made a feeble attempt to struggle against his bonds, but it was useless. His body was broken and refused to respond to his efforts with anything other than searing pain, though that receded the moment he lay still again. He'd always had a high threshold, even as a child, and his tolerance had only increased with age. It was the immobility that had him fucked.

'Just – get – it – over - with,' he sputtered when his captor returned.

'No, not yet ya fucker,' Liam cursed as he retrieved a chisel. 'Do you know something Peter? A man once told me that the most sensitive area on the human body is just under the collarbone, right where it joins the shoulder. Something to do with a load of bunched nerve endings, I seem to remember yer man saying. Do you believe that mate? Do you? He seemed to know what he was talking about, this feller, so shall we see if he was right?'

Liam's voice had lowered and his speech slowed with every word as he drew the chisel across the man's chest, making tiny incisions as he went. Nothing life threatening, just a precursor to the pain that should follow. He shoved his face close to Moore's, hissing, 'You ready for this, are ya, old pal? I'd take a deep breath now if I were you.'

He placed the chisel on the skin and pushed slowly. The sharp edge sank deeper until he heard it hit bone. Then he twisted and turned the tool several times in quick succession and, at last, he was rewarded by a small cry and a look of agony on the face below him.

'Shite, mate, that feller must be right. That must be really fuckin' painful if it makes a mad bastard like you cry out,' Liam told him before turning his attention to the other shoulder. Peter yelled once more before fainting again.

For a moment Liam thought he had killed him, but he checked and the heart was still beating. He sat back on the torso and grinned. 'Come on Peter, come back to me he hissed,' but the body was limp beneath him, the chisel still protruding from the chest. This could take some time.

Now that Moore's face had betrayed its torment, Liam finally felt in control again. This was proving a lot more challenging than he could ever have imagined and he looked at the broken body with respect and even pity. He quickly shook himself to exorcise the feelings and allow the hatred to flood back in as he deliberately remembered his Ma and the way this bastard had ordered her butchered and murdered. He couldn't allow himself any weakness here, but now he knew he wanted to do more than just inflict unbelievable pain. Of course the man must suffer, but that didn't seem enough any more. He needed remorse and he needed fear. He had to make the man talk to him.

There was still no sign of life so he rose and went to the kitchen to fetch water. A kettle stood to the side of the sink and suddenly all he wanted in life was a nice cup of strong tea. He knew it was strange, but the craving couldn't be denied. Besides, his throat was dry.

'Wakey wakey, Peter. Come on old son, you can do it,' Liam sang out a few minutes later as he poured water on the beaten face. This man had never looked normal in every day life, but now he looked positively moronic.

Moore came round slowly and felt the pain course through his body, but that was nothing compared to the shock he experienced as his eyes focused on the sight of a man calmly drinking tea from his favourite cup. Shite, he really was screwed.

'Ah, there you are,' said Liam. 'So, Peter, shall we have a little chat?'

'Fuck you Butch.'

'Now that's not very nice, is it?' Liam smiled, his tone conversational. 'Not very nice at all. I do think I can make you talk, you know. I mean, that's how I got me name after all. I'm sure you know the story of how I sliced off a man's ears and cut off all his fingers and toes, don't you? I took my time with him, slowly skinning his back and front. When I decided he could take no more, without dying on me, that is, I slit his throat and watched him bleed to death.'

Moore stared at him, but the expression seemed blank.

Liam drained his tea and smacked his lips. 'There now, that's better. Anyway, as I can tell you're so interested, this man talked all right, but he didn't know anything. He was one of the Shankill Butchers, you see, and back then I thought he was the one responsible for me Ma's murder. Weird thing is, as it turned out like, the Shankill crew had nothing to do with her killing, but then you knew that, didn't you Peter? You knew that all along, because you're the one who ordered her to be kneecapped and have her ankles smashed. Then, after she was beaten to a pulp, her throat was cut, but not until she had really suffered.'

Moore was blinking rapidly now, but still he said nothing.

'You see, to me that was overkill,' Liam said, a high, hollow laugh escaping him. 'So, that's why I took my time with that poor feller over in Belfast.'

He reached into his pocket and drew out *The Killer*, flashing the blade in Moore's face and keeping his voice level and calm as he continued. 'Everyone called me the Butcher of Belfast after that. Now, tell me Peter. If I could do that to the wrong guy, just what do you think I have in store for you, eh, you fuckin' murderin' bastard?'

'Go to Hell,' Moore spat.

'Oh I'm sure I will,' Liam agreed, 'but you'll be there long before me. Do you think you'll be needing all your fingers and toes down there, or do you reckon that won't matter any more?'

'Just go ahead and do what you gotta do, you fuckin' wanker,' Peter threw back at him, the grin on his face now looking more like a death mask as his lips were drawn back over broken teeth.

'Oh don't worry, me old pal, I will,' Liam assured him, 'but what I don't get, you see, is what a bastard like you got out of it. I mean it's not like you did it yourself. You just wrote a death warrant and let someone else do your dirty work. That strikes me as cowardly, Peter old son. On top of that, you didn't even tell Willy what you'd done. He reckons you're a psycho, did you know that?'

'Does he really?' Moore hissed as he attempted to raise his head before his eyes flickered and closed.

Liam was quickly slapping his face again. 'No you don't, ya fucker. No more fainting. You're going to stay with me while I finish the job.'

Over the next thirty minutes, Moore was in and out of consciousness as Liam carried out his threat, slicing off his ears and removing the fingers from his hands.

'Is that all you've got, you weak little fucker?' Peter managed in one moment of clarity.

'No, me old head, I've got more. Fuckin' loads more,' Liam informed him. 'You've still got all your toes, haven't you? Or how about I take my pound of flesh?'

He slid *The Killer* to the man's chest and began slicing until a long, thin strip of skin curled round its blade. There were no sounds from his victim now, not even small groans, and Liam sat back on his heels and tutted.

'Look Peter, either your body's gone into shock and you're totally beyond pain, or the stories are true and you simply are a fuckin' lunatic. But, do you know what, I couldn't care less which it is, because I'm bored. Do you hear me, Mr. fuckin' Moore? You are a fuckin' boring bastard and I reckon it's time for you to go.'

He moved his blade to the man's neck and stuck it slowly into the side.

'Wait,' croaked Moore. 'I've - something to - say.'

'What? Now you fancy a little chat? No, too late for that me old skin,' Liam hissed as the knife dug deeper.

'No – please.'

'Please, is it?' asked Liam, the blade stopping in its tracks. 'Well I have to say I do like the sound of a wee bit of beggin', even if it is a little late. Go on, then. What do you have to say?'

'I'm – not – begging. I've – been – waiting.'

'Waiting? What the fuck for?' It was a genuine question and Liam was caught off guard. 'Why the fuck would you wait and go through all that when you knew you had something to say?'

'No – security.'

'What? You're making no sense, man. What are you babbling on about?'

'Ask – Nolan.'

'Nolan? Willy? Ask Willy what?' Liam felt his heart beating faster and then his head swam as an unearthly noise assaulted his ears.

The body beneath him was anchored to the floor, but now the head was moving wildly from side to side, pushing itself against the blade of *The Killer*, forcing Liam to relax his grip. From deep inside Moore's chest the sound bubbled up and erupted in a hiccupping shriek as the pitch rose, higher and higher.

Liam grabbed the broken shoulders and shook him violently. 'Ask Willy what?' he yelled.

The deranged laughter continued and Liam returned one hand to the knife, the other attempting to still the maniacal head as he brought his own closer and stared into the mad eyes.

'Ask Willy what?' he said again slowly, his voice now hardly above a whisper.

'Nolan – knew. He – could – have – stopped – it,' came the croaked reply before the demonic cackling took over again. 'Take – that – to – Hell.'

Liam felt his body freeze, as Moore's head took on a life of its own again and thrust itself against *The Killer*. Liam quickly released his grip, but the blood was already spurting from the wound and the laughter was replaced by a deep gurgling.

'No! Fuck no,' he screamed as he pulled on the knife, but it was too late. The head began to twitch and the noise lessened and then stopped altogether. Liam stared for a second until his eyes blurred and the fury rose to his chest. He grabbed *The Killer* once more and started to saw furiously across Moore's neck until his head was almost removed from his body. There was another sound now and, only when Liam recognised his own scream, did the butchery finally come to an end.

He stood slowly and looked at the horrendously mutilated body on the ground, the face that had once grinned at him now contorted and unrecognisable. He spat on the corpse and let out a long, deep sigh as he realised he was absolutely exhausted. He felt emotionally drained and – completely numb.

As he turned he jumped at what looked like a poster from a bad horror movie, until he recognised his own reflection in a long mirror. He was covered in congealed blood. 'Bastard,' he cursed at Moore before dropping *The Killer* and heading to the bathroom. It took fifteen minutes of scrubbing and rinsing before he felt clean and he dried himself on a blindingly white towel.

He moved round the room slowly, his brain seeming capable of only one thought at once. Right now it was the need for deodorant, something to take the bad smell from his nostrils. 'Ah, Mandate, my favourite,' he muttered when he found what he was looking for. 'You may have been a lowlife, murdering scumbag, Peter, but at least you did know your fragrances, didn't you old pal?'

He strolled, naked, back to the body, looked down and felt – nothing! 'Jeans,' he said to the corpse. 'Got anything I could borrow? I ripped mine.'

There was little in the wardrobe, Moore's clothes probably packed for the removal men, but a small pile of discarded stuff on a shelf provided what he needed as he found a pair of jeans from his victim's slimmer days. He'd have to go commando, though. He certainly wasn't about to search through the man's underwear.

He cleaned off *The Killer* and his tools before balling up his Y-fronts and ripped jeans and throwing them in a corner. When the police found them and tested the blood, it would all be Moore's. He'd heard something recently about a new technique that could identify someone's DNA. Ah, what the fuck did he care? He'd be long gone before the police could do anything about it.

'Bye Peter,' he said softly as he walked through the apartment, deactivated the alarm and went out into the hall. His tread was robotic as he headed to the exit, then he stopped short as he caught himself whistling. "There was a wild colonial boy, Jack Dug..." He laughed involuntarily. He always used to whistle that when he'd won a bar fight. He'd won here tonight, finally, after four years, but he didn't feel as victorious as he should.

'Nolan knew. He could have stopped it.' The words flooded his brain. No, it couldn't be. Nolan had sworn he only found out after the event and Liam had known Willy a long time. Willy, the boss. An honourable man; a man who wouldn't lie to his face. Compare that with the meaningless pile of shit he'd just done away with and the truth was obvious. Moore had tried to take his final revenge by planting the seeds of doubt in his mind.

'Won't work, old son,' Liam said under his breath before walking to the exit and out into the cold night air.

'It's done Ma,' he breathed.

39

The Message

'What the fuck's that smell?' Gates whispered after Liam's low whistle had alerted him to his arrival.

'Mandate.'

'Ponce.'

'Fuck you.'

'You've been a while.'

'Aye,' Liam confirmed. 'Thanks for seeing to the guards.'

'What guards?' Gates asked. 'Been out here on me own for bleedin' hours.'

'No guards?' Liam was confused. 'But, surely…'

'No time for that now,' Gates hissed as they arrived back at the car. 'I've got a radio message from Turner.'

'A message?'

'Yes. It doesn't mean anything to me, but he says you'll get it.'

'Go on then,' Liam urged as he took the passenger's seat.

'Turner says: O'Leary said that Nolan signed the warrant.'

'You - fuckin' - what?'

The ferocity of Liam's response was so surprising that Gates stalled the car. 'Jesus, man,' he yelled, 'what are you tying to do? Give me a heart attack or something? Christ.'

The engine turned over at the second attempt and the sergeant looked across at his companion. It was too dark to see the colour of the man's face, but the rigid body and hands clamped on the dashboard were all too evident. 'So, I guess it does mean something to you, then?' he ventured.

There was no reply and Gates headed back to the road.

'Where are we going?' Liam finally asked after several minutes of silence, his voice barely more than a whisper.

'To the chopper, of course. Why?' asked Gates.

'Change of plan,' Liam told him. 'We're heading south.'

40

South Armagh, Northern Ireland

For the next two hours Gates drove and Liam sat in silence, chain smoking. His head was a jumble of names and thoughts, some which made sense and some that didn't.

Jonny O'Leary, contract killer, admitted murderer of his Ma.

Willy Nolan, trusted friend.

Peter Moore, murdering, scheming, lying bastard.

Larry O'Brien, Martin McMurphy, Sean Hogan – all signatories, all dead.

Willy Nolan, the boss.

Moore: "He could have stopped it." A final, vengeful damnation on his killer, or the truth? Revenge? Truth?

Jonny O'Leary, soldier: "I had no choice."

Willy Nolan, man of his word, giving him twenty-four hours to get out.

Witness protection. Jonny O'Leary in witness protection.

Turner: "I might have a way to garner more intelligence on Nolan and any connection to your mother."

Words of a dying man: "Nolan knew." Revenge? Truth? Revenge? Truth?

Turner could get to anyone. Turner always found out the truth.

Jonny: "It was a direct order."

Willy, the boss. Willy, always in charge.

Turner. O'Leary. Nolan signed.

Moore: "Nolan knew." Revenge? Truth? Truth? Truth. Truth!

Nolan knew. Truth.

FUCKING NOLAN SIGNED THE WARRANT. TRUTH!

***

A few miles outside the village of Crossmaglen, Liam broke his silence to give directions. His voice was calm and even and, to Gates' ears, over-controlled.

'Thanks, mate,' Liam said.

'What for?'

'Not asking questions.'

'Turner said it might change things,' Gates told him.

'He did?' Liam's voice finally took on some inflection. 'Did he say anything else?'

'No, just the message and that things might change.'

'Right.'

At Liam's instruction, Gates pulled the car up to the small break in the tree line and watched as Liam surveyed the scene.

'What now?' he asked.

Liam checked the clock on the dash. 'I reckon I've still got about half an hour to sunrise,' he mused. 'I could do with a little light, but not too much. We'll give it a few more minutes.'

'Then what? What do you want me to do?'

'Nothing. Just wait.'

Gates reached to the rear of the car to retrieve his rifle, pulling it from a dark canvas bag.

'What the fuck are you doing?' Liam hissed.

'If you think I'm going to sit here waiting for you, in the middle of fuckin' bandit country, with nowt in me hand but a bleeding' fag, you've got another think coming?' Gates snapped at him as he continued carefully rebuilding the weapon.

'And I'm tellin' you, you won't be needing a fuckin' gun. You're just to wait here for me and you'd better be ready to go when I get back. This place is going to get really fuckin' hot really fuckin' fast. So just keep that motor runnin' and fuck yer gun.'

'Aye, and fuck you too mate,' Gates said. 'Don't you worry, the motor'll be runnin' all right and I'll be here in it – with my gun! Just in case any of your Paddy mates happen by. You just go and do your fuckin' job and leave me to do mine.'

'Well, just remember one thing,' Liam said.

'And what's that?'

'If you do any shootin', make sure you know who you're aiming' at. I don't want to be shot by some trigger-happy, monkey hangin' blurt this time.'

'Oh, not that again. I told you I saw a movement in the shadows. I was watching your back, that's all.'

'Yeah, well, whatever. But seriously, like, if you hear someone come runnin' through the trees in a hurry, it's me. Got that?'

'Aye, bonny lad, I've got it,' Gates confirmed. 'Now shut the fuck up, get yerself gone and stop yer bleedin' moaning. Christ, I swear you whinge on like a bleedin' old woman. Anyway, how long do I give you?'

'Half an hour, tops. If I'm not back by then, go home to Turner and tell him I'm dead.'

'Dead fuckin' boring, more like,' Gates quipped, but a dark shadow crossed his face as he spoke.

Liam didn't respond, but he lit a fag, offering one to Gates, and checked his gun. He'd love to take his time with this, just as he'd done with Moore, but that wasn't an option here. He needed to face Willy, let him know that he knew, and then the kill would have to be quick. After that Gates would be on his way back to Turner to report his death, because he had no intention of returning to the car. He'd be out of there on foot and making a beeline for the nearest phone. He hoped to God that Laa Laa was ready for the call.

***

Liam stubbed out his cigarette under foot as he left the car in the faint morning light and made his way into the dense bush, crouching and pausing every few feet to listen for any unwanted sound. There was nothing, just the beating of his heart and the words running through his head. 'I'm coming for you, Willy, you fuckin' murdering, back-stabbing, lying bastard. You're a dead man.'

With around a hundred yards to go, a small noise stopped him in his tracks. Had that been a twig snapping? He froze, gun in hand, and listened. He waited for two minutes, unmoving, but there was nothing further. All he could hear was his own breathing and birds singing as they awoke to the dawn. 'Jesus, Mary and Joseph,' he whispered. 'You're getting paranoid, mate. Get yer act together, you bleedin' spanner.'

He set off again, three, four, five steps, and then he caught another sound. This time it was definite. Shite, there was some fucker back there.

Diving for cover he chambered a round as quietly as possible and was ready, gun aimed, as a slow moving shape disturbed the foliage. 'Whoever you are, you're a fuckin' dead man.'

In the next seconds the shape formed into a man carrying a rifle, and it was a man he knew. 'You fuckin' spanner,' he hissed as he breathed out in relief. 'What the fuck are you doing here?'

Sergeant Gates had also been aware of movement as a man broke from cover and appeared from behind a bushy tree. Now he froze, rifle aimed, then relaxed and smiled as he lowered his weapon.

'Jesus Christ,' Liam whispered. What was going on? Gates should be waitin' in the car, the fuckin' idiot. Just what did the bleedin' halfwit think he was doing?

Confusion gave way to dismay and Liam swallowed hard as he saw the lopsided smile leave Brian's scarred face and the rifle rise again. Now he stared back into the sergeant's dark, brooding eyes.

'What…' he began, but the question hung unfinished as the impact of a bullet knocked him backwards, clean off his feet and Gates was sprinting towards him.

***

It was several seconds before Liam could comprehend what had happened. His mind was blank and everything around him went dark. His mother's smiling face swam before his eyes followed by Montse's, tears on her cheeks. Then, as he refocused, the real face in front of him, just inches from his own, was heavily scarred and grinning.

'You with me, bonny lad?' hissed the sergeant.

'What – the – fuck?' Liam managed through ragged breaths, his hands on his stomach, feeling the dampness of his blood. He was gut shot and propped against a tree.

'Welcome home Paddy,' Gates laughed. 'You're back in Ireland now and this is where you're gonna stay.'

'You fuckin' bastard,' Liam groaned.

'Didn't see that comin', did ya, you fuckin' murderin' Paddy tosser? Now I guess you're wonderin' why, aren't you, ya dumb cunt?'

Liam swallowed hard. 'Yes,' he gasped.

'Why? That's for our Victor.'

'What? Who? Victor? Victor? Who the fuck is Victor?'

'No, you don't even know his name, do you? He was just some young squaddie who didn't matter. Is that right?'

'Who? I don't…'

'Well, he mattered to me you see,' Gates explained. 'He was my kid brother. Well, half brother really, and I didn't even know about him until a few years back. Doubt even Turner knew, 'cause all my records have me as an only child, but there he was sure enough. He was all the family I had and you killed him.'

'I didn't… I don't,' Liam mumbled, trying to concentrate.

'Declan O'Brien, then,' Gates suggested, his voice harsh but controlled. 'That name mean anything to you?'

'What? O'Brien? No. Yes. I don't know. There's something.'

'The I.R.A. shot him as a traitor on the Falls Road in 1981. Bring back any memories?'

'Aye,' breathed Liam, his mind flashing back to his sniper position as he waited for the British troops to appear.

'And do you remember what happened next?'

Liam closed his eyes tightly and another face appeared in his brain. The face of a young, excited, eager British recruit arriving with his squad at the site of the execution. The face he had picked on. The target he had chosen. The life he had ended. The face he had seen in his dreams many times as it contorted in agony, dying from the wound he had inflicted. A shot to the stomach. A gut shot.

As the memory hit him full force, so the shock that had taken over his body receded and he felt the onset of his own pain. A searing, agonising sensation that tore through his core as the blood oozed from his belly. He heard the scream come from his lips before a hand was clamped firmly over his mouth.

'Shut the fuck up and take the pain,' Gates hissed. 'Take it.'

Liam's breath came in short, ragged gasps as he tried to gulp air through the man's fingers. He pushed down hard on his stomach, feeling the blood seep more strongly from the wound and his head swam as blackness threatened to engulf him. He fought hard to remain conscious, the pain helping to focus his mind. He wasn't going to fucking die. Not here. Not like this. The blood flow was slow and he could have hours yet. He had time. He had time.

'Got him now, have you?' Gates snarled as he slowly removed his hand. 'Just a casualty of war, was he?'

'I'm – sorry,' Liam said as clearly as he could, and it was true. Just a few hours earlier Moore had referred to his mother in exactly the same way. 'I – didn't – know.'

'Bit late for apologies now, isn't it?'

'You should go,' Liam said hurriedly. If he could get rid of this man, he still had a chance. 'Someone will have heard the shot. Someone will have heard me scream. They'll be coming.'

'No they won't.'

'What?'

'They'd have been here by now, don't you think?'

'I…I don't…' Liam tried to concentrate, but it was hard to fight the waves of pain and make his brain function at the same time.

'Nobody's coming. Nobody cares. I've got all the time in the world.'

The conversational tone that Gates had now adopted was terrifying. He had used the same tactic himself with Peter Moore when he knew he wouldn't be disturbed. When he knew that there was no one coming.

'There were – no guards,' he stammered. Why hadn't that rung alarm bells? Why hadn't he paid more attention to it at the time? It had all been too easy, too good to be true, just like Turner had said.

Turner. Oh, God, no. Turner. It had to be. When had he set all this up? But no, that didn't make sense did it? Did it? He couldn't think straight. How could Turner…? Here? No. Why was no one coming? How could he…?

Gates was sitting back on his heels, smiling, the growing light of dawn clearly illuminating the scarred face. 'I'm glad I didn't take you out earlier when I could have,' he said. 'Wouldn't have been nearly as satisfying.'

'Newcastle?'

'Aye. I thought about killing you then, but I probably wouldn't have got away with it and I'd have been doing it for free. Much better this way with a paying customer. Besides I didn't know who you were then.'

'You didn't?'

'No. Back then you were just some Paddy twat and I hated 'em all. I couldn't get to the man who had killed our Vic, because he was already dead. Except you weren't, were you?'

'When – did – Tuner – tell – you?' Liam asked, immense sadness fighting with intense pain for control of his body.

'Turner?' Gates' surprise was genuine. 'What the fuck's Turner got to do with this?'

'It wasn't…'

'Ah fuck,' Gates spat. 'I missed that opportunity, didn't I? Shite. I could have sent you to Hell with that in your head. Fuck.'

'So…Aargh,' Liam screamed, as a new wave of pain coursed through his body. Oh Christ, this was agony, but he had to hold on. He had to keep alert. He leant forward, taking quick short breaths until he had himself under control again. 'So, who?' he managed eventually.

'I don't know,' Gates informed him. 'Now isn't that something?'

Liam said nothing. He couldn't make any sense of this and, for now, his main concentration was on bringing Gates back into focus. He seemed to have moved into some sort of black tunnel and the trees around him had disappeared, just as the pain was receding. A cold fear threatened to take the last of his senses. This wasn't good. This wasn't good at all. He needed his pain again. Pain let him know he was alive. Without it… oh fuck!

'Are you still with me, bonny lad?' Gates was shaking him now. 'Can't have you dying on me just yet.'

The agony engulfed him once more and he was back.

'Call yourself a hard bastard, do ya?' Gates was continuing. 'Christ, I've bleedin' shit better. I've been shot four times meself and I don't reckon I cried out like a bleedin' baby.'

'You – must – know – something,' Liam pressed, ignoring the taunting.

'Well, you see, I don't know which would be worse,' Gates considered. 'Knowing what I know, which isn't much I have to confess, or dying without knowing. Hmm, it's quite a dilemma.'

'Tell – me,' Liam croaked.

'You know, I think I will,' said Gates. 'After all, it was your idea.'

'What – the – fuck?'

'You remember. It was in that little café where the guy was threatening that bonny waitress. You told me then that I should look for some extra work so I could earn enough money to buy that flat in Spain after me wife had pissed off.'

'I…' Liam began, but Gates silenced him with a hand to his mouth once more.

'No, I'm tellin' the story here. No interruptions,' he went on. 'So I got my chance last year when there was all this talk of some guy with a crescent shaped scar who was scaring the shit out of the boys in Ireland. Well, I'm no Sherlock Holmes, but it had to be you, right? So I made a few calls and got a bit of dosh for me trouble, with the promise of a lot more to come. Then, some time last week, I got the news that you were the Butcher of Belfast. The fuckin' murderin' bastard who had shot our Vic.'

Gates' voice had begun to rise and he took a moment to calm himself before continuing. 'Then I had to let them know when you would be coming over. They said something about making it easy for you and killing two birds with one stone.'

'What?' Liam began

'No, I didn't get it either, but I didn't give a fuck to be quite honest with you. All I had to do was volunteer for the mission and then give you that message. You know, "O'Leary said that Nolan signed the warrant". That's what I had to say.'

'But you said Turner,' Liam managed, every reserve of strength now focused on trying to make sense of this.

'Now when have you ever known Turner to use names over the radio, you stupid twat? They just told me it had to come from someone you'd trust. To be honest, I wasn't sure you'd fall for it. I added that bit about Turner saying it would change everything just for good measure.'

Liam dropped his head to his chest and bent double, his arms now drenched in blood as he held them across his stomach with the gaping wound all too visible in the strengthening sun. Gates was right; he had been stupid. 'So Nolan didn't sign?' he groaned.

'Christ, man, don't you get it? I don't know who the fuck Nolan is and I don't know what the fuck he signed or didn't sign. All I know is that message was guaranteed to bring you here and then I could take you out and no one would bother me. And, well, they haven't.'

'Moore? Two birds. No guards.'

'What? You're rambling now, mate,' Gates told him pleasantly, his enjoyment obvious.

'I don't… Moore… Nolan – the boss…'

'The boss. Aye, that's the feller,' Gates interrupted him. 'He isn't just *a* boss, I don't think. It seemed to be his code name.'

There was a whooshing in Liam's head now that reminded him of childhood visits to the dentist when he'd been given gas. Gates' voice was echoing, as if in a chamber, and the words and thoughts were disjointed. Moore, he was the other bird. Sacrificed? Had he become a liability? That's why there were no guards. The Butcher of Belfast and Peter Moore. Two birds.

Suddenly he was aware of Gates bending over him, saying something about the end being near while he went through his pockets. He vaguely saw his money stolen and then *The Killer* in the other man's hand as the whooshing intensified in his head. He felt Gates move from him and he watched as he seemed to walk into the tunnel again, everything else disappearing. He was cold. He was so fuckin' cold.

Then Gates with a radio, the man seeming far away while the voice was right over his head. 'Renegade,' he heard. 'Golf Lima Golf Twenty confirmed.' A pause. Some crackling. 'Will do.'

Now Gates, back at his side, his lips right next to his ear, the voice booming and fading. 'Onnnne laaaast messsssage,' it droned. 'Willeeeeee saaaaaays gooooooooodbyyyyye.' Then blackness.

***

Brain Gates was nearly out of the woods when he stopped in his tracks. A man in a camouflage jacket, dark sunglasses and a scarf covering his face, stepped from the bushes. He was aiming an AK47 at him. For several heart stopping seconds the men stared at each other, then the AK was lowered and the camouflaged guy nodded and walked briskly away back into the dense undergrowth.

Gates held onto a tree and caught his breath. 'Fuck me,' was all he could manage.

Eventually he made it back to the car and, after quickly disassembling and packing away his rifle, drove off. He was heading for the coast, the ferry and England. Just on the outskirts of Dundalk he spotted a pay phone and parked alongside it.

'Hello,' said a voice as it answered his call.

'Renegade.'

'Go ahead Renegade.'

'Golf Lima Golf Twenty.'

'We already have confirmation.'

'Aye, well maybe you have, but I haven't got confirmation about me money.'

'The money is being transferred now and you have a green light to the coast. None of our boys will bother you.'

'Fine, I'll call again with a new contact number when I reach Spain,' said Gates. He hung up the phone, jumped back in the car and headed to the ferry.

***

In a small farmhouse in Catalunya, two brothers watched in concern as their sister stared at the silent phone. They didn't know what was going on, but they were worried for her. 'Beeline,' they heard her say. 'Please tell me Beeline.'

***

Up in the foothills a man with an eye patch paced, radio in hand. 'Where is he, Mamma?' he asked the wizened old lady in the kitchen. 'Where is my brother?'

***

'Are you sure there's been no message for me yet, Tony?' asked the young man in the leather jacket, the word "Druids" emblazoned on the back.

'I'm not your secretary,' huffed the barman. 'Now, are you having another beer?'

'Just one more,' Tommy agreed as he sat in the *Sunbrite Bar*, New York with the Rolling Stones playing loudly on the jukebox behind him.

***

'W…w…where are you B…B…B…Butch?' said the man hovering by the phone that didn't ring.

41

The Report

Anthony Turner sat alone in the darkened office. He hated receiving bad news. He had always found it deeply troubling. He killed time by carefully cleaning and repacking his pipe as the memories of this latest loss flooded his mind: the hatred, the anger, the arguments, all of which had eventually given way to a simple acceptance and, he hoped, a modicum of friendship. He was still deep in thought when a knock came to the door and shook him back to the present.

'Come,' he shouted.

A corporal entered and saluted. 'He's here sir.'

'Show him in will you, please.'

A uniformed soldier walked briskly through the door, marched up to Turner's desk and saluted. 'Sah, Sergeant Gates reporting as ordered, Sah.'

'Sit down Sergeant, and at ease if you please.'

Gates took a seat, removed his cap and waited.

'I have your report here Sergeant, but I would like to hear it in your own words. What happened exactly? Oh, and remember, do please speak freely.'

'Sah, when O'Neil had finished the job he said he had new information and we drove south. When we arrived close to the house I was ordered to wait in the car, sah. After around fifteen minutes I heard two gun shots ring out. I knew they were from both a rifle and a pistol. So, I left the car and ran into the woods to assist Mr. O'Neil. However, sah, when I arrived I found him on the ground, dead. He'd been shot once in the stomach and once in the head. The kill shot came from under the chin, blew the top of his head clean off it did. I performed a fast sweep of the area, but the gunman, or men, had disappeared. There was nothing I could do but leave and report the mission as a failure to you, sah.'

'I just don't bloody well believe it,' whispered Turner flatly.

'Sah?' questioned Gates with a frown.

'Oh no, not you old boy. I simply meant that I can't believe that an experienced operative such as Liam could be caught out like that. Not on his own ground. It seems impossible, that's all. Someone must have been expecting him. I have long wondered if we had a mole. I am not doubting your word of course, not for a single moment Sergeant.'

'Sah.'

'That's it Sergeant, you can leave.'

Gates stood and turned, then momentarily paused as he looked at the troubled man.

'Oh and thank you for this, Sergeant,' Turner said quietly. He smiled sadly as he held *The Killer* gently between his fingers.

'Sah, I'm sure Mr. O'Neil would have wanted you to have it.'

'Yes, quite. Anyway, Sergeant, that was a very considerate gesture. Thank you.'

Gates once more saluted, spun on his heel, and, with a small smirk on his face, left.

Turner looked at the switchblade again. It was six inches long, slim, flat and heavy with brass fittings at each end of the solid wood handle. In the centre, a row of raised brass letters spelled the word *Matador.*

He flicked it open, staring at the razor-like blade. 'What an absolute shame,' he muttered. 'Another young life snuffed out forever.'

He shook his head sadly and unlocked a desk drawer to reveal a short, fat lock-knife, a cutthroat razor, a meat cleaver and a heavy brass knuckle-duster. He placed *The Killer* gently alongside them. 'All those young men gone for good,' he sighed, as he locked the drawer once more. 'Where will it end?'

'It'll never fuckin' end, Mr. T.'

Liam's voice was so loud in his head that Turner looked round sharply, seriously believing for a second that he could be standing next to him. 'What the f…' he began, before quickly checking himself as he noticed another person in the room. 'Edwards, old chap, you startled me. Didn't hear you come in.'

'You all right there, Turner?' asked the suited man leaning casually against the wall. 'You look like you've seen a ghost.'

'Deep in thought, that's all,' Turner assured him. 'What can I do for you?'

'Well, we've had him for two days and he's still not talking. I think it's time you had a go. Oh, and look what we found on this one.'

Turner reached out his hand to take the offered item and dropped it on the desk in front of him. 'An ice pick? Really? Oh goodness me, how gruesome. Ah well, I suppose I'd better go and meet him.'

He followed Edwards down the long corridor and entered a room at the end. A young man with a bloodied, beaten face was strapped to a chair in the centre.

'Hullo, young fellow, my name is Turner,' he smiled as he picked up a file from the table. 'And you are Shane, I believe?'

When the youth didn't answer, Turner continued. 'Well, I bet you've had quite a day, haven't you. Would you care for a nice cup of tea, dear boy?'

'Tea? Do I want some fuckin' tea?' yelled the Irishman as he spat a mouthful of blood on the floor. 'Fuck you and fuck your tea, you fuckin' British bastard.'

'Oh dear, dear, dear, such anger and such foul language. That really won't get us anywhere, you know,' Turner tutted.

He strolled to the corner of the room and put the kettle on. There was no further sound from the young man as he turned back to him with a friendly smile. 'Biscuit?' he offered.

THE KILLER

To survive the violent streets of Belfast in the 1970s, young Darren McCann learns to fight. The IRA are interested in recruiting him but, though he is a Catholic, he refuses to take sides until a family tragedy allies him with "the cause".

His specialist training turns him into an efficient sniper and covert operative. One brutal interrogation earns Darren the reputation as "The Butcher of Belfast" and pairs him with his infamous knife, The Killer. After a high profile assassination, he takes refuge in Spain where he works with ETA terrorists and takes part in an audacious bank raid.

He returns to Ireland to continue the fight, but the seeds of doubt are planted in his mind by a British MI6 officer with shocking information and plans to turn him into a double-agent.

"This fast-paced chronicle of death and double-cross kept me glued to my seat from first page till last..."

Clifford Thurlow, author of Making A Killing.

"This is the fastest paced book I have ever read. I kept thinking I would come to a point where I could put it down for the evening, but that never happened."

Janie, Amazon.com

Buy the ebook from Amazon, or receive 10% off the price of the paperback with this code: PMAXENFU at CreateSpace:

www.createspace.com/3901544

Find out more about Jack Elgos and The Killer Trilogy at YELLOWBAY:

www.yellowbay.co.uk/the-killer